THE FIRST MOUNTAIN MAN:
PREACHER'S FURY

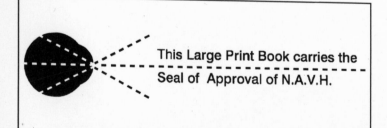

THE FIRST MOUNTAIN MAN: PREACHER'S FURY

WILLIAM W. JOHNSTONE
WITH J. A. JOHNSTONE

THORNDIKE PRESS

A part of Gale, Cengage Learning

GALE
CENGAGE Learning·

Detroit • New York • San Francisco • New Haven, Conn • Waterville, Maine • London

GALE
CENGAGE Learning®

LIBRARY OF CONGRESS CATALOGING-IN-PUBLICATION DATA

Johnstone, William W.
  The first mountain man. Preacher's fury / by William W. Johnstone with J.A. Johnstone. — Large print ed.
    p. cm. — (First mountain man) (Thorndike Press large print western)
  ISBN-13: 978-1-4104-5140-8 (hardcover)
  ISBN-10: 1-4104-5140-2 (hardcover)
  1. Revenge—Fiction. 2. Mountain life—Fiction. 3. Large type books. I. Johnstone, J. A. II. Title. III. Title: Preacher's fury.
  PS3560.O415F85 2012
  813'.54—dc23
                                  2012020989

Published in 2012 by arrangement with Pinnacle Books, an imprint of Kensington Publishing Corp.

Printed in the United States of America
1 2 3 4 5 6 7 16 15 14 13 12

THE FIRST MOUNTAIN MAN:
PREACHER'S FURY

CHAPTER 1

The trading post was called Blind Pete's Place. The proprietor wasn't blind, and his name wasn't really Pete. He was a German named Horst Gruenwald.

But he preferred to be called Pete, and since he was more than six feet tall and almost two hundred and fifty pounds of pure muscle, folks didn't argue with him.

His eyes were his only weakness, and the thick spectacles he wore allowed him to see well enough to crack a troublemaker's head open with a ham-like fist if he needed to.

Preacher wasn't the given name of the man riding down a pine-covered hill toward the trading post, either, but it was what he had been called for a number of years, ever since he had saved himself from torture and death at the hands of his Blackfoot captors by preaching constantly for days and nights on end, thereby making them think he was crazy. Most Indians wouldn't kill a crazy person for fear that his spirit would return to haunt them, and the Blackfeet were no different.

Preacher was still young enough to be a vital, active man, but old enough that strands of silver had begun to appear in his thick black hair and beard. Years of exposure to the elements had tanned his visible skin to the color of old saddle leather. A hard life as a fur trapper in the Rocky Mountains had left him with a lean, muscular body under his buckskin shirt and trousers.

He balanced a long-barreled flintlock rifle across the saddle in front of him, and tucked behind his belt were a pair of loaded and charged pistols. Another brace of pistols rode in sheaths strapped to his saddle. In addition to the guns he carried a razor-sharp hunting knife.

Preacher was widely regarded as one of the most dangerous men in these mountains. He could kill a man in any number of ways, including with his bare hands.

Some of the tribes knew him as White Wolf, because he resembled a dangerous lobo, while others called him Ghost Killer because of his almost supernatural ability to slip into a camp, slit the throats of his enemies, and get back out again without anyone even knowing he was there until it

8

was too late to help his victims.

At the moment, however, Preacher didn't feel like killing anybody. He was tired and thirsty. He wanted a drink, maybe some hot food, and then he would find himself a place to camp near the trading post. Recently he had spent several months down in Santa Fe, recuperating from some injuries, so he'd had plenty of having a roof over his head for a while.

A big, shaggy, wolf-like cur padded alongside the rangy gray stallion Preacher rode. He called the dog Dog and the horse Horse. Simple was best, in Preacher's book.

When Dog looked back over his shoulder and whined, Preacher said, "Go ahead, you varmint. I know you're itchin' to get there and say howdy to your sweethearts."

Tongue lolling happily, Dog bounded on down the hill ahead of Preacher and Horse. Blind Pete had a couple of wolfhound bitches, and Dog was eager to get reacquainted with them.

Preacher didn't feel the same need for female companionship right now. Having a woman around was like having a roof over his head. He'd had plenty of that while he was in Santa Fe. A pretty señorita named Juanita had nursed him back to health, and she'd had it in her mind that Preacher would spend the winter with her.

When the wild geese began to fly, though, he knew it was time to head north. The mountains called to him.

"You been to this place before?"

Preacher looked over at the small, elderly black man who rode beside him. He nodded to Lorenzo and said, "Yeah, a heap of times."

"Folks around here got anything against colored fellas?"

Preacher grunted disdainfully.

"You could be colored green or blue and it wouldn't make a lick of difference. Out here in the mountains we judge folks by what they do, not what they look like."

"Well, that's the way it oughta be, I reckon. But that ain't always how it is."

"I wouldn't worry," Preacher said.

"I'll take your word for it."

Preacher had met Lorenzo back in St. Louis, where he had gone to settle a score with an old enemy. They had been traveling together ever since. Lorenzo had never been West before, and he was enjoying the journey.

The two riders reached the bottom of the hill and started across a stretch of open ground toward the trading post, which was built near a fast-flowing creek. It was a sturdy, sprawling log building with a stockade fence around it that also enclosed a barn and corral. Watchtowers rose at each corner of the fence. The place was laid out with defense against attack in mind.

Preacher recalled that there had been a few skirmishes between Pete and the Indians in the early days after the German had established the trading post, but for the most part the tribes left him alone now. As a young man, Horst Gruenwald had been a Hessian mercenary and served as a cannoneer in the Revolutionary War, fighting in the employ of the British.

When it became obvious to Horst that he was on the side destined to lose, he had taken off for the tall and uncut and declared himself an American. Years later, when he decided to go West and see the frontier, he had somehow gotten hold of a three-pounder and hauled it out here with him.

After a few war parties had been shredded by canister rounds from that cannon, the rest of the Indians in the area had gotten the idea that it might be wise to avoid Blind Pete's.

Things were peaceful enough these days that the gate in the fence stood wide open. Dog was already inside the stockade. Preacher and Lorenzo followed, trailing the

11

pack horses behind them. Preacher lifted a hand in a lazy wave to a man lounging in one of the guard towers.

Preacher and Lorenzo intended to move farther north, and they needed to replenish their supplies while they had the chance. That was why they were stopping here at Blind Pete's Place.

A number of horses milled around in the corral. Preacher studied them, thinking that he might recognize a mount he knew. None of the animals seemed familiar to him, though.

But that didn't mean much. He had been away from the mountains for a while, and in that time, trappers he knew could have changed horses. Some friends of his might be inside the trading post, even if he didn't see their horses in the corral.

Some of his enemies might be in there, too. Preacher was just as interested in that possibility.

But he never went in anywhere without being careful about it. Blind Pete's would be no different.

Preacher didn't intend to spend the night here, so he and Lorenzo rode to the hitch rack in front of the main building instead of the corral and dismounted. The mountain man looped Horse's reins around the rack and tied the pack animals there as well.

He had just stepped up onto the porch when he heard a deep, powerful voice he recognized coming through the open door.

"Now thou hast but one bare hour to live, and then thou must be damned perpetually! Stand still, you ever-moving spheres of Heaven, that time may cease, and midnight never come."

Lorenzo frowned in confusion and asked, "What's that fella goin' on about?"

"Not much tellin'," Preacher said with a grin. "He's always got somethin' to say, though."

"You know him?"

"Yep. Fancies hisself a orator."

Lorenzo shook his head. Preacher didn't say anything else. It would all become clear to his companion soon. The two of them stepped into the trading post.

The main room was a big, low-ceilinged chamber. To the right were a bar and several tables, to the left shelves and crates and barrels full of merchandise with a counter at the far end of the room. The floor was made of rough puncheons hewn from split logs. Planks sitting on barrels formed the bar, and the tables and benches were as rough as the floor, which meant a fella had to be careful when he sat in order to avoid getting splinters in his behind.

One of the benches had been pulled into an open area of floor. The man who had been spouting words as Preacher and Lorenzo entered stood on the bench with one arm lifted over his head in a dramatic stance.

He was only about three and a half feet tall, but his brawny shoulders and full beard testified that he was a man full-growed, or as full-growed as he was going to get, anyway. His eyes widened at the sight of the tall, lean figure in the doorway, and he exclaimed, "Preacher!"

"Good to see you again, Audie," Preacher said with a nod.

Nimbly, the little man hopped down from the bench and hurried toward the newcomers. He held out a hand and shook gravely with Preacher.

With his other hand, he jerked a thumb toward a blanket-wrapped shape sitting in a corner.

"I'm afraid my recitation from *Dr. Faustus* has put Nighthawk to sleep. The unenlightened fellow never has had much appreciation for the works of Marlowe. He's more partial to the Immortal Bard, although of course there are some scholars who make the claim that Marlowe actually penned

14

those words attributed to the actor from Stratford-on-Avon. But I'm positive that he'll be quite pleased to see you when he awakens. Nighthawk, I mean, not Bill Shake-a-lance."

Preacher grinned over at Lorenzo, who stood there openmouthed in awe.

"Yeah, he does like to go on a mite," Preacher said. "Audie, meet Lorenzo. Him and me been travelin' together for a spell."

Audie grabbed the stunned Lorenzo's hand and pumped it heartily.

"The honor is mine, sir. Any boon companion of Preacher's is a boon companion of mine."

"Uh, sure," Lorenzo said. "Pleased to meet you, too."

"The Crow over yonder in the blanket is Nighthawk," Preacher went on. "He don't say much, so he sorta balances Audie out when it comes to talkin'."

"We're a fine pair indeed," Audie agreed. "You're not wintering in St. Louis this year, Preacher?"

The mountain man grimaced and shook his head.

"I've had enough of that damned St. Looie to last me for a long time," he said. "I might just spend the rest of my life in these here mountains."

"There are much worse places to be, that's indisputable. Nighthawk and I have been giving some thought to spending the winter with Chief Bent Leg and his band of Assiniboine. Perhaps you and Lorenzo would care to join us."

"That ain't a bad idea." Preacher turned to Lorenzo and went on, "Ol' Bent Leg's a pretty good fella, and his people are friendly to the whites."

"You maybe got so used to bein' around me, Preacher, that you don't notice no more, but I ain't exactly white," Lorenzo pointed out.

"To the Assiniboine you are, or might as well be. That's one thing about the tribes . . . To their way of thinkin', there's them, and then there's everybody else. The names of the tribes usually translate to 'The People' or 'The Real People' or 'The True People.' Some of 'em are more tolerant of us lower classes than others. Like Nighthawk's people, the Crow, generally get along with most other folks except for the Blackfeet. Those two bunches don't cotton to each other at all."

"Umm," Nighthawk said from the corner without looking up.

Audie started toward one of the tables and motioned for Preacher and Lorenzo to follow him.

"I think we could all use a libation —" he began.

That was when a man at one of the other tables stood up and said in a loud, angry voice, "Hey, Little Bit, you can't just stop in the middle of a poem like that. You need to finish up your recitin', damn your midget hide."

Preacher stiffened and said, "Aw, hell," under his breath.

"What's wrong?" Lorenzo asked.

"I don't know who that fella is, but now he's gone and done it."

"Done what?"

Preacher recalled something he had heard Audie quote once. He said, "He done cried havoc, and let slip the dogs o' war."

CHAPTER 2

Audie stopped short and stood very still as he looked at the man who had spoken to him. The man was tall and rawboned, with a lantern-jawed face and long, dark brown hair that fell lank and greasy down the back of his neck. He wore a broad-brimmed black hat, a linsey-woolsey shirt, a patched and faded frock coat, and whipcord trousers tucked into tall black boots. The butt of a pistol jutted out from where it was tucked behind his belt on the left side.

Five other men were at the table where the man had been sitting. Some were in buckskins, some in town clothes that had seen better days. But they were all armed and all looked tough and ornery.

Audie finally said, "Were you speaking to me, sir?"

"You're the only damn sawed-off runt in this place, ain't you?" the man said. "Shoot, don't take offense, Little Bit. I liked your poem. I wanta hear the rest of it."

"I'm glad you have an appreciation for the finer things in life, sir. Unfortunately, that doesn't negate the fact that you're an ass."

The man frowned in surprise and anger and said, "What'd you call me?"

Preacher glanced into the corner at Nighthawk. The Crow hadn't moved and still appeared to be half-asleep, but Preacher saw how Nighthawk's eyes were slitted in close observation of what was going on. If trouble broke out, Nighthawk was ready to move.

And trouble seemed inevitable, because Audie said, "I called you an ass, but I'm sorry for that."

The man grunted in satisfaction and said, "Oh, you are, are you?"

"That's right. I inadvertently insulted all the honest, hard-working asses in the world by comparing them to a sorry pile of dung such as yourself."

The man's eyes widened in rage, but before he could do anything, Audie sprang forward and drove a punch into his belly, burying his small but rock-hard fist almost to the wrist.

Audie was short in stature, but his arms and shoulders were better developed than those of many normal-sized men. The blow he landed was so powerful that it caused the man to double over, and that brought his hair within Audie's reach.

Audie grabbed the dangling strands with both hands and jerked down. At the same time, he brought his knee up. Knee met chin with a loud crack. The man fell to his knees, half-stunned.

That put him at the perfect height for the haymaker that Audie uncorked on him. The man pitched to the side, out cold.

The whole thing had taken only a few heartbeats. It all happened so fast, in fact, that the unconscious man's companions were left sitting at the table trying to figure out what had happened.

But as soon as they had, a couple of seconds later, benches were shoved back, the men sprang to their feet, and one of them yelled, "Get that little varmint!"

Preacher glanced at Lorenzo.

"You game to take a hand in this?"

"You know I am!" Lorenzo said.

They stepped up, flanking Audie, as the five men rushed to the attack. At the other end of the room, Blind Pete yelled from behind the trading post counter, "You break anything, you bought it, *ja!*"

The five ruffians had forgotten about Nighthawk. The big warrior came swooping out of the corner like his namesake, throwing aside the blanket in which he'd been wrapped so that it fluttered behind him like wings. He caught two of the men by the neck and banged their heads together. They collapsed limply, out of the battle before it had truly begun.

That meant Preacher, Lorenzo, and Audie were no longer outnumbered. They took on their opponents evenly now. Lorenzo was spry for his age, and Audie had already demonstrated that he could hold his own in a fight. They waded into two of the men, punching and gouging.

Preacher blocked a punch from the other man, who was shorter than the mountain man but seemingly as broad and sturdy as a redwood's trunk. Preacher hammered a fist to the man's belly, but it was like hitting a wall.

He couldn't completely avoid the blow the man hooked at his head. It grazed his jaw with enough force to jerk Preacher's head around. He caught himself and shot a jab into the man's face. The blow landed cleanly but barely made his head rock back.

No, not redwood, Preacher thought. The son of a gun was made of granite.

The man's fist thudded into Preacher's chest and knocked him back a step. While

Preacher was a little off balance, the man tackled him, coming in low and catching him around the waist. Preacher suddenly found himself going backward with his feet off the floor.

The two men crashed into a pile of crates and knocked them over. They sprawled on the floor as Pete yelled, "Hey, be careful, damn it!"

Preacher was on the bottom. Sensing that his opponent was about to try to drive a knee into his groin, he twisted his body and took the vicious blow on his thigh instead. He hammered his right fist into the man's left ear.

That didn't seem to do much damage, either. Preacher jerked his head aside as a blocky fist came at his face. The punch missed completely, so the man wound up hitting the floor instead. For the first time, he grunted in pain.

Preacher grabbed the front of the man's buckskin shirt and hauled hard on it, throwing the man to the side. Preacher rolled after him and hit the man in the belly again three times fast, his arm drawing back and striking like a piston in its cylinder. He was finally doing some damage to the varmint, Preacher thought.

The next second, the man drew up a foot,

planted it in Preacher's belly, and levered the mountain man up and over him. Preacher let out a yell as he found himself flying through the air.

The flight didn't last long. He landed on top of a barrel. The impact drove the air from his lungs and left him gasping for breath.

His stocky opponent was already up. He grabbed the back of Preacher's shirt and slung him into some shelves, drawing another angry shout from Blind Pete. The German's policy was to stay out of any brawls that broke out in his place, but he might take a hand in this fight since it was threatening his merchandise.

Preacher caught himself against the shelves before he fell again. The man he was battling might not look all that impressive physically, but he was tough as whang leather and obviously an experienced, brutal brawler.

A little too confident, though. He seemed to think Preacher was just about done, so he rushed in to finish off the mountain man.

Preacher met him with a hard, straight right that landed square on his nose and pulped it. Blood spurted over Preacher's knobby knuckles. The man reeled back as a crimson stream flowed from his ruined nose.

Preacher kicked him in the belly and then planted another savage blow on the varmint's beezer. This fella wasn't the only one who could fight hard and mean. Preacher let him have a left and then a right, lambasting him and driving him backward. The mountain man didn't ease off now that he had seized the advantage, either. He followed, slugging hard and swift with both fists.

The man crumpled. He might be made of granite, but he had finally been worn down by Preacher's iron fists.

As the man lay there bleeding on the floor, the breath rasping and wheezing through his swollen and misshapen nose, Preacher swung around. He had been too busy to keep up with how Lorenzo and Audie were doing against their opponents. He hoped his friends were all right.

They were more than all right, Preacher saw. They had emerged from the battle triumphant. Audie, in fact, was standing with one foot on the chest of an unconscious man, dusting his hands off against each other in obvious satisfaction.

A few feet away, Lorenzo leaned against a table and grinned. His hat had been knocked off and he had a few scrapes on his face, but he seemed to be fine otherwise.

"What a fine display of pugilistic excellence!" Audie said.

"Is he sayin' we whupped 'em good?" Lorenzo asked.

Nighthawk stood nearby with arms folded. He nodded and said gravely, "Ummm."

Preacher had lost his hat during the fight. He looked around, saw it lying on the floor, and picked it up. The broad-brimmed, brown felt headgear was pretty shapeless to start with, but it was even more crumpled now because it looked like it had been stepped on a few times. Preacher punched it back to the way it was supposed to be and settled it on his head.

Pete stalked out from behind the counter and came along the aisle toward them. He stopped, planted his fists on his hips, and said, "Somebody will have to pay for these damages, *ja?*"

Preacher swept a hand toward the unconscious men.

"They started it. I reckon you can check their pockets."

Pete jerked his shelf-like jaw at the man Preacher had knocked out and asked, "Do you know who that is?"

"Nope, and I don't care."

"His name is Willie Deaver. That one is Caleb Manning." Pete pointed at the long-haired man Audie had knocked out to start the ruckus. "I do not know the names of the other men, but they are the same sort as Deaver and Manning. Bad men. You would be wise to leave before they wake up, Preacher."

The mountain man bristled.

"I ain't in the habit of runnin' away from trouble. Fact is, the last thing I run away from was my folks' farm, and that was a hell of a long time ago."

"You would not be fleeing," Pete said. "You would be saving my place from even more damage."

Preacher shrugged.

"Fine. Lorenzo and me didn't plan to stay the night here, anyway. We just wanted to pick up some supplies."

"I will give you a good price if you tell me what you need, so you can load them up and leave."

Preacher looked at Audie and Nighthawk.

"What about you fellas? Are we all ridin' together and headin' for Bent Leg's village?"

"That strikes me as a more than agreeable course of action," Audie said. Nighthawk just nodded.

"All right, Pete," Preacher said. "We need flour, salt, dried apples, beans, maybe a little coffee and molasses if you got it, and some salt jowl."

Pete nodded and said, "I will put everything in a bag."

"We'll go saddle our horses," Audie said. "Come on, Nighthawk."

Ten minutes later, the four men were ready to ride out. Preacher had settled up with Pete for the supplies.

"Much obliged," Preacher said after he'd swung up into the saddle on Horse's back. "Too bad about the trouble."

Pete waved that off as he stood on the trading post's porch. He glanced back over his shoulder. Deaver, Manning, and the other three men were still out cold, but they would probably be coming around soon.

"Men like that, trouble always follows them," he said. "You should watch your back, Preacher."

"I always do," Preacher said with a smile. He lifted a hand. "So long, Pete."

"Guten tag, mein freund," Audie called.

"You talk that Dutch lingo?" Lorenzo asked as they rode toward the gate.

"Ein bischen," Audie answered.

"No, I ain't bitchin'," Lorenzo said with a frown. "I don't care what you talk."

"Nein, nein."

"Ten," Lorenzo said. "That's what comes

27

next. What're we countin', anyway?"

"You might as well give up," Preacher told him. "He'll pick at you all day if you let him." He turned in the saddle and let out a piercing whistle. Dog came running from somewhere in the compound. "Sorry if you didn't get to do as much visitin' as you'd like," Preacher told the big cur. "But we got places to go."

They rode out of the stockade, putting the trading post behind them and heading north toward a range of snow-capped mountains. A cool breeze blew in Preacher's face. It smelled good.

CHAPTER 3

Blind Pete leaned on the counter as he laboriously entered numbers in the ledger book that lay open before him. He chewed at the graying blond mustache that drooped over his mouth. He had learned to cipher as a young boy in Dusseldorf, but it had never come easy to him.

Despite what Preacher had said, Pete hadn't taken any coins from the pockets of Deaver, Manning, and the other men to pay for the damages caused by the brawl. If Deaver had woken up to find someone rifling his pockets, there would be hell to pay. Besides, there really hadn't been that much damage.

Pete made sure to have a loaded shotgun lying on the counter in front of him when the men regained consciousness. As they came around, groaning and cursing, Pete had told them, "Preacher and the others are gone. There will be no more trouble here, *ja?*"

Caleb Manning had looked like he wanted to take out his anger on the proprietor, but Deaver had stopped him.

"Let it go," Deaver said. "It ain't Pete's fault that Preacher and his friends jumped us. If there's a score to settle, it's with them."

That reasonable attitude had surprised Pete, but he welcomed it. He was even more surprised a few minutes later when Deaver laid a five-dollar gold piece on the counter and said, "That's for the whiskey we drank and the trouble we caused. Are we square, Pete?"

Pete's first impulse was to pick up the coin and bite it to make sure it was real, but he suppressed that and nodded instead. "*Ja,* we are square."

"So we're welcome back here?"

Pete understood now. Deaver didn't want to be banned from the trading post, a ban that Pete could enforce with his cannon if he chose to.

"*Ja,* of course."

"Obliged." Deaver had turned to his companions and snapped, "Come on. We're ridin'."

Night had fallen now. The trading post's other customers had gone on their way,

30

except for a couple of trappers who were spending the night in the little rooms at the back of the building. They would be moving on come morning. The gate in the stockade fence was closed and barred, and one of the men who worked for Pete was on guard duty. The other three workers were probably asleep in their quarters in the barn by now.

The only light in the main room of the trading post was the candle that burned on the counter and cast its flickering light on the ledger. Pete dipped his pen in the inkwell and wrote a few more numbers in his cramped, precise script.

The front door swung open.

Pete looked up in surprise. It was rare for him to have customers this late. And the guard in the tower would have blown on the trumpet that was kept up there to announce visitors. Anyone who rode up in the dark would be challenged before they were let into the compound.

Clearly that hadn't happened, because two men strode into the trading post and started toward the counter where Pete stood.

Through the thick spectacles that perched on his nose with a ribbon attaching them to his collar, he recognized the newcomers. Deaver and Manning. Seeing them here again made a cold ball of apprehension form in the pit of Pete's ample belly.

"Mein herrs," Pete greeted them. "I did not expect to see you again so soon."

"I'll bet you didn't," Deaver said. His hat was thumbed back so that his thatch of straw-colored hair stuck out from under it. "I realized that we forgot something when we left this afternoon."

"Oh? What was that?"

"We forgot to ask you if you know where Preacher and his friends are goin'."

Pete placed both hands flat on the counter and leaned forward slightly. He shook his head from side to side, even though he had heard Preacher say that they were going to the village of Chief Bent Leg of the Assiniboine.

If he told that to Deaver and Manning, though, they might follow Preacher and the other men and cause more trouble. Pete didn't want that.

"They never mentioned where they were going," he said. "They just bought some supplies from me and rode out."

"Did you see which direction they headed?"

"Nein. No."

Deaver smiled and shook his head.

"Now, see, Pete, I've got a problem. I

32

think you might be lyin' to me."

"You have no right to speak to me in such a way," Pete said with an angry glare.

"Oh, I'll talk to you any way I want, you big fat Dutchman." Deaver flicked a glance at Manning and nodded.

Pete knew he was in trouble. He started to straighten and reach under the counter for the shotgun he had placed there earlier, but before he could move, Manning whipped out a hunting knife and plunged it down into the back of Pete's right hand. The point of the blade penetrated cleanly all the way through the hand and buried itself in the wood, pinning Pete to the counter.

Pete let out a bellow of pain and tried for the shotgun with his other hand. Before he could reach it, Deaver brought out a pistol and fired.

The heavy lead ball smashed into Pete's left shoulder, shattering the bone. Pete roared. The agony he felt might have caused him to collapse, but the knife holding his hand on the counter kept him upright.

"Now, see, you should have convinced me right off that you were tellin' the truth," Deaver said. The ugly smile never left his face.

One of the trappers who was renting a

bunk came running into the trading post's main room, drawn by the yelling and the shot. He carried a flintlock rifle slanted across his chest and wore only a pair of long underwear.

Before the man could even demand to know what was going on, Manning pulled a pistol with his right hand. He used his left to keep the knife planted firmly in Pete's hand, which had blood puddling under it. Manning lifted the gun and fired, the dull boom of the shot filling the room.

The ball punched into the chest of the man who had just run into the room. He staggered back a step, dropped his rifle, and fell to his knees as a bloodstain bloomed vividly on the long underwear. He pitched forward on his face and didn't move again.

"My men . . ." Pete rasped. "They will —"

"They won't do a damned thing," Deaver said. "The rest of the boys have finished cuttin' their throats by now. You should've posted a better guard, Pete. That poor fella up in the tower was wearin' a bloody grin from ear to ear before he knew what was happenin' to him."

Pete groaned. His employees were dead, and so was one of his customers. He didn't know where the other trapper was. Probably hiding, hoping these vicious animals would overlook him.

"I'll ask you again, and you better not lie to me," Deaver said. "Where was Preacher goin'?"

"I don't —" Pete began.

Manning leaned on the knife and twisted it. The razor-sharp blade cut deeper in Pete's hand. Pete couldn't hold in the scream that welled up his throat.

His wounded shoulder was bleeding heavily. He felt the hot flow dripping down his arm as it dangled uselessly at his side. He knew he would pass out soon, so if he was going to fight back, it had to be now.

He suddenly jerked back as hard as he could with his right arm, putting his considerable strength behind it. The knife sliced through muscle and bone and filled Pete with pain worse than any he had ever known existed, but abruptly his hand was free. He had forced the knife to cut its way right out.

He couldn't make a fist with that ruined hand, but he could swing his whole arm. He threw himself forward over the counter and crashed his forearm against the side of Manning's head. The blow knocked Manning into Deaver, and both of them got tangled up for a minute. That gave Pete time to roll off the front of the counter and land on his feet.

He kicked Manning in the groin and barreled into Deaver, knocking the smaller man off his feet. If he could get outside, Pete thought, he might be able to give Deaver's men the slip in the darkness. He would probably still bleed to death, but at least he would have a chance to get away.

He was only halfway to the front door when a pistol roared behind him. Something smashed into the back of his left knee, knocking that leg out from under him. He tumbled to the floor, knocking over some boxes that clattered down around him.

Pete tried to lift himself, but neither of his arms worked well enough now. Deaver rushed up and kicked him in the jaw. Stunned, Pete rolled onto his back.

Deaver leaned over him, cursing.

"I'll kill you, you blasted —"

"Wait a minute," Manning croaked. He stumbled into Pete's view, which was blurry now because his spectacles had fallen off. Pete could still see well enough to know that Manning was clutching himself where he'd been kicked, and Pete felt a little bit of satisfaction from that, anyway.

Manning went on in a pain-wracked voice, "Let me . . . work on him. He'll tell us . . . what we want to know."

"Yeah," Deaver said. "That's a good idea. Let's cut these trousers off of him."

Pete started to bellow in outrage even before he felt the touch of the cold steel. Once he did, the bellows turned to shrieks of pain.

And in the end, of course, he told them how the mountain man and his companions had talked about spending the winter in the Assiniboine village. Deaver and Manning believed him this time. After being tortured like that, no man could have uttered anything except the truth.

Pete knew there was no hope for him now. He was hurt too badly to recover. But he managed to husk out, "Go ahead . . . and kill me."

Deaver shook his head and grinned.

"I don't think so. That'd be too easy. There are some knives over there in a case, Caleb. Get a couple of them and we'll stake him out."

They spread his arms, and Manning drove a knife through the palm of each hand, then used a maul to hammer the blades even more deeply into the floor.

"What about his feet?"

Deaver shook his head.

"He ain't goin' anywhere, just like that." He jerked a thumb at the rooms in the back.

"Go check those out and make sure nobody else is back there. We're not leavin' anybody alive except for the Dutchman here, and he won't be alive for very long once we burn this place down around him."

Pete groaned. Bad enough they were going to kill him, but did they have to destroy the business he had worked so hard to build, too?

Clearly, nothing was beyond the viciousness of animals such as these.

A moment later, through the red haze that was beginning to fill his head, Pete heard a pistol shot. He knew that Manning had just murdered that other fur trapper. Now no one would ever know what had happened here or who was responsible for this atrocity.

"I threw around some coal oil," he heard Deaver say. "Get that candle. We'll light it and get out of here."

A moment later, Pete heard the *whoosh* of flames and felt their heat against his face. In a matter of seconds, they were all around him, rapidly turning into an inferno.

The roaring blaze behind them turned the night sky an ugly, garish shade of orange as Deaver, Manning, and the other three men rode away from the trading post. Manning shifted uncomfortably in his saddle, and Deaver asked, "Feelin' any better?"

"Not much. That old man deserved everything he got."

"Yeah, but at least he told us where to find Preacher."

Manning hesitated, then said, "We don't have time to go after him right now, Willie. You know that. We've got to rendezvous with those other fellas. I was willin' to come back here tonight, but —"

"Don't worry," Deaver broke in impatiently. "I haven't forgotten about that business we have to take care of. But Pete said Preacher was plannin' to winter with Bent Leg's bunch of redskins. And our business won't take us all winter. There'll be plenty of time later on to teach that son of a bitch and his friends a lesson they'll never forget."

"All right," Manning said with a grin and a nod. "I like the sound of that."

They rode on as the flames leaped high behind them, consuming Blind Pete's Place and everything in it.

Yes, sir, Deaver thought, it was going to be a long winter.

Especially for Preacher.

CHAPTER 4

A storm roared down out of Canada a few days later, bringing with it a biting wind and hard pellets of sleet that pelted down, making life miserable for man and horse alike.

Because of that, Preacher considered them lucky to have found a cave where they could get out of the weather. It was empty, so they didn't have to share it with a hibernating grizzly bear.

People had used the chamber in the side of a rocky hillside for shelter in the past. That was obvious because of the charred ring on the floor where campfires had been built. The ceiling of the cave had a crack in it that ran all the way to the surface of the hill to carry away smoke. Nighthawk built a fire, and the heat from the flames, along with that put out by the horses, warmed the cave so that it was quite comfortable.

"Have you ever been here before,

Preacher?" Audie asked as the four men sat around the fire that first night.

"Not that I recollect," the mountain man answered. "I recall ridin' through this valley before, but I must not've stopped and looked around any. How about you?"

Audie shook his head and said, "No, it's all new to me as well."

Nighthawk said, "Umm."

Audie turned to him.

"What's that you say? You've been here before? Eight winters ago?"

"Umm."

Lorenzo frowned and asked Preacher, "How's he do that? I never heard that Injun do nothin' except make that sound like he's tryin' to pass somethin' that hurts."

"They got their own way of communicatin', I reckon," Preacher said.

"Yes, I agree that it's a fine place," Audie went on. "We should be able to wait here until the storm blows over." He turned to Lorenzo. "Why don't you tell us how you and Preacher came to meet, my friend?"

"It's a long story," Lorenzo said, "and it ain't a particularly pretty one."

Audie smiled and spread his hands.

"Until the weather gods smile upon us again, we have nothing but time."

"Well, I reckon that's true enough." Lorenzo looked at Preacher. "You mind if I tell the story?"

Preacher waved a hand.

"Like Audie says, we got nothin' but time."

"Well, it was back in St. Louis, you see," Lorenzo began, "and I was workin' for a fella who was nothin' but a lowdown, dyed-in-the-wool varmint."

"You were his slave?" Audie asked.

"No, sir. I'm a freed man. But Mr. Shad Beaumont, he was as bad or worse than any plantation owner who might've put me to work pickin' cotton."

Lorenzo continued with the story of how Preacher had come to St. Louis to settle a score with Shad Beaumont, the criminal who was responsible for causing a lot of trouble for Preacher and some of his friends on the frontier. Because of Beaumont, people Preacher cared about had died, and the mountain man couldn't let that pass. It just wasn't in him.

Preacher's enmity for Beaumont hadn't extended to all the folks who worked for the man, however, and he had found an unexpected ally in Lorenzo. They had been traveling together ever since, along with another former employee of Beaumont's, a young woman called Casey, who had formed an attachment with Preacher, too. Along with the members of a wagon train, the three of them had made a perilous journey over the Santa Fe Trail.

Casey had married one of the young men from the wagon train and remained behind in Santa Fe, and Preacher was glad of that. She'd had it in her head for a while that she ought to marry him, and that never would have worked out. He wasn't the sort of hombre to get hitched permanent-like, although he enjoyed the company of women and had spent more than one winter in temporary marriages to women from various Indian tribes. None of them expected him to stay in one place for more than a few months.

"It certainly sounds as if you've had some thrilling adventures," Audie said when Lorenzo finished his tale. "As for Nighthawk and myself, we first met Preacher a while back down in the Sangre de Cristo Mountains, while he was looking for an ancient Spanish treasure."

"You're a treasure hunter, Preacher?" Lorenzo asked. "I didn't know that."

"I was just helpin' some other folks look for it," Preacher said. "I can't think of nothin' much worse'n windin' up a rich man. Too much money'll weigh a man down ever' bit as much as chains will."

"I wouldn't know. Wouldn't mind gettin' the chance to find out one o' these days, though."

"People like to cite Scripture and claim that money is the root of all evil," Audie said. "Actually, that's an incorrect quote. The verse actually says that the *love* of money is the root of all evil."

"I don't love money," Lorenzo insisted. "I'm just passin' fond of it, that's all."

They talked until the fire burned down, then Preacher, Lorenzo, and Nighthawk rolled up in their blankets to sleep. Audie stayed awake to take the first turn on guard duty, nursing a cup of coffee as he sat beside the glowing embers of the fire.

With the storm howling outside, it was unlikely that anybody was out and about to bother them, but folks who had lived in these mountains for very long knew that it was never wise to take unnecessary chances. Later, each of the other men would take a turn standing watch.

The clouds had blown on by morning, leaving behind air cold enough to make a man gasp when he took a deep breath, as well as a landscape that glittered so brightly in the sun that it might as well have been covered by diamonds. The ice storm had coated the ground as well as the trees and bushes.

"Lordy, it's beautiful," Lorenzo said as he looked out from the mouth of the cave. "We used to get sleet back in St. Louis, but it never left the place lookin' anything like this."

"Like an ice castle from a fairy tale," Audie said.

Lorenzo shook his head.

"I wouldn't know nothin' about no fairy tales. But this here is right pretty."

"And slick as it can be," Preacher put in. "A hoss might slip and bust a leg on that stuff. We'll stay here until it melts off."

That happened the next day, when the wind turned back around to the south and blew strongly. By mid-morning the temperature had warmed above freezing and water was dripping everywhere as the ice melted, making its own peculiar and beautiful kind of music.

The four men rode north again, climbing toward a saddle between two peaks. Preacher didn't know how they were designated on maps, but he called the mountains the Sleeping Woman and Old Baldy, because that's what they reminded him of. On the other side of the mountains lay a valley that stretched for twenty miles north and south

45

and was about five miles wide.

That valley was the domain of Chief Bent Leg's band of Assiniboine. There was plenty of game, and another range of mountains at the northern end gave it some protection from the weather. It was a good place to spend the winter.

They camped that night at the base of Old Baldy and climbed to the high pass the next day. Even though Lorenzo was riding, he began to breathe harder the higher they climbed.

"Lord, there ain't much *air* in the air up here, is there?" he asked when they stopped to rest the horses.

"You get used to it when you spend much time in the high country," Preacher told him. "Don't try to gulp down so much of it at a time. Just breathe more shallow-like."

Lorenzo tried to follow the advice and soon felt a little better.

"Just imagine what it must be like to try to breathe at the summit of some of the great mountain ranges of the world like the Alps," Audie said. "And I've heard it said that there are some even taller, at the edge of the Orient."

Lorenzo shook his head.

"Never heard o' them places. This is plenty high for me. Remember, I'm a flatlander." He pointed back to the south. "Land's sake, you must be able to see for a hundred miles up here!"

"Probably not that far," Preacher told him. "You can see for a good ways, though. And it's a right pretty view, too."

"That it is," Audie agreed. "Never thought I'd see the likes o' that in all my borned days."

They pushed on and made it through the pass by late afternoon. There was just enough light left for them to descend a short distance into the valley and find a place to camp. They did that on a little bench that backed up to a rocky bluff so they would be out of the wind.

"With any luck we'll find Bent Leg's village tomorrow," Preacher said that evening as he fried some salt jowl over a small fire.

"What's this fella Bent Leg like?" Lorenzo asked. "I reckon it's safe for me to assume that he's got a bent leg?"

"Yeah, it got broke in a fight with the Gros Ventre when he was a youngster," Preacher explained. "Didn't heal back right, so it's always had a funny kink to it ever since. It didn't stop him from gettin' around, though, and he grew up into quite a warrior. He's gettin' on in years now, but he's been a good leader for his people."

"Who are the Gros . . . Gros . . . what'd you call 'em?"

"Gros Ventre. That's another tribe, lives west of here a ways. They don't get along with the Assiniboine. Any time tribes don't cotton to each other, they raid back and forth, and it was durin' one of those raids that Bent Leg got hurt. The Gros Ventre stole some horses and took some captives to make slaves out of 'em."

"I don't think I like these Gros Ventre folks, and I ain't even met any of 'em yet," Lorenzo said.

"Because they take slaves?" Audie asked. "Almost every tribe has been known to do that, at one time or another. Not only that, but . . . Were you born in this country, Lorenzo?"

"I sure was. Born and bred in Missouri."

"Well, your ancestors in Africa almost certainly had slaves from other tribes there with which they were at odds. It's an accepted form of warfare across the entire world."

"That don't make it right," Lorenzo insisted.

"No, certainly not. But it's a matter of historical record that the African tribes were quite proficient at capturing slaves from other tribes and selling and trading them to the Americans who sailed slave ships to their shores, especially during the last century."

"How come you know so much?" Lorenzo asked with a frown.

Preacher said, "Audie used to be a teacher at one of them colleges back East before he chucked all that and became a fur trapper."

"Why would you want to do that?"

"Because the color of one's skin is not the only means by which people discriminate," Audie said. "I was tired of being judged solely by my stature, or lack of same, and not by what was in my heart and my head."

"Reckon I can understand that. I'll be honest with you, you looked a mite funny to me at first, but now you're just Audie. I don't even think about the other no more."

"Nor does your Moorish coloring bother me, my friend."

"No, I told you, I'm from Missouri."

Preacher was about to chuckle when some instinct warned him. Maybe he had heard a faint noise from atop the bluff at their backs. Whatever it was, it brought him to his feet in a swift, sudden move. He started to turn and reached for one of the pistols tucked behind his belt.

Before he could draw the gun, a shape plummeted down from the top of the bluff and a bloodcurdling cry split the night. The

49

figure crashed into Preacher and drove him to the ground. The pistol slipped out of his fingers and skittered across the rocks. Preacher was stunned, but not so much that he couldn't see the savage, twisted face of the man who had tackled him, or the tomahawk that was lifted high, poised to fall and dash his brains out.

CHAPTER 5

A gun roared before the tomahawk could swoop down and end Preacher's life. It was the Indian who died instead, as the ball from Audie's pistol smashed into the side of his head, bored through his brain, and exploded out the other side of his skull in a grisly spray of blood, brain matter, and bone chips.

The attacker wasn't alone. Rifles blasted from the top of the bluff. The balls thudded into the ground as Audie, Nighthawk, and Lorenzo scrambled in different directions.

Preacher flung the dead Indian's body aside, snatched up the tomahawk the man had dropped, and sent it spinning toward the bluff top with a flick of his wrist.

He aimed the throw just above one of the muzzle flashes but didn't really expect to hit anything. He just wanted to make one of the attackers duck for cover.

Instead, a man suddenly pitched over the

edge and plummeted to the ground, landing next to the fire. The light from the flames revealed that the tomahawk was buried deeply in his forehead.

Preacher had never been one to turn down good luck. He rolled toward the base of the bluff, where the men on top of it would have a harder time drawing a bead on him because of the angle.

He pushed himself to his feet and planted his back against the rock wall. From there he could see that Audie, Nighthawk, and Lorenzo had reached the cover of the trees that grew around the clearing where they had made camp. They opened fire, peppering the top of the bluff with rifle balls.

Preacher had been about to draw his pistols and try to get a shot, but now he decided to leave the guns where they were for the moment. Instead he turned and faced the bluff. It was steep, but not quite sheer. Rocks stuck out from it here and there to form handholds, and a few hardy plants grew on it as well.

Preacher looked at the trees where his friends had taken cover and grinned. He pointed at himself and then jerked a thumb upward.

Reaching as high as he could, he found a handhold, got one of his feet on a rock lower down, and started to climb.

The men on the bluff and the ones in the trees continued to trade shots while Preacher made his ascent. He could tell from the way three different rifles sounded in the trees that all three of his friends were still in the fight. One or more of them might be wounded, but they were still alive.

Preacher had gotten a good enough look at the two dead Indians to know that they weren't part of Bent Leg's band of Assiniboine. He could tell by the decorations on their buckskins and the way their faces were painted that they were Gros Ventre. They had probably ventured this far east to raid Bent Leg's village.

As Preacher neared the top of the bluff, he stopped long enough to pull one of his pistols from behind his belt. Then he grasped one of the small, sturdy bushes and lifted himself higher as a rifle blasted a short distance above him. He could see flame spouting from the barrel.

The warrior started to reload. Preacher pushed with his legs and drove himself up. His head and shoulders cleared the rim. The Gros Ventre was on one knee, ramming a fresh load down the barrel of his rifle, when Preacher appeared and took him by surprise.

Preacher jammed the pistol under the warrior's chin and pulled the trigger.

The weapon went off with a flesh-muffled boom. The Indian was thrown backward. His head had exploded so that not much of it was left as he landed on his back with his arms and legs thrown out to the sides.

The Gros Ventre hadn't expected to find Preacher among them. He rolled onto the bluff and came up with his other pistol in his left hand.

A few yards away, one of the surprised warriors let out an angry screech and tried to swing his rifle toward the mountain man. Preacher's pistol roared before the Indian could pull the trigger. The ball smashed into the warrior's chest and knocked him sprawling.

Preacher heard a rush of footsteps behind him and whirled to see one of the warriors charging him and swinging a tomahawk. Preacher ducked under the slashing blow and crowded against the man. The empty pistol in Preacher's right hand smashed against the warrior's temple. Preacher felt bone crunch under the impact. The man dropped like a stone.

He twisted away as another Gros Ventre thrust a knife at him. The blade brushed Preacher's side, but it didn't penetrate his buckskin shirt. He dropped both pistols, clamped his hands on the Indian's arm, and heaved. With a startled yell, the warrior flew off the bluff and into empty air. His crashing impact as he landed below near the fire cut off the outcry.

Preacher drew his knife and crouched, ready to continue the fight, but all the shooting had stopped now and no one came at him. There were three dead men down below and three more corpses up here on top of the bluff. It was possible those half-dozen warriors made up the entire raiding party.

Preacher listened intently for the sounds of anyone fleeing, but he didn't hear anything. The violence had even silenced any birds or small animals nearby.

"Preacher, are you all right?" Audie called from below.

"Yeah. That seems to be all of 'em."

"You killed everyone up there?"

"Seemed like the thing to do at the time," Preacher replied.

He sheathed his knife, picked up his pistols, and swiftly reloaded them. He tucked away one of the weapons but held the other one ready as he checked on the three Gros Ventre up there. All of them were dead, which he had thought to be the case, but it never hurt anything to make sure.

The raiders' horses had to be somewhere nearby. He went to look for them and found them tied in a stand of trees about fifty yards away. There were only six ponies, confirming Preacher's guess about the size of the raiding party.

The Gros Ventre must have smelled the smoke from the campfire and decided to investigate. Then one of them had gotten carried away and jumped Preacher, probably figuring he could take the mountain man by surprise and kill him.

That had come close to happening. Audie's fast reaction had saved Preacher's life. That wasn't the first time, either.

He untied the ponies, gathered their reins, and led them along the bluff, looking for a way down. He left the dead warriors where they had fallen.

A couple of hundred yards away, the slope fell away at a gentler angle. Preacher was able to lead the ponies down it. He started back toward the fire, and as he approached, he called, "Hello, camp! It's just me, so don't get antsy."

When he walked up leading the horses, he found Audie and Lorenzo standing there, alert and watchful for trouble, while Nighthawk dragged the corpses of the other Gros

Ventre into the trees.

"We ain't gonna bury these fellas?" Lorenzo asked.

"I ain't in the habit of goin' to the time and trouble to bury folks what try to kill me and my friends," Preacher said. "The wolves'll take care of 'em for us."

"Fine by me," Lorenzo said. "I was just askin'."

"Gros Ventre, by their markings," Audie said. "We were just talking about them. Do you think they came looking for Bent Leg's village, Preacher?"

"That'd be my guess. They either didn't find it yet, or else their raid didn't go so good. They didn't have any prisoners or stolen ponies with them."

Nighthawk came back from disposing of the bodies in the woods. He pointed to the top of the bluff and said, "Umm."

"I didn't hear anything," Audie said. "Did you, Preacher?"

"Nope," the mountain man said. "I reckon everybody up there is dead —"

He stopped short as the sound of a muffled cry reached his ears.

"Doggone if you ain't right, Nighthawk," Preacher said. "Somebody *is* alive up there. Don't know who it could be, though. All six of the Gros Ventre are accounted for, and they only had six ponies."

"A prisoner could have been riding double with one of them," Audie pointed out.

Preacher nodded.

"That's sure enough true. Lorenzo, you and Nighthawk stay down here, and be ready for more trouble. Audie and me will go have a look."

"I'm not sure I can climb that bluff," Audie said.

"There's an easier place over yonder a ways," Preacher told him, pointing.

He led Audie to the spot where he had brought the ponies down from the bluff. They climbed to the top without any trouble and started back along the rim. Preacher heard several more muffled cries and steered toward them. They seemed to be coming from some thick brush, not far from where the Gros Ventre ponies had been tied.

"Somebody's in there, all right," Audie said. "You want me to take a look, Preacher?"

"Naw, I can do it."

"I'm smaller. I can get through that brush easier than you can."

Preacher couldn't argue with that. He said, "All right, but be careful. You don't know what you're gonna find in there. Might even be a bear."

"It doesn't sound like a bear to me," Audie said. He handed his rifle to Preacher and drew a pistol instead. The short gun would be much easier to use in that brush if Audie had to shoot.

Audie pushed some of the branches aside and disappeared through the small opening he had made. Preacher heard the crackling sounds as Audie moved through the brush. After a moment they stopped.

Preacher's nerves grew taut as he waited. Several more seconds went by, and then Audie said, "Preacher, you're going to want to look at this. Just push the brush aside, there's nothing to worry about."

Preacher trusted the little trapper with his life, so he did as Audie said. He set Audie's rifle on the ground, then used the barrel of his own flintlock to make a path for himself. It didn't take long to reach a tiny clearing surrounded by undergrowth.

Audie knelt there next to a shape Preacher couldn't quite make out in the darkness.

"Just a moment and I'll have this loose," Audie said, and Preacher got the sense that Audie wasn't talking to him. It was starting to look like the Gros Ventre had had a prisoner with them after all.

"There you are," Audie went on. "You should be able to breathe easier now that

that gag is gone. I'll cut these bonds on your hands and feet — Whoa!"

The startled exclamation made Preacher stiffen. He lifted his rifle and said, "Audie, are you all right?"

A woman's voice came out of the darkness, warning him, "Back away, white man, or I will cut this child's throat."

CHAPTER 6

"Madam, please," Audie protested croakingly, indicating that there was some pressure on his throat. "I'm not a child. And I give you my word that I didn't intend to touch you in such an indelicate fashion. I was simply trying to determine your circumstances."

"By pawing me all over?"

"It was too dark to see."

Preacher didn't know whether to chuckle or curse. He settled for saying, "Take it easy, ma'am. If you were a prisoner of that Gros Ventre raidin' party, then we're your friends. We're the ones who done for 'em."

After a moment's hesitation, the woman asked, "Are they all dead?"

"That's right," Preacher told her. "Six of 'em, and I'm pretty sure that was the whole bunch."

"It was," she said.

"Audie, I reckon the lady grabbed your

knife away from you as soon as you cut her
hands loose?"

"Yes, and I'll thank you not to tell Nighthawk about this. He'd never let me hear the
end of it."

The woman had been speaking English,
but the slight accent in her voice told
Preacher that it wasn't her native tongue.
He said, "Ma'am, you wouldn't happen to
be Assiniboine, would you? One of Bent
Leg's people?"

"You know Bent Leg?" she asked, sound-
ing surprised.

"For a good many years now," the mountain man said. "My name's Preacher."

"Preacher!" she repeated.

"That's right."

"I am sorry."

Audie said, "Ah, thank you for taking that
knife away from my throat, my dear. It was
getting a bit nerve-wracking having it there.
My Adam's apple was rather jumpy."

Preacher heard the woman moving. After
a moment, she said, "Here is your knife.
Are you sure you are not a child?"

"Quite certain," Audie told her. "And
again, I apologize for any inadvertent impro-
prieties."

"Someone help me up."

The gal was good about giving orders,

Preacher thought. But he stepped forward and extended a hand.

"Here," he said.

A second later he felt her fumbling in the darkness for his hand. He wrapped his fingers around her wrist and lifted her effortlessly to her feet. That brought her closer to him, and even in this bad light he could make out the shape of her face and the long wings of dark hair that framed it.

"Thank you," she murmured. She let go of his hand and tried to take a step, but her balance deserted her and she leaned toward him suddenly. Preacher slipped his arm around her waist to steady her.

That brought her even closer to him. He smelled the bear grease on her hair and the slighty musky but pleasant scent of her skin. Her waist was trim and warm where his arm encircled it.

"You've been tied up for a while, haven't you?" he asked. "Your legs don't want to work right just yet."

"I'm fine," she insisted. "You can let go of me now."

"Are you sure?"

"I am certain."

Preacher took his arm away and stepped back. The woman seemed to be steady on her feet now.

"We have a camp down below," he told her. "You can get some hot food in you and then tell us what happened to you."

"What will you do with me?" she asked, and he heard worry and suspicion in her voice.

"Why, we'll return you to your home as soon as it gets light tomorrow, dear lady," Audie said. "Isn't that right, Preacher?"

"Yep," the mountain man said. "We'll take you back to Bent Leg's village."

"Thank you," she said again, but Preacher couldn't tell if she completely believed them. She would have to see it for herself.

"Come," he said. "There's a path over yonder where we can get down the bluff."

He led the way, holding the branches aside so the Assiniboine woman could get through the brush easier. Stepping to the edge of the bluff, he called to Nighthawk and Lorenzo, "We're comin' down. We found a prisoner up here."

A few minutes later, the three of them walked into camp. Nighthawk had built up the fire so the flames cast a large circle of light. When the woman stepped into that reddish-gold glow, Preacher got his first good look at her.

She was a sight worth waiting for.

She was medium height and well-shaped

in the buckskin dress she wore, with wide hips, muscular calves, and high, firm breasts. Her face was slightly rounded. Long hair the color of midnight surrounded it and flowed down over her shoulders. Her cheekbones weren't quite as high as those of most Indian woman, and her skin was a slightly lighter shade of copper. Those were indications that she had some white blood in her, and her dark blue eyes confirmed that. Probably her father or grandfather had been white, either an American or a French-Canadian fur trapper, more than likely.

And she was as downright pretty a woman as Preacher had seen in a long time.

As they all stood by the fire, Preacher told her, "You already know who I am. This is Audie, Lorenzo, and Nighthawk." He nodded to each of the men in turn.

"I am called Raven's Wing, or simply Raven," the woman said. Preacher figured she'd been named for the color of her hair. "Thank you for helping me. It might have taken me a long time to get free if you had not found me."

"Nighthawk, you reckon you can rustle up some grub for Raven?" Preacher asked.

"Umm," the Crow replied. He went to their supplies and set to work.

"Did the Gros Ventre capture you when

they raided your village?" Audie asked.

Raven nodded.

"Yes. I was the only captive they managed to get away with. Even though they took us by surprise, our warriors were able to make them flee. They didn't even get any of our ponies."

"Just one woman," Preacher said.

Raven looked at him with a challenging expression in her dark eyes.

"Yes," she agreed. "Just one woman."

"And when they smelled our smoke and decided to have a look, they tied and gagged you and stashed you in that brush?"

"Yes. They warned me that if I tried to escape, they would come back and cut my throat." With a look of savage satisfaction, she added, "Now they are the ones who are dead."

"You have Preacher to thank for that," Audie said. "He did for five of them."

Preacher said, "Yeah, but I wouldn't have had the chance to do that if you hadn't shot that varmint who was about to brain me with a tomahawk."

"Nighthawk and me helped keep 'em busy," Lorenzo put in.

Preacher nodded.

"You sure did," he said, then asked Raven's Wing, "How come you didn't make any noise when I first came up there lookin' for their ponies?"

"I did not know who you were," she explained. "You might have been someone even worse than the Gros Ventre. I thought I could get loose on my own after you left." She shrugged. "But then I tried and realized I was tied too tightly. If no one found me and freed me, I might have died of thirst. So I started making noise in hopes that you would return." She smiled. "And you did, along with this little one . . . and his hands."

Audie said hastily, "I told you, Miss Raven's Wing, how sorry I am that I —"

"I think she's joshin' you now, Audie," Preacher drawled. "She's got a mischievous look about her."

"That is right," Raven admitted. "I know you were just trying to help me. I thank you for that."

"Oh, well, uh, you're welcome," Audie said. For once he wasn't as glib as he normally was.

Nighthawk fried some salt jowl and heated a couple of biscuits left over from their supper. When he gave Raven the food, she knelt beside the fire and ate hungrily, washing down the food with water from Preacher's canteen.

"Why are you men in the valley of the

Assiniboine?" she asked when she had finished licking the last of the grease from the salt jowl off her fingers.

"We came to see if Bent Leg would be willin' to let us spend the winter with you folks," Preacher said. "I know he's let trappers do that before."

Raven looked at him with increased interest.

"You have never wintered with the Assiniboine before. I would remember if you had." She glanced around at the other men. "That is true for all of you."

"This is my first winter out here," Lorenzo said, "so I ain't never stayed with any of the tribes."

"And Nighthawk and I have spent most winters with his people, the Crow," Audie said.

"Why do you not go to the Crow this winter?" Raven asked.

Audie shrugged.

"A man likes to do something different now and again."

Raven snorted and said, "I know what men want different. You want a different squaw to share your blankets every year."

She wasn't that far wrong, Preacher thought, but he said, "We're just lookin' for a place to get out of the weather. The first

68

snows will fly in a week or two."

"This is true," Raven admitted. "My people's village is less than half a day's ride from here. You can present your request to Bent Leg and see what he says. If he refuses, you will still have time to look elsewhere."

"Fair enough," Preacher said. He hunkered on his heels and picked up the coffeepot to pour a little in his cup. "If you don't mind my askin', where'd you learn to speak English? You seem to savvy it pretty good."

"My father was a trapper who came up the Missouri River to Fort Lisa," she explained, naming the outpost that the first American fur trappers had founded. "He remained in the mountains for the rest of his life. He married my mother and taught me the white man's tongue."

"What was his name?" Preacher asked. "I've been out here for a good many years myself. Maybe I ran into him at a rendezvous or somethin' like that."

"His name was George Harris."

Preacher grinned.

"Ol' Georgie? Shoot, yeah. I never knew him well, but we shook and howdied a few times." He grew more solemn. "You say he's crossed the divide?"

"Two years ago," Raven said with a nod.

"A fever took him."

"Well, I'm right sorry to hear that. He was a good man, and I never heard anybody say any different."

"Thank you."

"He did a good job teachin' you white man's lingo, too."

"Yes, indeed," Audie agreed. "Have you ever given any thought to going East to attend a real school, Raven?"

She gave him a look like he had gone mad.

"Everything I need is in these mountains," she said.

"But with an actual education, you could —"

Preacher silenced Audie with an outstretched hand. He had heard something in the trees. He knew better than to think it was the Gros Ventre raiders come back to life. Noises meant flesh and blood. He reached for his rifle.

As Preacher touched the weapon, a man stepped out of the trees holding a bow and arrow. The bowstring was drawn back tautly, and all it would take to send the arrow driving deep into Preacher's body was the slightest motion of the man's fingers.

CHAPTER 7

Raven's Wing spoke sharply in Assiniboine. Preacher was fairly fluent in the language, so he had no trouble translating the words.

"Two Bears, no! These strangers are friends. They rescued me from Snake Heart's men!"

The bow and arrow didn't budge a fraction of an inch in the warrior's hands. Preacher didn't make any threatening moves. He told his companions, "Better stay still as you can be, fellas. I'd bet this ol' hat of mine there are more of 'em in the trees, just waitin' to turn us into pincushions."

The warrior Raven had called Two Bears was a big, husky man with a couple of feathers in his slicked-down black hair. From the looks of the way he was glaring at Preacher, he had taken a dislike to the mountain man right off.

"Two Bears," Raven said, still speaking Assiniboine, "the raiders are all dead. This man killed five of them by himself. He is the one called Preacher."

Two Bears' eyes narrowed.

"Preacher?" he repeated in a guttural voice.

"That's right," Preacher said, also speaking the Assiniboine tongue. "It's been a while since I've visited Bent Leg, Two Bears, but you ought to remember me. And this is Audie and Nighthawk, you ought to know them."

"The Little Man," Two Bears said as he looked at Audie.

"I know you mean no insult by that," Audie said, also in Assiniboine.

"Could somebody maybe tell me what's goin' on?" Lorenzo asked in English. "Are we all gonna die?"

"Eventually," Preacher said dryly, "but I got a hunch it ain't gonna be tonight."

Two Bears slowly lowered his bow and let the tension off the string. He made a curt motion, and one by one, nearly a dozen more Assiniboine warriors stepped out of the trees. Their bows were still raised and ready to launch their arrows.

"Lord have mercy," Lorenzo muttered. "We was in a fix, all right."

"Still might be," Preacher told him. "Stay calm and follow my lead."

"Easier said than done when you start jabberin' in that redskin talk and I don't have no earthly idea what you're sayin'."

"Stay where you are," Preacher said. He stood up and moved deliberately toward Two Bears, keeping his hands in front of him so it was obvious they were empty. He confronted Two Bears and went on, "I have always been friends with the Assiniboine. And the Gros Ventre and their cousins the Blackfeet are my enemies. The people who live in the mountains know that."

Two Bears nodded.

"This is a thing that is known."

"You probably already found the bodies of the three Gros Ventre raiders in the trees. There are three more atop the bluff. They attacked us, and we killed them. Then we found the one called Raven's Wing, who was their prisoner."

"He speaks the truth, Two Bears," Raven said.

"Then the people of Bent Leg owe you a debt," Two Bears said, "for saving one of our fairest maidens."

Preacher couldn't argue with that assessment of Raven's beauty. Instead he held out his hand and said, "The friendship of Two Bears and the rest of the Assiniboine is ample payment of that debt."

Two Bears hesitated, but only for a second. He gripped Preacher's hand, then ordered the other warriors to lower their weapons.

"Should I be heavin' a sigh of relief about now, Preacher?" Lorenzo asked.

"I reckon you could do that," the mountain man said. "We're all friends now."

"Thank the Lord for that. I was about to mess my drawers when all them Injuns stepped outta the woods like that."

The Assiniboine warriors hunkered near the fire, except for a couple who moved off into the trees at Two Bears' command. Preacher knew they would stand watch, although it was unlikely there were any more enemies in this valley who would attack such a large group.

Two Bears himself sat close to Raven's Wing, and Preacher sensed the possessiveness in the man. He didn't exactly act like Raven was his wife, but he had it in mind that she might be one of these days, thought Preacher.

"After the Gros Ventre raided your village, you pursued them?" he asked.

Two Bears nodded solemnly.

"At first Bent Leg said we would not give chase, since they stole no ponies, but I persuaded him that we should pursue them anyway."

"To rescue Raven's Wing, you mean."

"Yes. She is his niece, and he did not think it was right to risk the lives of his warriors for one prisoner, even though he is her uncle."

Preacher understood. As chief, Bent Leg's first responsibility was to the entire band, and he couldn't be seen to be playing favorites because one of his relatives was in danger.

"But you changed his mind."

"I had no choice. Raven's Wing could not live her life as a slave to the filthy Gros Ventre."

Yeah, he was definitely sweet on her, Preacher thought. Well, there was nothing wrong with that. He wouldn't have wanted to let the raiders get away with Raven, either.

"In the morning, we will return to the village," Two Bears went on. "The people will celebrate that Raven's Wing is safe. And there will be a feast of thanks for Preacher and his friends."

"Preacher wishes to spend the winter in our village," Raven said.

Two Bears frowned a little at that, but he said, "That will be for Bent Leg to decide."

After the events of the evening, everyone

75

was tired. Preacher, Audie, Nighthawk, and Lorenzo rolled up in their blankets to sleep. They didn't have to worry about standing guard tonight. The Assiniboine would take care of that.

"They ain't gonna murder us in our sleep, are they, Preacher?" Lorenzo asked quietly from his bedroll before Preacher dozed off.

"Not likely," Preacher replied. "If they wanted us dead, they could've done it before now. Some folks think that Indians are tricky, but they really ain't, leastways when it comes to killin'. They're pretty straightforward about that."

"Oh, well, I'll sleep really good now," Lorenzo said.

Preacher tilted his hat down over his eyes. "I intend to."

And he would have, too, except for some reason he kept thinking about Raven's Wing.

The lodges of the Assiniboine village were built along the banks of a creek that flowed through the valley. When winter clamped its frigid grip on the land, the stream would freeze over and the people of the village would have to chop down through the ice to get water and fish. But it would help sustain them through the long, gray, cold months.

Right now, even though the air was chilly, there was no snow on the ground, and all the evidence of the ice storm several days earlier had melted and vanished. The creek still bubbled along, making its merry music. Winter was almost close enough to reach out and touch, but it wasn't here yet.

Two Bears was right about the celebration. Happy cries went up from the people of the village when the group rode in the next day and they saw Raven's Wing on the back of Two Bears' pony, riding in front of him. Women and children pressed around the riders, reaching out to touch her as if they couldn't believe she had been returned safely to their midst, and dogs barked and added to the commotion. The warriors who hadn't been part of the rescue party stood to the side, arms crossed, nodding in grave satisfaction that the mission had been successful.

There were plenty of curious looks cast toward Preacher and his companions, too, but since they had ridden in with Two Bears and the other warriors, the rest of the band was inclined to give them the benefit of the doubt and assume they were friendly.

The crowd around Two Bears' pony parted so that Bent Leg could limp through the opening. The old chief embraced

Raven's Wing as she slid from the pony's back to the ground.

"The one who is like a daughter to me has returned," Bent Leg announced. That wasn't really necessary, since everybody could see her with their own eyes, but important occasions such as this demanded a certain formality. When Two Bears had dismounted, Bent Leg gripped his hand.

Then the chief turned toward the new-comers, who had swung down from their saddles, and said loudly, "Preacher!" He threw his arms around the mountain man and pounded him on the back.

Preacher returned the enthusiastic greeting.

"It is good to see Bent Leg again," he said.

"Many winters have passed since last you visited. We have each of us grown old since then."

"Maybe I have," Preacher said with a grin. "You still look the same as you always did, Bent Leg."

"You lie like a white man." Bent Leg threw back his head and laughed. He turned to Audie and said, "Little Man, another of my old friends. The village of Bent Leg is truly blessed today to have such visitors."

He bent to embrace Audie with another round of back-slapping. Bent Leg's greeting for Nighthawk was more reserved. The Crow and the Assiniboine were not enemies, but they were not the same, either. The tribal differences were minor, though.

Bent Leg turned back to Preacher.

"Did Two Bears and the others find you when they sought Raven's Wing?"

"They did," Preacher said.

Raven spoke up, saying, "It was Preacher and his friends who rescued me from the Gros Ventre."

Bent Leg looked surprised, and Two Bears scowled a little. He had planned to save Raven's Wing, but circumstances hadn't worked out that way.

"We owe you a great debt, my old friend," Bent Leg said to Preacher.

"It's already paid," Preacher told him. "But there is a great courtesy you could do for me and my friends, if you would."

"Speak it, and it shall be done," Bent Leg assured him.

"We're lookin' for a place to spend the winter, and we can't think of anywhere we'd rather do that than right here with the Assiniboine."

Bent Leg nodded.

"So shall it be. You will be our honored guests until the spring comes."

"Thank you, old friend."

"There are widows in the village whose husbands had no brothers," Bent Leg said with a twinkle in his eye. "And some unmarried women as well."

There wasn't much pretense to these people. They had their societal rules, of course, and Preacher respected them. But they didn't go out of their way to repress folks' natural instincts and appetites, like most of the so-called civilized societies did. Preacher had always found their honesty refreshing.

Right now, though, he was more interested in having a place to wait out the winter than he was in finding a woman to warm his blankets during those cold months. That would come in time, in the due course of events.

"We will see," he told Bent Leg, who nodded gravely.

"Well, what's the verdict?" Lorenzo asked in English. "They gonna let us stay?"

"Yep," Preacher said. "For the next six months or so, Lorenzo, this is gonna be home, sweet home for us."

CHAPTER 8

More than a week had passed since the trouble at Blind Pete's Place. During that time, an ice storm had forced the five men to hole up for a couple of miserable days, but then they had been able to ride on, heading north toward the Canadian border.

Willie Deaver was pretty sure they had passed the border by now and were actually in Canada. The men they were supposed to meet ought to be waiting for them somewhere close by.

Unless St. John and his people had grown impatient and left. Deaver wasn't going to be happy if that happened.

So it was with a sense of relief that he spotted a thread of smoke curling into the sky up ahead as he and his men rode along a twisting hogback ridge. That was the signal he'd been looking for during the past two days.

Deaver pointed out the smoke to Caleb

Manning and said, "That's got to be them."

"Or else it's comin' from some fur trapper's cabin," Manning said.

Deaver shrugged.

"We'll be able to tell when we get there."

They followed the smoke and soon descended from the ridge, entering a small valley where a cold wind whipped down from the north. Deaver led the way with Manning riding behind him.

Bringing up the rear were Cy Plunkett, Darwin Heath, and Fred Jordan. Plunkett was a rotund little Englishman who was much tougher than he looked. Heath was thin and dark, with a narrow face deeply pocked by the childhood illness that had almost killed him. Jordan was a big, blond man who was always grinning, no matter what sort of terrible thing he was doing at the time.

All five men had come West several years earlier to make their fortunes as fur trappers. Like plenty of others, they had discovered pretty quickly that the only people getting rich off the fur business were the traders and the business owners back East who made hats and coats from those furs. The trappers, the men who carried out the hard, dangerous jobs and did the actual work that made the whole industry possible, always got paid the least.

The five of them, who hadn't known each other starting out, gradually had drifted together and decided that they would be better off taking the spoils of somebody else's labor rather than grubbing for themselves.

Since then they had robbed and killed parties of trappers smaller than themselves, raided a couple of wagon trains, and looted a few trading posts. They had cleaned out all the money and gold in Blind Pete's Place before setting it on fire.

But that had been an opportunity that presented itself, so Deaver and the others had taken it. They had other plans that would allow them to leave their hand-to-mouth existence behind. They were going to be rich men.

Of course, some people would have to die in order for that to happen, but Deaver didn't care about that.

Plunkett, being an Englishman, was the one who'd put them in contact with Odell St. John, a fellow Britisher, during one of the gang's periodic trips back to St. Louis. Deaver wasn't sure exactly what St. John's game was — maybe he was just out to make some fast money, or maybe he was working for the British government — but again,

Deaver didn't care. The payoff was all that mattered.

Deaver and his men rode through a thick stand of trees, and when they emerged from the woods they saw a camp beside a small stream. Half a dozen tents were pitched not far from the creek, and the smoke rose from a little crackling fire nearby. Some saddle mounts were penned in a rope corral, along with several large, heavily-built pack animals. A number of crates were stacked on the ground beside the tents and covered with a large piece of canvas. The ends of the crates peeked out so that Deaver could tell what they were.

Most of the men in the camp wore buckskins or homespun work shirts and corduroy trousers, like Deaver and his companions. One individual, though, stood out from the others. He wore a dark suit, including a swallowtail coat, high-topped black boots, a white shirt, and a cravat. He was bareheaded as he strode forward to meet Deaver. The wind ruffled his brown hair, which matched his close-cropped beard.

"Mr. Deaver!" the man said. "How utterly splendid to see you again!"

Deaver grunted and said, "Yeah." Cy Plunkett sounded like an Englishman and that had never bothered Deaver. Something about Odell St. John's oily accent rubbed him the wrong way, though.

"You're late."

Deaver motioned for his men to dismount. He swung down from the saddle before saying, "Ice storm caught us a few days ago. It wasn't safe to travel until the ice melted off."

"I understand. We've had a bit of inclement weather up here as well. I told the men that was probably what delayed you." St. John rubbed his hands together. "But you're here now, eh, and ready to do business?"

"That's right. *If* we're satisfied with the quality of the goods you brought with you."

"Oh, you will be," Deaver promised. "There'll be plenty of time for you to examine the merchandise. First, though, how about a drink?"

"That sounds mighty good to me," Manning put in. "It's been a long, thirsty ride."

Deaver frowned. The ride hadn't been all that thirsty. They had taken several jugs of whiskey from Blind Pete's, too.

He didn't like Manning butting in like that, either. *He* made the important decisions in this bunch, by God!

But the men were all licking their lips, and Deaver was a canny enough leader to know that he might be facing a mutiny if he told them to forget about the whiskey. And Caleb Manning was a good man to have on your side, second in viciousness only to Deaver himself, so he'd cut Manning some slack . . . this time.

St. John was looking at him, one dark eyebrow arched quizzically. Deaver jerked his head in a curt nod and said, "Sure. A drink will be fine."

"Excellent!" St. John turned and called to one of the other men, "Brutus, bring the jug!"

They all gathered around the fire to pass the jug from man to man. St. John counted and then said, "I see there are thirteen of us here, all told. A somewhat less righteous band of apostles than the original, eh?"

Deaver took the jug from Manning, tilted it to his mouth, and downed a slug of the fiery corn liquor. He passed it along to Plunkett and wiped the back of his left hand across his mouth.

"I don't know about callin' us apostles," he said. "They weren't rich, from what I remember of my ma readin' to me from the Good Book a long, long time ago, and I intend to be a rich man."

"The prospect of passing a camel through the eye of a needle doesn't trouble you, eh?"

"Not one damn bit," Deaver said, "and it probably wouldn't even if I knew what in blazes you were talking about."

That brought a laugh from St. John. The jug went around the circle again, and then the Englishman said, "Very well, down to business."

He led the way to the stack of crates and threw back the canvas so that one of the long wooden boxes was revealed. With a snap of his fingers and a sharp "Brutus!", St. John had the man who was evidently his lieutenant use a heavy-bladed knife to pry up the lid nailed onto the crate.

A number of long, oilcloth-wrapped shapes lay in the box. Brutus picked up one of them and unwrapped it, revealing a long-barreled flintlock rifle. All the brasswork on the weapon gleamed with newness.

St. John took the rifle from Brutus and passed it to Deaver, saying, "The finest rifle of its kind to be found anywhere in the world, my friend. Direct from the factory in England to this backwoods Eden."

Deaver examined the flintlock closely. Its mechanism appeared to be in perfect working order. It might have never been fired.

"How'd you get your hands on 'em?" he asked.

"I don't believe that information was included in our arrangement." St. John gave an eloquent shrug. "However, I don't mind saying that there are always means by which to make certain a shipment of goods goes astray and never arrives at its intended destination. In this case, that destination would be a British army garrison in Ontario. A little bribery, the judicious use of blackmail . . . arrangements can be made, you understand."

"Sure," Deaver said with a nod. He handed the rifle to Manning. "What do you think, Caleb?"

Manning looked the flintlock over.

"Mighty fine weapon," he declared. "Does it shoot true?"

"See for yourself," St. John invited. "You're welcome to load and fire it."

Manning looked at Deaver, who thought about it for a second and then nodded. Manning used his own powderhorn and a ball from his shot pouch to charge the rifle.

When it was ready to fire, Manning lifted it to his shoulder. He hesitated, then swung the barrel around swiftly until it was lined on St. John's chest.

"How about I see just how well it works on a real target?" he asked with a savage grin.

Odell St. John didn't seem worried.

"If you did, you'd be dead a split-second later yourself," he said coolly. "Brutus is standing behind you with an axe in his hands. It would be interesting to see how far your head flies after he cleaves it off your shoulders."

"Stop it, you crazy bastards," Deaver grated angrily. "Caleb, point that thing somewhere else. St. John, tell your man to back off."

St. John made a languid motion as Manning lowered the flintlock.

"Sorry," Manning muttered. "I didn't mean nothin' by it. I was just havin' some sport."

"Give me that," Deaver snapped. He took the rifle out of Manning's hands, turned, and aimed at a tree branch on the other side of the creek. The tree was a good fifty yards from him. He drew in a breath, held it, and squeezed the trigger.

The rifle boomed, and the branch at which Deaver had aimed went flying, cut off cleanly. Deaver squinted as the powder-smoke stung his eyes a little.

He gave the rifle back to St. John and said, "It shoots true, all right. And the rest are all the same?"

"One hundred rifles, brand-new, just as we agreed six months ago in St. Louis," the Englishman said. "And here's the really intriguing bit . . . I can lay my hands on more of them, if you like. As many as you want."

That offer convinced Deaver more than ever that St. John was lying about stealing those rifles. The man was working for the British government. The English had been carrying a real grudge ever since ol' George Washington and his friends had booted them out more than fifty years earlier.

They had raised hell in the former colonies on numerous occasions since then, sometimes openly, like back in 1812, but often in secret. More than once they had tried to disrupt the fur trapping business and make things hot enough on the frontier that the Americans would pull back.

Deaver figured this was just more of the same. St. John had to know these guns would wind up in the hands of the Indians. That was exactly what the Englishman wanted.

"Well," St. John went on, "do we have a deal?"

"I want to take a look at every gun," Deaver said. "You've got powder and shot, too?"

St. John looked a little annoyed, but he forced a smile onto his face and nodded.

"Of course. And you're welcome to examine the merchandise. Actually, I've thrown in some extras: two dozen jugs of whiskey for our coppery-hued friends."

Deaver couldn't help but chuckle when he thought about how much havoc a bunch of liquored-up redskins with brand-new rifles could wreak. There wouldn't be a fur trapper between here and halfway to Bent's Fort who was safe. It could turn into a bloodbath, all right.

But it would put plenty of money in his pockets, or at least it would once he sold all the furs that the Indians would trade him for these guns.

"If everything is the way you say it is, St. John, then yeah, you've got a deal."

The Englishman grinned at him, took the open jug away from one of the other men, and lifted it.

"Then here's to a long and prosperous partnership, my friend!"

CHAPTER 9

The first few days in the village of the Assiniboine passed pleasantly for Preacher and his companions. Bent Leg gave them an empty lodge to use, although it was understood that the men would probably wind up spending the winter with some of the unattached female members of the band in their lodges.

Preacher was in no hurry to do that, although Lorenzo soon made the acquaintance of a plump, middle-aged widow and began talking about moving in with her.

"Of course, I don't understand a word the gal is sayin', but she's right friendly and I figure we can get to where we communicate all right in other ways, if you know what I mean. And I think you do," Lorenzo said. "Besides, a fine figure of a woman like that is bound to be a good cook, and Lord knows she could keep a man from freezin' to death on them cold, cold nights."

"What's her name?" Preacher asked dryly as they sat beside the fire in the lodge they were sharing for the moment.

"Name?" Lorenzo repeated. "I don't know her name, exactly. I've taken to callin' her Honey Gal, and she seems to answer to it all right."

"You seem to have everything settled," Audie said. "I'm glad for you, my friend."

"What about you?" Lorenzo asked. "I've noticed that several of these ladies been flockin' around you since we been here."

"Audie's got a reputation," Preacher drawled. "Reckon those gals are curious if it's true."

"Reputation? What sorta reputation?"

"Well, you know how they call him Little Man?"

Lorenzo nodded.

"Yeah?"

"Let's just say that in one particular respect that name don't fit him at all."

"I don't quite get what you're — Wait just a doggone minute. Are you sayin' that . . . well, that he . . . I mean . . ."

Audie smiled across the fire and said, "The word you're looking for is prodigious."

Lorenzo held his hands up quickly.

"No, sirree, I ain't lookin' for nothin', and you can be mighty sure about *that!*"

The corners of Nighthawk's mouth moved about an eighth of an inch, Preacher noted. That was as close as the Crow ever came to a grin.

The next day, Lorenzo moved in with the widow he called Honey Gal. Audie, being fluent in the Assiniboine tongue, didn't have to guess the name of the woman he chose to warm his blankets for the winter. She was called Wildflower, and she was pretty enough to deserve the name. Nighthawk paired up with a widow named Otter's Pelt who was just about as quiet as he was. If they didn't go loco from the silence, they would probably have a pretty good winter together, Preacher thought.

That left him alone in the lodge Bent Leg had given them, except for Dog.

He had seen Raven's Wing around the village a few times since they'd been here, but he hadn't spoken to her. Sometimes the warrior Two Bears was with her, and sometimes she was with the other women. The mountain man was surprised but pleased when the deerhide flap over the lodge's entrance was pulled back and he looked up to see Raven standing there.

"Preacher," she greeted him. "You are well?"

He got to his feet and nodded.

"Yes'm, I reckon I'm fine. How about you?"

"It has been good to be back, after being captured by Snake Heart's warriors."

Preacher frowned slightly.

"I've heard mention of this fella Snake Heart. Gros Ventre war chief, ain't he?"

"That's right. He has risen to power among them in recent years by leading successful raids against the Assiniboine and other tribes. His war parties have captured many horses, many prisoners. And he has killed many of his enemies. Some say he would rather kill than capture."

"But he didn't come along on this latest raid."

Raven shook her head.

"No. And for that I count myself lucky. You might not have prevailed against him, Preacher."

"I'll take my chances," Preacher said.

"But in this case, it would have been my life you were wagering with, as well as your own," she pointed out.

"Yeah, you got a point there," he admitted. He gestured toward the bearskin robe spread on the ground. "You want to sit for a spell?"

She thought it over, but not for long. She sank gracefully onto the robe with her legs tucked under her. Preacher sat cross-legged nearby, close but not improperly so. Dog lay on the other side of the lodge, his chin resting on his paws as he watched them.

"You have not found a woman with whom to spend the winter," Raven said.

"Not yet. But I ain't been in any big hurry."

"Your friends have all moved in with others."

"Yep. I'm glad for 'em. But that's them, not me."

Raven smiled.

"You do not want a woman?"

"I never said that." Preacher tried to steer the conversation in another direction. "How's ol' Two Bears doin'?"

She frowned.

"Why would you ask me?"

"Well, I've seen the two of you spendin' time together, and I figured —"

"Perhaps you figured incorrectly," Raven said.

"Maybe so."

"Two Bears is my friend, and as far as I know he is well. I have not spoken to him for several days."

Preacher nodded slowly.

"All right. I got the feelin' from the way he acted that it was more than that. He was the one who persuaded Chief Bent Leg to send men after you when the Gros Ventre carried you off."

"And I am grateful for that," Raven said. "But as for it being anything more . . . I cannot control what is in Two Bears' heart, any more than I can control what is in . . . mine."

She gave him a frank look, and it would have been pretty hard not to see what she meant by it. Preacher saw, all right, and under different circumstances he probably would have welcomed it.

It was true that he was considerably older than her, but she was a woman full-growed and perfectly capable of making her own decisions. She was smart and pretty and would be a pleasure to spend time with, in more ways than one.

But if he moved into her lodge, or if she moved into this one with him, there might be trouble with Two Bears. Whether it was true or not, the warrior thought he had staked a claim, and he wouldn't appreciate some other fella moving in on it.

Preacher wanted to spend the whole winter here with Bent Leg's people, and that wouldn't be easy if one of the band's leading warriors had a grudge against him.

"Raven, I appreciate that," he told her,

"but I ain't so sure it'd be a good idea."

"You do not find me comely?"

Dang it, he'd insulted her, he thought. He had worried about that, too.

"You know good and well I do. Any man'd have to be plumb blind and a tarnal idjit on top of it not to find you comely, Raven's Wing. But I came to your village to spend a nice peaceful winter, not to have a fight on my hands."

"You are afraid of Two Bears?"

"Not hardly," Preacher answered honestly. He wasn't really afraid of any man. "But I respect him," he went on, which was also the truth. "I don't want to have trouble with him, and I don't want your uncle havin' to deal with problems like that."

"What about what I want? What about what you want in your heart?"

"It ain't just me I've got to consider," he tried to explain to her. "If I had to leave this village, then my friends would probably have to go, too. They're happy here. I don't have any right to ruin that for them."

"I thought you had more courage," she said, giving him a scornful look.

He shrugged.

"You can think whatever you want. I still got to do what I believe is best."

Raven got to her feet. Preacher followed suit.

"I am sorry you feel the way you do."

"Believe me, Raven's Wing," he said, "you ain't any sorrier about it than I am."

Saying that was a mistake, he saw as soon as the words were out of his mouth. They gave her hope that she could still change his mind. He could tell by the way her eyes lit up, even though she was still a mite angry with him.

He was going to say something else to try to disabuse her of the notion, but before he could, she moved with swift grace to push the entrance flap aside and step out of the lodge. Preacher stepped out of the dwelling as well and watched her walk away.

She didn't look back.

Feeling eyes on him, he glanced to his right. Two Bears stood about fifty feet away.

There was no way the warrior could have missed Raven's Wing leaving Preacher's lodge. Judging by the scowl on Two Bears' face, he had jumped to the wrong conclusion.

Preacher muttered a curse. It wouldn't do any good to go over there and try to explain things to Two Bears. If he did, likely it would just make things worse. Maybe when Preacher and Raven's Wing didn't move in together for the winter, Two Bears would figure out that he was wrong about things.

Preacher hoped so, anyway.

The next day the sky was overcast, the sort of gunmetal-gray sky that presaged a winter storm. The snow was probably still a few days away, but it was out there and it would arrive relatively soon. Preacher was resigned now to spending a chilly winter by himself. If he invited another woman to share his blankets after refusing Raven's Wing, she would just be more insulted.

He sat cross-legged outside the lodge with Lorenzo, Audie, and Nighthawk.

"I was thinkin' that we might ought to go huntin' tomorrow or the next day," Preacher said. "Probably be a good idea to lay in a supply of fresh meat before the storm blows in. We're liable to be stuck here for a while."

"All the ice from that other storm melted off pretty quick," Lorenzo pointed out.

Preacher shook his head.

"The storm that's comin' won't be like that. This'll be snow, not ice, and it's liable to dump a couple of feet on us. It'll take a good while for it to melt off, too."

"Of course, we can still get around even after it snows," Audie put in, "but it'll be more difficult. If we have plenty of food, though, we won't need to. We can just hole ter."

"Bein' stuck inside with Honey Gal for a week or so don't sound so bad," Lorenzo said. "I reckon we could find plenty o' ways to pass the time."

Audie smiled.

"Yes, there's nothing like cold weather to bring out the friskiness in a woman."

"Umm," Nighthawk said.

"I reckon that means the three of y'all are gettin' along all right with your gals?" Preacher said.

"Fine and dandy," Lorenzo replied. "I'm even startin' to pick up some of the lingo. For instance, I know how to say —"

What Lorenzo had learned how to say went unspoken as a commotion erupted on the other side of the village. Preacher looked up as he heard the sound of excited voices.

"We'd better find out what that's all about," he suggested as he got to his feet.

The four men walked across the village to find Chief Bent Leg, Two Bears, and a number of the other warriors gathered around a young man. The youngster's face was bloody from a cut on his forehead. He was in obvious pain as he talked in a halting voice.

"What's goin' on?" Lorenzo asked quietly

101

as he leaned close to Preacher.

"More trouble," the mountain man replied. "The Gros Ventre are back."

CHAPTER 10

Preacher kept up a low-voiced, running translation for Lorenzo's benefit.

"That young fella and some of his friends had the same idea we did. They went out huntin' to lay in a supply of fresh meat. But while they were over toward the western side of the valley, some Gros Ventre jumped them. They killed a couple of the Assiniboine boys and captured the rest. This younker is the only one who got away, and he got walloped in the head by a glancin' blow from a tomahawk before he could manage to."

"What are they gonna do with the prisoners?" Lorenzo asked. "Makes slaves out of 'em?"

"They make slaves out of women and kids," Preacher replied grimly. "The warriors they captured today may be young, but they're old enough to provide some entertainment for the rest of the band once the Gros Ventre get back with 'em."

Lorenzo's eyes widened as he said, "You mean they're gonna *torture* 'em?"

Preacher shook his head.

"The Gros Ventre ain't big on torture. Not like, say, the Comanch' down in Texas. But they're cousins to the Blackfeet, so they got plenty of meanness in 'em. Likely they'll kill those prisoners by burnin' 'em at the stake, just like the Blackfeet planned to do to me once."

"You was gonna be burned at the stake?"

Audie said, "I'll tell you the story sometime, Lorenzo, if Preacher doesn't want to. Right now, though, there are more pressing concerns."

"That's right," Preacher said. "I reckon Bent Leg will send some of his warriors after those varmints to try to rescue the boys who got grabbed, and I think we ought to go with 'em."

"Volunteer to help, you mean?" Lorenzo asked.

"They're lettin' us spend the winter with them. That makes us part of the band as long as we're here, to my way of thinkin'."

"I ain't disagreein' with you," Lorenzo said. "I was just makin' sure what was goin' on, that's all."

Preacher looked over at him.

"Might be a good idea for you to stay here. We'll be movin' fast."

"And you think I'm too old to keep up, is that it?" Lorenzo asked, puffing up a little in anger. "Think I'm just some feeble ol' codger who can't take care of hisself in a fight? Hell's fire, Preacher, you oughta know better'n that!"

"That ain't what I said at all," Preacher replied . . . although the sentiments expressed by Lorenzo were exactly what he had been thinking. "I just figured it'd be a good idea for one of us to stay here and keep an eye on things in the village. This whole thing could be a trick. If there's one bunch of Gros Ventre raiders in the valley, there could be another."

"A trick, eh?" Lorenzo repeated. "Like the first bunch wanted to lure most of the warriors away from the village, and then the second bunch could swoop in and raid the place?"

"Exactly," Preacher said. He didn't really believe that was the case, but now that Lorenzo had put it into words, it was sort of a worrisome possibility, Preacher thought.

"Well, then, I reckon I can stay here to help out if I'm needed."

Preacher clapped a hand on Lorenzo's shoulders.

"Good. That's a load off my mind."

Now that the wounded young man had told his story, the warriors were already making plans to go after the raiders. Two Bears seemed to be taking charge. Even though Bent Leg was the chief of the band, in times of trouble a younger man could assume command as a war chief. Obviously that was Two Bears' role.

Followed by Audie and Nighthawk, Preacher approached Two Bears and said in the Assiniboine tongue, "The three of us are coming with you."

Two Bears scowled at the mountain man. "No one asked you to accompany us."

"No one has to ask," Preacher said. "For as long as we are here with your people, our hearts are Assiniboine."

"No white man's heart can be Assiniboine," Two Bears snapped. He looked at Nighthawk. "Nor any Crow's."

"Wait," Bent Leg said. "You would turn down the help of a true warrior such as Preacher? Little Man and the Crow are respected fighters as well."

"They are not of our people!" Two Bears insisted.

"A wise man does not go into a fight with less strength than he might have had otherwise, solely because he is stubborn." Bent

Leg's voice was hard as flint. Two Bears might be in charge of the war party, but Bent Leg's tone left no doubt as to who was the ultimate authority in this band of Assiniboine.

"Very well," Two Bears said through clenched teeth. "The white men and the Crow will go with us."

Bent Leg crossed his arms over his chest and nodded solemnly.

"But I will not save them at the cost of Assiniboine blood," Two Bears added with a fierce look.

"Nobody's askin' you to," Preacher said. "We'll take care of ourselves, don't worry about that."

"If that's settled," Audie said, "we'd better go gather our gear and say farewell to the ladies."

"Umm," Nighthawk agreed.

Preacher returned to his lodge to get his rifle, powderhorn, shot pouch, and extra pistols. By the time he reached the brush corral where the horses were kept, Audie and Nighthawk were there, too, readying their mounts for the trip. Dog padded along behind Preacher, going wherever the mountain man went, as usual.

Horse greeted Preacher with a toss of his head. After a few days here in the Assiniboine village, the rangy gray stallion appeared to be ready to get out and stretch his legs. Preacher felt the same way, which was why he had suggested the hunting trip.

Unfortunately, they were going to be hunting men, and he wished that breaking the routine of village life hadn't come at the cost of two young men's lives.

It didn't take long to saddle Horse. The three men led their mounts back to the center of the village where the rest of the war party was gathering.

The warriors were saying good-bye to their women. Preacher spotted Raven's Wing moving through the crowd and thought she was probably there to tell Two Bears to be careful and wish him well.

Instead, she stepped up to Preacher, facing him from a distance of less than a foot. She lifted her arms and put them around his neck, then pressed her mouth to his in the sort of kiss that white men and women exchanged.

Raven's actions took Preacher by surprise. He supposed he could have avoided her embrace if he had tried hard enough. Maybe deep down he didn't want to, he thought as she kissed him. He had been leading Horse, but now his left hand dropped the stallion's reins, and that arm went instinctively around Raven's waist. She moved closer, pressed her body into his.

"White man!"

The loud, angry voice belonged to Two Bears. The warrior's exclamation didn't surprise Preacher. He figured that was exactly the sort of response Raven intended to provoke when she kissed him in front of everybody like that. She was declaring herself to be Preacher's woman.

He wasn't expecting Two Bears to grab him, though, and that was what happened. Two Bears' hand came down hard on Preacher's shoulder and jerked him around, tearing him away from Raven's embrace.

The warrior wasn't content with breaking them apart, though. He threw a fist at Preacher's face.

The mountain man reacted to that as instinctively as he had to Raven's actions. He pulled his head aside so that Two Bears' fist shot past his ear. That missed blow threw Two Bears off balance and made him stumble forward a step.

Preacher hooked a punch of his own that landed solidly on Two Bears' jaw. The impact twisted the warrior's head to the side but didn't put him out, or even knock him down.

Instead, Two Bears caught himself and

roared in anger as he lunged forward and grabbed Preacher, locking his arms around the mountain man's torso as he drove Preacher backward.

Preacher's feet came off the ground. Two Bears was a big, powerful man, and he had some momentum behind him. Preacher chopped at his attacker's head, but he couldn't stop Two Bears from slamming him to the ground. Two Bears landed on top of him, and that weight drove the air from Preacher's lungs.

Over the pounding of his own pulse in his ears, Preacher vaguely heard the shouts of the crowd. He figured most of the Assiniboine were rooting for Two Bears in this fight.

But the whole thing was crazy. They shouldn't even *be* fighting, he thought. They were on the same side, and they had prisoners to rescue.

Meanwhile, Two Bears pressed his left forearm across Preacher's throat, keeping him from drawing in the air he needed to replace what he'd lost. Preacher hammered a fist into Two Bears' ribs, trying to dislodge him, but the warrior shrugged it off.

Two could play at this choking game. Preacher's right hand shot up and the fingers locked around Two Bears' throat.

Using that grip as leverage, he was finally able to throw Two Bears to the side and get the man's crushing weight off his chest. They rolled over, and Preacher dragged some air back into his lungs at last.

He drove a knee into Two Bears' belly and hung on to the warrior's throat. Two Bears slugged and kicked at him, but Preacher hung on. He got his other hand around Two Bears' neck, and with that grip he was able to lift the man's head and slam it back into the ground a couple of times. Two Bears' struggles became weaker, but they didn't stop completely.

"Preacher! Preacher, that's enough!"

Slowly, Preacher became aware of the urgent voice yelling at him. He recognized it as Audie's. Blinking, Preacher shook his head and looked around. Audie and Nighthawk flanked him protectively, but they were all surrounded by the Assiniboine warriors, most of whom looked angry.

"Preacher, you'd better let him go," Audie went on. "If you choke him to death, things aren't going to go well for us."

Audie was right, of course. Preacher knew that. He had just let his own instincts and the battle fever that gripped him get the best of him. Whenever somebody attacked him, he fought back. That reaction was as much a part of him as breathing.

And he usually fought back to kill, because most of the time the varmint he was fighting with wanted to kill him.

In this case, though, it was just jealous rage that had prompted Two Bears to jump him. Preacher let go of the warrior's throat and heaved himself to his feet. Two Bears lay there, dark of face because of his near-suffocation, and heaved rasping breaths.

Bent Leg stood nearby, glaring at him.

"I'm sorry, Chief —" Preacher began.

Bent Leg silenced him with an upraised hand.

"It is not your fault," he said. "Two Bears attacked you. You merely fought back. I would expect nothing less for a warrior of the Assiniboine, even a . . . winter warrior." The chief looked around at the others and raised his voice as he continued, "This was a fight between two men over a woman. Nothing more. They will settle it between themselves . . . *but not now.* Now, two of our young men are dead, and others are in danger, captives of the hated Gros Ventre. Have you all forgotten this?"

Two Bears struggled to his feet.

"My apologies, Bent Leg," he said in a hoarse voice. "If you wish me to remove myself as war chief —"

"No!" Bent Leg's voice was firm. "Go, and bring back our young men. Punish the Gros Ventre! And there will be no more trouble over the affections of my niece while this is going on. Do you understand?"

Two Bears bent his head.

"Your word is law, my chief."

"I'm agreeable to that, too," Preacher said.

"Very well." Bent Leg motioned toward the eastern part of the valley. "Our enemies are fleeing, even as we speak. Find them! Kill them!"

"We ride," Two Bears told the members of the war party. He started toward his horse.

The others followed suit. As Preacher mounted up, he looked around for Raven's Wing. He didn't see her. Maybe she was ashamed of what she had done and was hiding her face because she was embarrassed.

He had a hunch she wasn't all that ashamed, though. He had a hunch she was the sort of woman who knew what she wanted and figured it was her right to go after it, any way she pleased.

And if that meant raising a little hell along the way, so be it.

Nighthawk lifted Audie into the saddle and then swung up onto his own pony. The three visitors fell in with the war party. Two

Bears gave Preacher a grim nod.

Preacher understood what the warrior meant by that. Two Bears wouldn't go against Bent Leg's orders. For now, Two Bears and Preacher were allies, and each of them could trust the other with his life.

But when this rescue mission was over, if both of them returned alive to the village, then it would be a different story. A very different story . . .

One that might well end in blood.

CHAPTER 11

The wounded young Assiniboine, whose name was Stormbreaker, was in no shape to go with the war party to show them where he and the others had been attacked.

He was able to give good directions to the spot to Two Bears, though, and since the war chief knew every inch of the valley, he would have no trouble finding it.

The warriors took enough provisions with them to last for several days, in case the pursuit turned into a lengthy one. Preacher's saddlebags held a good supply of jerky, flat-bread, and pemmican. There was plenty of game in these mountains, too, if it turned out that they needed fresh meat. They might not want to risk a shot, but snares could always be set for rabbits.

In most situations, Preacher just naturally took the lead. That wasn't the case here. He didn't push himself to the front of the group. He was content to ride in the middle of the bunch with Audie and Nighthawk and let Two Bears lead the way.

A couple of hours after leaving the village, they reached the site of the ambush. The bodies of the two fallen Assiniboine young men were still there, each riddled with arrows. Two Bears picked out a couple of men to take the bodies back to the village, and then the others pushed on.

It was impossible to flee quickly through these woods without leaving some sign, and after taking prisoners, the Gros Ventre had been more interested in speed than stealth. So the trail wasn't difficult to follow. After a while, Preacher realized that it was leading generally in the direction of a notch in the rugged ridge that formed the western boundary of the valley.

No matter how Two Bears felt about him, Preacher didn't want to ride into anything blind. He pushed Horse up alongside Two Bears' mount and said to the war chief, "It's been a while since I've been in these parts. Refresh my memory. What's on the other side of that ridge?"

"Badlands," Two Bears replied curtly. "Many gullies and more ridges. There are paths that lead through, but it is easy to get lost if one does not know the way."

"And beyond that?"

"The area controlled by the Gros Ventre."

Preacher nodded. Something else had occurred to him, so since Two Bears seemed willing to talk right now, he went on, "Those two young men back there were killed with arrows."

"Yes. Gros Ventre arrows." Two Bears' voice was full of anger and bitterness.

"The bunch that attacked us, the ones who captured Raven's Wing, they were armed with rifles."

Preacher knew it might be a mistake to bring up Raven's Wing, but he really wanted to satisfy his curiosity.

Two Bears' face hardened at the mention of the woman's name, but he said, "The Gros Ventre possess a few old rifles. Trade muskets. Not very good. Since Snake Heart was sending those men into Assiniboine territory, he must have armed them with the best weapons he had."

"We shouldn't be outgunned too badly, then, once we catch up to them."

"If they have rifles, there will only be one or two. And they may blow up when they are fired."

Preacher nodded. If Two Bears was right about that — and Preacher had no reason to doubt the war chief's word — it was possible that the rifles and pistols carried by the two white men and the Crow might be enough to swing the odds in their favor, even if the raiding party outnumbered them.

Preacher knew how much damage a man armed with a bow and a quiver full of arrows could do — he was a pretty fair hand with a bow himself — but powder and shot usually trumped arrows.

They began climbing toward the notch. Preacher wasn't sure they would reach it before nightfall, and the Gros Ventre had a lead on them. If their quarry made it into the badlands today, the Assiniboine might not be able to follow them.

"Can you get through that mess you told me about in the dark?" he asked Two Bears.

The war chief shook his head.

"No one can, not even the Gros Ventre. They will make camp somewhere on the other side and wait for daylight."

"You're sure about that?"

Two Bears glared.

"You asked me a question, white man, and I answered it."

"Fair enough," the mountain man said.

"But we will continue to climb," Two Bears went on. "By morning they will not be far ahead of us."

Preacher nodded. It sounded like a reasonable plan, although it meant they would be traveling in darkness, which was often a risky proposition.

Preacher and his companions, along with the Assiniboine, were very watchful as they pressed on during the slate-gray afternoon. It was possible, though unlikely, that the Gros Ventre would double back and try to ambush them.

There was a much better chance the raiders had lit a shuck out of the valley as soon as they grabbed those prisoners. They probably wouldn't try anything fancy. Only a fool didn't keep his eyes open, though.

Given the time of year and the overcast skies, it was still early when the light began to fade. Dusk started to settle down when the war party was still a couple of miles shy of the notch.

True to his word, though, Two Bears kept the men moving. They were lined up on the gap in the ridge that was their destination, and as long as they kept going in a straight line, they ought to reach it without much trouble.

Another worry started to nag at Preacher. He had considered it unlikely that the Gros Ventre would double back and ambush them here in the Assiniboine valley . . . but that gap up there was another story. He tilted his head back and took a good look at it before all the light faded away, and what he saw confirmed his hunch.

That gap in the ridge was a perfect place for a trap.

It was only wide enough for a few riders to pass through it at a time. Once the war party, some thirty strong, was strung out, even a much smaller force could do considerable damage to it in a short period of time.

If the Gros Ventre were smart, they could split their force and send some of their warriors ahead with the prisoners, while the rest found hiding places that commanded a field of fire in that gap.

Then all they would have to do was sit and wait for the Assiniboine to show up. A couple of volleys of arrows would thin their ranks in a hurry.

Preacher had fallen back to ride with Audie and Nighthawk, but now he pushed ahead to come alongside Two Bears again.

"Are we gonna stop and make camp this side of the gap?" he asked.

"I told you, we must cut down their lead. We will stop on the other side of the gap."

"You're gonna ride through there in the dark?"

Two Bears didn't look over at Preacher, but the sneer was evident in his voice as he said, "Are you afraid of the dark, white man?"

"No, but what's in it can make me a mite nervous sometimes. What if the Gros Ventre split up and left some men behind to ambush anybody who rides through the gap?"

Two Bears shook his head.

"They are too stupid and cowardly for that. Now that they have prisoners, they want only to get back to their own land as soon as they can."

"You seem mighty certain about that."

"They are my enemies, not yours. I know them better than you do."

"They're pretty much the same thing as Blackfeet, and I know Blackfeet. They can be tricky critters when they want to."

"We must catch them before they get through the badlands. We will keep moving as long as we can."

Preacher saw that it wasn't going to do any good to keep arguing. In fact, it might have been a mistake for him to even say anything to Two Bears. The war chief was going to disagree with whatever he said, just on general principles. He was too mad at Preacher to listen and really hear.

With a sigh, Preacher fell back again. Audie asked, "What were you and His Nibs talking about?"

"He plans for us to ride on through the gap in the ridge tonight and make camp on the other side."

Audie frowned.

"I'm not sure that's such a good idea."

"I'm not, either," Preacher said, "but he pretty much told me to go climb a stump."

"Because he's angry with you over Raven's Wing."

"And because he's a proud, stubborn varmint to start with."

"Umm," Nighthawk said.

"Indubitably," Audie agreed. He hesitated. "Are we going to keep going with them, or pull out?"

"I reckon you know the answer to that," Preacher said.

"Yes, I suspect that I do. Two Bears isn't the only one around here who is proud and stubborn."

"Difference is, I don't let it make me do damn fool things."

"Oh?" Audie asked with lifted eyebrows.

Preacher had to chuckle.

"We're stayin' with 'em," he said. "And if they wind up in a heap of trouble, we'll do our best to pull 'em out of it."

"In other words, business as usual."

"Call it what you want." Preacher narrowed his eyes as he looked up at the notch.

It was close now, because the war party had been climbing for a while, but the light would be gone in another half-hour, maybe less.

They pushed on, and soon it was dark enough that Preacher could barely make out the man riding in front of him. He checked the pistols tucked behind his belt to make sure they wouldn't hang up if he had to unlimber them in a hurry. The pistols in the saddle holsters were loaded and charged, too, as was his rifle. All he had to do was cock and fire.

As the war party reached the gap, the two sections of the ridge loomed above them, visible as dark, hulking shapes even in the thick shadows. Earlier, Dog had roamed away from the war party, but now that it was dark the big cur padded along in his customary place right beside Preacher. A low growl rumbled deep in Dog's throat as the riders started through the opening.

A shiver of apprehension rippled along Preacher's spine. Dog's instincts told him this was a bad idea, too. Preacher guided Horse with his knees and lifted the flintlock in both hands, looping his right thumb over the hammer so he would be ready to pull it back in a hurry if he needed to.

The war party kept moving, with Two

Bears in the lead and Preacher, Audie, and Nighthawk riding together about the middle of the pack. The thud of hoofbeats echoed back from the walls of the gap. Preacher's head tilted back a little and swiveled back and forth on his neck, but there was nothing to see up there above them. Nothing but darkness.

Then suddenly, balls of garish red light flared into being in several places and fell out of the night like huge drops of crimson rain. Preacher's eyes, adjusted to the darkness, narrowed involuntarily as the glare struck them almost like a physical blow. Up and down the line of riders, men exclaimed in surprise as the blazing orbs fell among them and lit up the notch.

A second later, bloodcurdling screeches ripped out, and the whistle of flying arrows filled the air along with the war cries.

CHAPTER 12

Preacher knew what the Gros Ventre had
done. They had gathered tinder-dry brush,
rolled it into balls, and bound it together.
Then they had ignited those giant, makeshift
torches and kicked them over the edges of
the cliffs that formed the gap.

The blazing brush served two purposes. It
blinded the Assiniboine and their allies, and
it gave the Gros Ventre enough light to aim
their arrows. Preacher heard some of the
Assiniboine warriors crying out in pain as
arrowheads drove deep into their bodies.

He might not be able to see very well, but
he could hear just fine. One of the Gros
Ventre *yip-yip-yipped* a war cry not far above
his head. Preacher lifted the rifle to his
shoulder and fired in the direction of the
sound.

He didn't know if he hit anything, and
there wasn't time to wait for his eyes to
adjust. The best thing to do was to bust out

of this trap if they could, so he drove his heels into Horse's flanks and sent the gray stallion leaping ahead in a burst of speed.

"Everybody keep goin'!" Preacher yelled in Assiniboine. "Keep movin'!"

Hoofbeats pounded around him. He felt an arrow pluck at the fringe on his buckskin shirt as it narrowly missed him. Leaning forward in the saddle to make himself a smaller target, he galloped toward the other end of the notch.

The brush was burning itself out now. Darkness began to gather, and as Preacher emerged from the gap he found himself surrounded by thick shadows once more. He hauled Horse to a stop and said in a quiet but urgent voice, "Dog?"

An answering growl came from nearby. Preacher felt relief go through him at the knowledge the big cur had survived the ambush.

But that left him with other worries. More riders milled around him.

"Audie!" Preacher said. "Nighthawk!"

"Here!" Audie said. "Preacher, are you all right?"

"Yeah. How about you?"

"I'm not much of a target. They missed me. But Nighthawk's not here!"

Fearing that the Crow might have been

skewered by an arrow back in the gap, Preacher started thinking about a counterattack. In Assiniboine, he asked, "How many are here?"

A number of men spoke up; then Two Bears' rumbling voice said, "I am war chief here!"

"Then you better take command," Preacher snapped. He was in no mood to worry about Two Bears' feelings after the man had ignored his warning about riding through the gap in the darkness.

"We are between the Gros Ventre who attacked us and the rest of their party," Two Bears said. "They will come at us again."

Preacher thought that was probably right. But in the meantime they had wounded men back there in the notch. Wasted time might mean lost lives.

"You can wait here and block the trail so the Gros Ventre can't get through," he said. "Audie and I are goin' back to see about the survivors."

"You will ride right into the enemy!"

"That's our problem, not yours," Preacher said. He heeled Horse into motion again.

With Dog bounding along beside him and Audie riding just behind, Preacher headed for the gap. He slid the empty rifle into the fringed and beaded sheath strapped to the saddle and pulled both pistols from behind his belt.

It didn't take long to run into trouble. Riders loomed up on the trail and charged them, yelling again. Preacher was grateful to the Gros Ventre for announcing themselves. He sent the stallion plunging into their midst.

Preacher felt the wind from a tomahawk that swept past his head in a slashing blow. He thrust out his right-hand pistol at the shadowy figure who had swung the weapon and pulled the trigger. For a split second, the muzzle flash illuminated the hate-filled face of a Gros Ventre warrior before the heavy lead ball smashed the man's features into a red ruin.

An arrow struck his saddle and lodged there, the shaft trembling. Preacher twisted in the direction it had come from and fired the left-hand pistol. The Gros Ventre who had launched the arrow went backwards off his pony as the shot struck him.

Preacher heard Audie's guns booming behind him, and Dog snarled and snapped furiously. When one of the Gros Ventre let out a hideous gurgling scream, Preacher knew the big cur had knocked the man off his pony and ripped his throat out.

With the empty pistols behind his belt

again and the two guns from the saddle holsters in his hands, Preacher fired into the chaos of shadowy figures crowding around him. The double-shotted charges ripped into the Gros Ventre and cut down several more of them like scythes.

More hoofbeats thundered in the night. Preacher's charge had broken the back of the attempt by the Gros Ventre to get past the Assiniboine. The trap had backfired on the raiders. They had done some damage, but then they themselves had been trapped. Now Two Bears and the rest of the Assiniboine were closing in to finish off the Gros Ventre.

Preacher left them to that task and galloped into the notch, followed by Audie and Dog.

"Nighthawk!" the mountain man shouted. "Nighthawk, where are you?"

A weak "Umm" guided him to a dark shape sitting propped against one of the cliffs. Preacher dismounted quickly and dropped to a knee next to the Crow. He put out a hand and rested it on Nighthawk's shoulder.

"How bad are you hit?"

Nighthawk took Preacher's hand and moved it to his side. Preacher felt the warm, wet blood soaking into Nighthawk's buckskin shirt. There didn't seem to be a lot of it, which was a good sign. Nighthawk was wounded, but maybe not fatally.

"How is he?" Audie asked anxiously from the back of his horse. It wasn't easy for him to dismount. Nighthawk usually lifted him down from the saddle.

"Not too bad, I hope," Preacher replied. The shadows were thick and virtually impenetrable in the gap now. "We could use some light."

Somewhere not too far off, Two Bears called, "White man!"

"Over here," Preacher responded. "We need some fires."

Two Bears gave orders. This gap in the ridge was barren of vegetation except for the balls of brush that had already burned to ashes, so a couple of the Assiniboine warriors rode back down the slope they had climbed earlier to look for firewood.

While they were gone, Preacher worked by feel, easing Nighthawk's shirt up so he could check the wound itself. It seemed to be a long, fairly clean slash in the Crow's side, deep enough to be more than a scratch but probably not life-threatening.

The men came back with brush and broken branches that Two Bears used to make a fire. He struck sparks with flint and steel and set the tinder alight. Soon flames leaped up and cast their reddish-yellow glow over the interior of the notch.

The light confirmed Preacher's estimation of Nighthawk's injury. The Crow had lost enough blood to weaken him, but he would be all right once the arrow wound was bound up and he'd had some time to recover.

Some of the other members of the war party hadn't been as fortunate. Five Assiniboine warriors were dead, and another half-dozen were wounded.

That brought the number of men healthy enough to continue the pursuit of the captives down to eighteen. They didn't know how many warriors had been in the Gros Ventre raiding party — Stormbreaker had estimated about forty — but a good number of them were now dead, wiped out in the fight tonight.

The odds were close enough to even, Preacher thought.

So did Two Bears. The war chief said, "Those who are not badly injured can stay behind and care for those who are. The rest of us will go ahead, after the other Gros Ventre and the prisoners."

"You said they wouldn't be able to make it through the badlands in the dark,"

Preacher reminded him. "That means they're probably not too far ahead of us."

Two Bears' head jerked in a nod.

"So?"

"So they must be close enough to have heard the shots and maybe even the yellin'," Preacher said. "They'll know the warriors they left behind ambushed us. And when those men don't show up to join them, they'll know that we won this fight."

"You are saying they will be on their guard."

"Yep . . . but not until morning. Because they won't expect us to try to make it through the badlands by night, either."

Two Bears snorted.

"A man would be a fool to attempt it. He might get lost and wander for weeks. We should wait for dawn so we can see where we are going."

"I know somebody who can make it through, or at least find the Gros Ventre camp for us."

With a sneer, Two Bears said, "You think very high of your abilities, white man."

Preacher shook his head.

"Not me. Him."

He pointed toward Dog, who sat nearby beside Nighthawk.

"You would trust the lives of my men to

that animal?" Two Bears demanded.

"I'd trust *my* life to him, and I have many times. I reckon if it's good enough for me, it's good enough for you fellas."

"Preacher is right," Audie put in. "Dog has the keenest nose west of the Mississippi. He can track those Gros Ventre through any sort of maze and lead you right to them."

Two Bears frowned.

"If we could find their camp, we would take them by surprise. They would not expect any pursuit until morning."

"That's the idea," Preacher said. "What do you say?"

Two Bears looked around at the other warriors, but their faces were impassive. The decision was his to make.

After a moment, he nodded.

"If we wait, they may try to ambush us again," he said. "This way we can turn things around and fall upon them with no warning."

"It might be better if we went ahead from here on foot," Preacher suggested. "Hoofbeats would echo in those gullies and canyons."

Two Bears looked like he wanted to argue just out of habit, but instead he nodded again and said, "A good idea."

Nighthawk started to get to his feet.

Preacher rested a hand on his shoulder and held him down.

"You lost enough blood it'd probably be a good idea for you to stay here. Audie, reckon you can patch up Nighthawk and the rest of these wounded hombres?"

Audie frowned.

"I thought I'd come with you and the others, Preacher."

"Yeah, and I'd love to have you along, but these fellas are hurt, and if we don't come back, they're gonna need a good man to see to it that they get back to Bent Leg's village."

"If I didn't know better, I'd say you were just making an excuse to leave me behind, like you did with Lorenzo."

"Not hardly," Preacher said. "We've fought side by side often enough you ought to know better."

Audie thought about it for a second and then shrugged.

"You're right. If you'll help me down, I'll see what I can do about tending to the various injuries among these men."

A few minutes later, the group of warriors that would be going on after the Gros Ventre were ready to move out on foot, taking only their weapons. One way or another, this would end tonight, so they didn't really need the supplies anymore.

Preacher said so long to Audie and Nighthawk, both of whom wished him luck. He led Dog out of the notch and down the slope to the area where the bodies of the dead Gros Ventre littered the ground. Preacher cut an unbloodied piece of buckskin from one man's shirt and held it under Dog's nose.

"Find the rest of the bunch," he told the big cur. "You can do it, old son. Find!"

Dog trotted away, nose to the ground. He cast back and forth for a moment, then started on a fairly straight course, deeper into the badlands.

Preacher hurried on, and after him came Two Bears and the rest of the Assiniboine.

In a matter of moments, the night's shadows had swallowed them all.

CHAPTER 13

They hadn't gone very far into the badlands before Preacher felt the cold kiss of a snowflake against his leathery cheek.

That was fine, he thought with a grim smile. Let it snow. Dog would still be able to follow the scent of the Gros Ventres, and a coating of the powdery white stuff would muffle the sounds of their approach even more.

Whether Two Bears liked it or not, Preacher had taken the lead now. He was used to keeping up with Dog when the big cur was following a trail. He was able to keep Dog in sight, and Two Bears and the other Assiniboine followed him, trotting along single file as their path led through gullies, along ridges, and around massive piles of rock.

Finally Dog came to such an abrupt halt that Preacher almost tripped over him. He knelt and slipped an arm around the big cur, feeling how Dog's muscles were now tense. He felt as much as heard the growl that rumbled deeply inside the animal.

Two Bears crouched beside them.

"The Gros Ventre are close?" the war chief asked in a whisper.

Preacher sniffed the air and smelled wood-smoke.

"Yeah, they've built a fire. Probably too small to see unless you're real close, but I can smell it. Better let me and Dog go ahead and do some scoutin'."

"We will wait here, but not for long." Two Bears sounded like he didn't care for the idea, but he knew Preacher was right.

The snow was falling thickly now, and the ground was beginning to turn white, which made it a little easier to see where they were going.

On the other hand, the lighter background would make it easier for anybody to see them moving against it, Preacher thought as he and Dog slipped forward soundlessly. Their breath fogged in front of their faces.

Dog led the way into a narrow passage between two huge upthrusts of rock. Preacher could have put his hands out and brushed his fingertips against the rock walls on both sides. Those walls rose fifty or sixty feet and seemed to lean in oppressively.

The passage ran straight at first for a hundred or so yards, then began to angle back and forth. It would be impossible for the two groups to fight a battle in here, Preacher thought. There simply wasn't enough room for anything other than *mano á mano* combat.

The farther he and Dog went, the darker it got. Not much snow had fallen down here through the narrow crack above. Preacher reached down and grasped the thick fur at the back of Dog's neck so he and the big cur wouldn't get separated in the almost impenetrable gloom.

He stopped short and tightened his grip on Dog's coat as voices drifted faintly to his ears. A grim smile tugged at the corners of Preacher's wide mouth. Dog had done his job. He had brought Preacher right to their quarry.

Kneeling next to the animal, Preacher breathed in Dog's ear, "Stay."

Dog let out a tiny whine.

"I know, if there's a ruckus you want to be right in the middle of it. Don't worry, I'm just gonna go take a look."

Leaving the dog there, Preacher stole forward silently, guiding himself by touch as he kept his left hand on the stone wall. The voices got louder, and the smell of smoke from the campfire was stronger now as Preacher approached the spot where the rest of the Gros Ventre had stopped with their prisoners.

Even though the raiders probably didn't expect the Assiniboine to come after them tonight, they would still have at least one guard posted. It would be foolish to do otherwise. Preacher didn't like the Gros Ventre, but he knew they weren't fools.

So he moved inches at a time, being careful before each step to search the darkness around him with every sense he possessed. He relied on his keen instincts to warn him, as well.

It was a combination of those things that alerted him to the presence of one of the warriors in the narrow passage just ahead of him. He smelled the man first, then heard the faint sound of his breathing.

Preacher stood absolutely still until his eyes picked out the man-shaped patch of deeper darkness about six feet in front of him. The man was leaning against the rock wall. He was probably tired and having trouble staying awake.

Preacher waited, barely breathing.

After a while, the guard's head drooped forward a little and his breathing deepened. He had dozed off. That lapse lasted only for a second, though. He jerked his head up and muttered something to himself.

Preacher knew by the man's reaction to falling asleep that the Gros Ventre warrior had no idea he was so close to death. The mountain man stayed where he was, utterly motionless, and after a few more minutes had passed, the guard's head swayed forward again.

Preacher's hunting knife came out of its sheath without a sound. He moved swiftly, his left hand reaching out to clamp over the guard's mouth. At the same time, he struck with the knife, driving the blade up and into the man's chest. He felt a spasm go through the warrior as the razor-sharp tip penetrated his heart. Preacher pressed him back against the wall and held him there until he was sure the guard was dead.

Then he lowered the body slowly and carefully to the ground. He pulled the blade free and wiped the blood on the dead man's shirt. A few flakes of snow drifted down and landed on the man's face, but he could no longer feel them.

Preacher stepped over the corpse and moved deeper into the passage. Up ahead of him, someone laughed. The narrow trail through the rocks twisted again, and now he could see an orange glow from the campfire.

The passage opened onto a broad ledge that ran to the left. The ledge was about twenty feet wide, then it dropped off sharply into a deep ravine. The Gros Ventre had built their fire on that level ground. Rocks overhung the place, giving it some protection from the wind and the snow.

Preacher took his hat off and edged his head out a little more as he looked for the Assiniboine prisoners. He spotted them — seven or eight young men — sitting at the base of the wall that loomed over the ledge. From the way they were sitting, their hands were lashed behind their backs, probably with rawhide strips, and they looked angry, miserable, and afraid all at the same time.

He did a quick count of the Gros Ventre. Twenty-two warriors. Counting the sentry he had killed, twenty-three. That agreed with earlier estimates. So the Assiniboine were outnumbered, but not by a great deal.

And if he could free those prisoners, Preacher thought, that would tip the odds in their favor.

Unfortunately, he couldn't see any way to reach the captives. Their would-be rescuers couldn't count on their help.

Some of the Gros Ventre were asleep, but others were still awake talking. One of them

141

stood up, stretched, went over to the far side of the ledge, and relieved himself over the rim of the ravine.

Then he turned and walked toward the narrow passage where Preacher stood.

This fella was about to take over for the guard he had killed, Preacher thought. Which meant that discovery wasn't far off. He grimaced in the darkness. He couldn't take on more than twenty Gros Ventre warriors by himself, but there wasn't going to be time to go back and fetch Two Bears and the rest of the war party.

This was one time when that old saying about being stuck between a rock and hard place was literally true.

He could whittle the odds down by one more, though, he told himself as he moved deeper into the shadows and pressed his back against the wall of the passage. He drew his knife and waited as the unsuspecting Gros Ventre warrior ambled toward him.

The man entered the passage and called out in a soft voice. Preacher understood enough of the Gros Ventre lingo to know that the man was calling to the guard whose place he intended to take. Preacher grunted in response, the sort of sound that a tired man ready to turn in for the night might make.

The warrior came closer. Preacher was absolutely still and silent now. He didn't make his move until the unsuspecting man stepped past him.

Then, uncoiling like a striking snake, Preacher looped his left arm around the warrior's throat from behind, clamped down to cut off any sound, and drove his knife into the man's back. The Gros Ventre arched and shuddered as the knife slid between his ribs and sliced into his heart, stopping it. With a final spasm as life departed, the man went limp in Preacher's grip.

Preacher lowered the body to the ground as he had with the other guard. That left twenty-one raiders to deal with. If he could just figure out a way to get them to stroll into the passage one at a time, he could handle them, he thought with a grim smile.

They wouldn't do that, though. When neither of the guards came back to the fire, after a while they would start to wonder what was wrong. Then several of the men would come to investigate, more than likely. They might be able to attack two at a time, but considering the passage's narrow confines, it was more likely that just one man could charge in once they suspected that an enemy lurked in here.

And as soon as they knew that for sure, they would back off and send arrows whistling along the passage. Preacher was confident that he could take cover behind the first bend and be safe enough, but he couldn't free the prisoners from there.

It would be a standoff, and if that happened, ultimately the Gros Ventre would win. They could leave two or three warriors with plenty of arrows on the ledge. That would be enough to keep the Assiniboine bottled up in there until the rest of the raiders were long gone with the prisoners.

No, a surprise attack was the only chance he and his allies had, Preacher told himself.

Some tiny noises drew his attention. He turned back the way he had come from. Two Bears had warned him that they wouldn't wait long, and they hadn't. The rest of the Assiniboine rescue party was slipping through the passage toward him, quietly enough that only the keenest ears would hear their approach.

Preacher had ears that keen. He waited until he sensed that someone was near him, then whispered, "Two Bears."

He knew he was taking a chance. The men coming along the passage toward him might *not* be the Assiniboine.

But he didn't know who else they could

be, and sure enough, Two Bears whispered back, "White man?"

It annoyed Preacher that the war chief wouldn't call him by name, but that wasn't important now. He leaned closer to Two Bears and in a voice that couldn't have been heard more than a few feet away, he explained what he had found at the end of the passage.

An idea had begun to form in the back of his mind. He asked, "Are there any of your fellas who are good at climbin'?"

"You mean climbing a tree? There are no trees here!"

"I was thinkin' more of rock climbin'." Preacher pointed up, even though it was so dark in the passage Two Bears probably couldn't see the gesture. "If somebody could get above that ledge and drop down on it while the Gros Ventre were distracted, he could cut the prisoners loose so they could get in on the fight, too."

"Climb that cliff in the dark? It cannot be done."

"It's our best chance," Preacher insisted. "I'll do it."

"You will fall and die," Two Bears predicted.

"Well, then," Preacher said with a touch of bleak humor, "if I do, it'll be your problem figuring out how to rescue those boys, won't it?"

CHAPTER 14

Two Bears had to know just as well as Preacher that they didn't have much time to settle on a plan. After a moment, the war chief said, "What is this distraction you speak of?"

"If I'm doin' the climbin', the distraction will be your part," Preacher said. "If it was me, I'd just sorta saunter out onto the ledge and dare them Gros Ventre to come after me. They'll rush over here after you, and while they're busy doin' that, I'll drop down behind them and free the prisoners. Then we'll jump the varmints from that direction. When they swing around to see what in blazes is goin' on, that's when the rest of you come pourin' out. We'll hit 'em from both directions at once, and we'll have the odds on our side if I can get those boys loose."

For several seconds, Two Bears was silent in the darkness. Then he said, "It sounds like it might work. But how will I know when you are ready, so I can distract them?"

"That's a problem, all right. I'd let out a birdcall to signal you, but I don't reckon there are very many birds around these parts at this time of year."

"No," Two Bears agreed. "Not many. But can you howl like a wolf?"

Preacher grinned.

"Folks have accused me of bein' an old lobo. I can sound like one if I need to."

"Then that will be the signal. Go. There is no more time to waste."

"Nope, there's sure not."

Preacher had left his rifle with Horse, so he didn't have to do anything with it when he turned to the stone wall and began feeling for handholds. He wished he had gotten a good look at this cliff in the daylight. What he was setting out to do might be impossible, but he wouldn't know that unless he tried.

He found what seemed to be a sturdy grip.

"Listen for the wolf," he told Two Bears.

Then he began pulling himself up the steep rock wall.

This was the second time in recent weeks he had climbed a cliff to turn the tables on a bunch of Gros Ventre raiders. Heights didn't really bother Preacher — not much did — but it would be fine with him if this was the last time he ever had to imitate a blasted mountain goat.

Preacher moved as fast as he could, but it was inevitable that having to work completely by feel, in almost total darkness, slowed him down some. Despite that, he thought he was making pretty good progress. He angled in what he hoped was the right direction.

Getting down onto the ledge was going to be tricky. He thought about that as he climbed. If he'd had a rope, he could have secured it somewhere, dropped the other end off the edge of that overhanging rock, and shinnied down it without much trouble.

But he didn't have a rope, which meant he would have to hang from the rim and let himself drop. The ledge stuck out farther than the overhang, and the drop would only be about a dozen feet, so that ought to work.

If he miscalculated, though, or if he just flat-out missed, he might plunge right into that ravine, which had appeared to be forty or fifty feet deep. A fall like that could seriously injure a man or even kill him.

And it would certainly prevent him from freeing the prisoners, which meant the Assiniboine rescue party might wind up getting slaughtered, too.

Preacher forced those thoughts out of his mind and concentrated on his climbing. The rocks were cold and in some places slick with snow. He had never been one to brood about what *might* happen. Plan for it as much as you could, deal with it when it was happening, and go ahead. It was a simple philosophy, but one that had served him well.

Without warning, one of his feet slipped. He pressed himself to the rock as hard as he could as he started to fall. His fingers wedged in some tiny cracks, and for a second they had to support all his weight. Pain shot through Preacher's hands and along his arms. But he hung on, and after a few nerve-wracking seconds both feet found new purchase and took the strain off his fingers.

Preacher leaned against the rock wall and dragged in a deep breath. He would have liked to rest there for a few moments, but there wasn't time for that. He started hauling himself upward again.

A minute later, he spotted a faint orange glow in the sky to his right. That had to be coming from the campfire. He was getting there, he told himself. Not much farther now.

But time was running out. The Gros Ven-

tre warriors who were still awake were probably wondering by now why the guard who
had been relieved hadn't come to join them.
If they went to investigate too soon, the plan
would be ruined.

Preacher tried to move a little faster. Up
and to the right, up and to the right . . . As
long as he didn't encounter a stretch without any footholds and handholds, he could
make it, he told himself.

And of course, that jinxed him. It never
failed. He had to stop, and try as he might,
he couldn't find any other grips within
reach to his right.

Biting back a curse, Preacher tilted his
head back to study the rock wall above him.
He thought he could probably continue going straight up, but that wouldn't put him
any closer to the Gros Ventre camp.

That appeared to be his only option, so
he stretched one arm above his head and
found a small, protruding rock. He grasped
it tightly and felt around with a foot until
he found a little crevice that he could get
the toe of his boot into. With a tiny grunt of
effort from the strain, he hauled himself
higher.

Seconds ticked past, and with each one,
Preacher's nerves drew tighter. After a
minute or so he found a crack that angled

up and to the right, just the way he wanted to go. He wedged his toes into it and began sliding along.

It petered out after about fifteen feet.

But from where he was, with the glow from the fire helping him to see now, he could make out the giant slab of rock that overhung the Gros Ventre camp. It was about ten feet below him and three or four feet ahead of where he clung to the rock. An easy enough jump if he'd had a place from which to launch himself.

As it was, though, all he could do was let go, push off from the rock, and twist his body as he fell in hopes that he could reach the stone slab. If he missed, he would tumble helplessly down into the darkness. He didn't know what might be waiting for him there, but it couldn't be anything good. Probably fang-like rocks that would smash the life out of him.

But again there was no choice. Preacher took another deep breath, tensed all his muscles, and flung himself away from the cliff as hard as he could.

Twisting in midair, he reached out desperately for the rock where he wanted to land. For a terrible split second that seemed much longer, he thought he was going to miss it.

Then the edge of the slab hit him in the belly, knocking the breath out of him, and his hands slapped against the stone and began to struggle for purchase. He had landed half-on and half-off, and it would be very easy to slip back and fall.

The rough surface painfully gouged his palms and fingertips, but he hung on for dear life and stopped his slide before he went too far over the edge and fell. Gritting his teeth from the effort, Preacher pulled himself forward until all of his body was sprawled on the slightly slanting top of the massive rock.

As soon as he had caught his breath, Preacher sat up. He turned back toward the passage where he had left Two Bears and the other Assiniboine. Tipping his head back, he let out the wavering howl of a lobo wolf.

If the signal was going to be loud enough for Two Bears to hear, it had to be loud enough that the Gros Ventre would hear it, too. That couldn't be avoided. Preacher hoped that he sounded enough like a wolf to fool them.

It had to help that an answering howl came back, and the yowling *yip-yip-yip* was undoubtedly authentic. Preacher grinned. Good old Dog! He hadn't expected the big cur to pitch in and make the charade even more convincing. The Gros Ventre wouldn't be suspicious of a pair of wolves howling at each other across the badlands.

On hands and knees, Preacher crawled toward the other side of the rock slab. He went down on his belly the last few yards and took his hat off so he could peer over the edge. He couldn't see the prisoners from where he was, of course. He couldn't even see the campfire.

But he could hear just fine, and he recognized Two Bears' voice as the war chief stepped out of the passage and called in a loud, arrogant voice, "Gros Ventre! You dung-eating dogs! Let my warriors go!"

Instead, shouting angrily, the raiders charged along the ledge toward the mouth of the passage. Preacher swung around and slid backwards so that his legs dangled off the rock. If he dropped straight down, he would land about a yard from the ledge's rim. As long as he didn't over-balance and topple backward, he would be fine.

That was taking a big chance, though, and he knew it.

He pushed himself back and let his legs dangle until he was hanging full-length from his hands. More angry yelling came from the passage as the Gros Ventre tried to pursue Two Bears into it.

Preacher wasn't sure what he would run into down there, but there was only one way to find out.

He let go.

The drop took only a heartbeat, but it was a breathtaking instant anyway. Preacher's boots hit the ledge solidly, but his weight started to carry him backward. He windmilled his arms to catch his balance, and as he did that, he saw that the Gros Ventre hadn't left the prisoners unguarded when they chased off after Two Bears. Two of the raiders stood between Preacher and the captives, bows in hand with arrows nocked.

Preacher threw himself forward as one of the Gros Ventre fired. The arrow sliced through the air above his head, where his belly had been a second earlier. Preacher landed in a rolling dive that carried him into a somersault. As he came up, his knife was already in his hand.

The blade sliced into the belly of the guard who had fired the arrow and gutted the man. Preacher grabbed his arm and swung him around just as the other guard loosed his arrow. It struck the dying guard in the back with such force that the arrowhead went all the way through his body and burst out his chest to protrude bloodily from his buckskin shirt.

Preacher had already ripped his knife from the man's belly. He threw it over the dying guard's shoulder with deadly accuracy. The blade transfixed the other guard's throat, not only inflicting a mortal wound but also insuring that he couldn't let out a warning shout to the other members of his party.

Preacher shoved the first guard aside. The second guard had dropped to his knees and was pawing at the handle of the knife lodged in his throat. Preacher grabbed the handle and kicked the man in the chest. He went over backward, and as the knife came free, a crimson stream shot up like a geyser from his ruined throat.

Preacher bounded toward the prisoners, who watched him with wide, shocked eyes. All of them probably knew who he was, knew that he had been staying in the village of Bent Leg's people and was considered a friend, but still they might have experienced a moment of nervousness as this grim-faced white man holding a blood-dripping knife charged toward them.

Then Preacher was behind them. The blade severed the bonds holding them.

"Go!" Preacher told them in Assiniboine. "You're not prisoners anymore. It's time to teach those Gros Ventre a lesson!"

CHAPTER 15

The captives' hands had been tied, but their feet were free. They leaped up and charged toward the Gros Ventre clustered around the mouth of the passage. They were eager to avenge their friends who had been killed and to pay their captors back for the rough treatment they had received.

Their eagerness erupted in angry shouts, which warned the raiders that something else was wrong. A couple of them were able to swing around and loose arrows at the charging young warriors. One of the shafts missed, but the other thumped into the chest of a young man, causing him to stumble and fall.

But then the rest of the group slammed into their former captors, and the other Assiniboine warriors led by Two Bears came yelling and fighting out of the passage, and suddenly all hell was breaking loose on the ledge.

Preacher pulled the loaded pistols from behind his belt and stalked forward. The melee was so closely packed that he couldn't fire into it at the Gros Ventre without risking hitting the Assiniboine, too. So he held his fire and waited for clear shots.

He didn't have to wait long. One of the raiders grabbed one of the former prisoners, catching him by the throat and forcing him down. The Gros Ventre lifted his tomahawk. He was poised to smash open the young man's head when Preacher blew a hole in his back and sent him toppling forward.

Movement in the corner of his eye made him swing around instinctively just in time to see another of the Gros Ventre lining up an arrow that was aimed at Two Bears' back. The war chief had hold of one of the raiders and was choking the life from him, but he was about to be cut down from behind and didn't know it.

Preacher squeezed the trigger of his other gun before the warrior could send the arrow hurtling at Two Bears. The man toppled to the side as the ball ripped into his side and smashed through his lungs. His fingers let go of the arrow anyway, but it flew high and wide since he was already falling when he released it.

As Two Bears' opponent slumped in death, the war chief glanced around to see what the shot was about. His dark eyes widened slightly as he saw the smoke curling from the muzzle of Preacher's pistol and the dead Gros Ventre lying only a few yards away with a fallen bow next to him.

Two Bears was smart enough to figure out what had just happened, Preacher thought, and judging by the scowl on the war chief's face, he didn't like knowing that the mountain man had saved his life.

The Gros Ventre were being overwhelmed now. Preacher waded in and smashed the skull of one raider with an empty pistol, then tucked the guns away and used his knife to slit the throat of another. The men still struggling on the ledge had to wade through pools of blood to do so. This little corner of the badlands had become a charnel house.

In a matter of moments, the fight was over. All the Gros Ventre were dead. Two Bears used his knife to make certain of that as he stalked among the fallen enemies.

Five of the Assiniboine warriors had been killed, too, including two of the former prisoners. Preacher knew they would have considered their deaths to be for a good cause, and those deaths had been avenged.

Two Bears ordered his men to take the bodies of the Gros Ventre and throw them into the ravine.

"A feast for the wolves and the other scavengers," he growled. "It is all that such as them deserve."

In the morning, the bodies of the Assiniboine dead would be taken back to the village and laid to rest with the proper customs and respect.

Preacher whistled for Dog. The big cur bounded out of the passage a few minutes later. He had stayed where Preacher told him, and as a result he had missed the fight. Preacher would have sworn that the look Dog gave him was reproachful.

The snow was still falling. Preacher hadn't even noticed it during the battle. All his thoughts had been focused on staying alive and accomplishing what he'd set out to do.

Now as he looked up at the night sky, he thought the way the flakes swirled down through the orange glow from the fire was beautiful. It was like a brief dance in the light before they reached the flames and hissed out.

Sort of like the way men lived their lives, he thought as he reloaded his pistols.

By morning, the badlands were covered

with nearly a foot of snow. The stuff had come down all night, and even though it had stopped by the time Preacher and the Assiniboine left the ledge, the sky was still leaden with the promise of more.

At least with all the snow on the ledge, you couldn't see the dried blood anymore, Preacher thought as the group got ready to leave.

They reached the notch in the ridge by mid-morning. The going was a little slower now because they had to slog through the snow and the even deeper drifts. When they got there, they found Audie, Nighthawk, and the wounded warriors anxiously awaiting their return.

Audie hurried out to meet them. Nighthawk came along behind him, taking it easy because of the bandaged-up wound in his side.

"Preacher! You're all right?"

The mountain man nodded.

"Yeah, I didn't get a scratch. I was one of the lucky ones, though."

Audie grew more solemn as he said, "Yes, I can see you suffered some casualties."

"Two of the prisoners and three of the fellas who came with us," Preacher confirmed. "But all of the Gros Ventre are dead."

"Umm," Nighthawk said.

"I don't know," Audie replied, "but I'll find out. Was Snake Heart among them?"

Two Bears had to answer that one, since Preacher didn't have any idea what Snake Heart looked like.

The war chief shook his head and said, "No, that evil one was not among the enemy. He sits back in his village, sending forth his warriors to die."

"From what I've heard of him, he doesn't lack courage," Audie said. "You'll probably be seeing him again."

"Yes," Two Bears agreed. "In the spring, we will seek revenge on the Gros Ventre for the things they have done."

And then the Gros Ventre would be out for blood in return, and on it would go, thought Preacher. The way of the world on the frontier. No use debating whether or not it should happen like that. Things were what they were.

If the Assiniboine waited until spring to renew hostilities, though, there was a good chance he and his friends would be gone by then. They only planned to stay in Bent Leg's village through the winter. When the weather warmed up, they would be moving on.

As the reunited group mounted up and

started across the valley toward the Assiniboine encampment, Preacher saw more snowflakes start to drift down. Within minutes they were flying thicker and heavier.

Winter was closing in good and proper now, so the tribes would observe the usual truce until better weather. These recent raids were the last shots for now in the ongoing war.

When it was cold and the snow was several feet deep on the ground, nobody wanted to be out killing or being killed. It was better for a man to be in his lodge, curled up in his robes with a warm, willing female. That just made good sense.

But thinking about it reminded Preacher of the things left unsettled between him and Two Bears . . . and of Raven's Wing.

The Assiniboine knew every foot of this valley, so there was no danger of them getting lost, even in a blinding snowstorm. The drifts were really deep by now, so the horses didn't make much noise as they approached the cluster of lodges along the creek bank.

The dogs smelled them coming, though, and ran out barking to greet them. That alerted the village's human occupants that something was going on. Some of them began to emerge from the lodges.

Preacher saw one figure in particular hurry toward them, bundled in a bearskin robe. Raven's Wing let out a cry of recognition, tossed the robe aside so she could move faster, and broke into a run toward them.

She dashed right past Two Bears, who was riding in the lead, and came up to Horse instead, where she threw both arms around Preacher's left leg.

"You live!" she said.

"You were afraid I wouldn't?" he asked with a wry smile.

"I feared that the same spirits who brought you to me might take you away," she said. "You know how fickle they can be."

Speaking of fickle, he thought, then decided that wasn't fair. Raven had insisted all along that she had never promised herself to Two Bears. That was what *he* had decided would happen, and he hadn't consulted her about it.

But he still wasn't happy about Raven's decision, and he half-turned on his pony to glare at her and Preacher as more of the villagers gathered around the men who had just ridden in.

"Two Bears!" Bent Leg said exuberantly. "You brought back our young men!"

"Two of them are dead," the war chief

said, "along with five of the warriors who went after them. But all of the Gros Ventre are dead, and we brought their horses back with us." He waved a hand at the extra ponies.

Bent Leg nodded solemnly.

"You have done well."

Two Bears returned the nod, obviously pleased by the chief's praise even though he was upset about the situation with Raven's Wing and Preacher.

Preacher had dismounted by the time Lorenzo reached him. The old-timer had a big grin on his face.

"Well, you look all hale and hearty. Chasin' redskins must agree with you."

Lorenzo put out a hand. Preacher clasped it firmly and asked, "Any trouble here while I was gone?"

"Nope. There wasn't no second bunch of Gros Ventre raiders."

Preacher nodded.

"I'm glad to hear it. We had enough trouble with just the one bunch."

Bent Leg limped over to him.

"You are well, old friend?"

"I am well," Preacher replied with a nod.

"And so is Little Man. But the Crow is hurt."

"Umm," Nighthawk said disdainfully.

"He'll be fine," Audie said. "An arrow just ripped a gash in his side. I patched it up, along with the injuries suffered by the other men."

"You are a good friend to the Assiniboine, Little Man." Bent Leg raised his voice and lifted his arms. "We would have a feast to celebrate this homecoming, but the spirits have brought us this snowstorm instead. When the weather is better, then we will dance and eat."

Several of the warriors let out yips of appreciation and agreement.

Everyone dismounted to put away the horses and scatter to the various lodges. Raven's Wing took Horse's reins from Preacher and insisted on leading the rangy gray stallion. They walked through the deep snow toward Preacher's lodge with Dog padding along behind in the trail they had broken.

"I have moved my things into your lodge," Raven's Wing said quietly.

"Are you sure that's a good idea?"

She stiffened beside him.

"You do not want me?"

"I never said that. I want you plenty, if you want to know the truth."

The smile spread across her face again.

"You have me. I am yours."

Preacher looked across the village. Just as he expected, Two Bears was over there about twenty yards away, watching them. And the same hatred that had been etched on the war chief's face when he was battling the Gros Ventre was visible there now as he stared at Preacher.

Raven's Wing might be his woman right now, Preacher thought, but the trouble wasn't over between him and Two Bears.

Not by a long shot.

CHAPTER 16

When the snow began to fall, Willie Deaver and his companions were still fifteen or twenty miles from their destination. Deaver muttered a curse under his breath.

Why wouldn't the damn weather co-operate? First that ice storm that could have cost them the rendezvous with Odell St. John, and now this, which threatened to delay their plans for the rifles the Englishman had turned over to them.

Caleb Manning edged his horse up alongside Deaver's mount.

"Are we pushin' on, Willie?" he asked.

"What do you think?" Deaver snapped. "I want those pelts the redskins promised us. They'll be worth a small fortune when we sell 'em to the fur traders next spring."

"Yeah, but if this storm gets much worse, we won't be able to travel in it. Those pack horses can't make it through the drifts, carryin' the load they are."

Plunkett, Heath, and Jordan were leading the horses that had the crates of rifles strapped to their backs. The animals were tired. They all were, Deaver thought. He had been pushing everyone hard since they left Canada, including himself.

"Anyway," Manning went on, "we're liable to get lost. I don't know this area that well. Do you?"

"I'm not gonna get lost," Deaver said. "You can stop worryin' about that."

Manning shrugged.

"I just don't want us wanderin' around in circles until we starve or freeze to death."

Anger welled up inside Deaver. Manning had been a good lieutenant, but he got a little cocky sometimes. Deaver didn't like anybody challenging him, not even the man he considered closer to a friend than anybody else in the world.

Friend or not, Deaver wouldn't hesitate to put a bullet in Manning if it became necessary.

He waved a hand at their surroundings, which were rapidly becoming covered with snow.

"You see any place around here to hole up?"

"No, but —" Manning abruptly fell silent. He sniffed the air. "Smell that, Willie?" he asked with excitement in his voice. "Smoke!"

Deaver lifted his head and tested the air with his nose. Manning was right. The unmistakable tang of woodsmoke drifted on the wind along with millions of snowflakes.

"Smoke means a cabin," Manning went on.

"Or at least a campfire," Deaver said. "It might be in a cave or something like that."

"Right now even a cave would look good if it was warm inside and out of the storm."

Manning had a point there, Deaver had to admit.

"We'll follow the smoke," he said. "It's comin' from the direction we want to go anyway, so if we see there's too big a bunch for us to jump, we'll just go around 'em. No harm done and nothin' lost."

Manning nodded.

"Sounds good to me, Willie."

Deaver reined in and signaled for the others to do likewise. He explained what was going on to Plunkett, Jordan, and Heath.

"If the smoke is coming from a cabin, we'll just make ourselves at home, eh?" Plunkett suggested.

"What if the folks stayin' there object to that?" Heath asked.

With his usual grin, Jordan answered,

"Then it'll just be too bad for them, right, Willie?"

Deaver grunted.

"Right. Let's go."

They rode on, following the smoke through the increasingly heavy storm. The wind whipped around some, causing Deaver to worry that they would lose the scent. Without the trail of the smoke, they might wander around in this white maelstrom for hours, even days, never finding what they were looking for.

The smoke smell just grew stronger, though, telling Deaver that they were getting closer to its source. He felt excitement building inside him, along with a little anger.

Chances were, violence was in the offing, and that always made him go a little crazy. His head was like the boiler of a steam engine. All that pressure built up, and if he didn't let it out some way, he was sure he would explode.

A few minutes later, still riding in the lead, Deaver caught a glimpse of something through the swirling curtains of snow. It was dark against the whitening ground and trees.

A cabin, all right. It was small, more than likely just a single room. It probably belonged to a fur trapper who had built it so he could hole up here in the winter, instead of having to go back to St. Louis or spend the cold months with a bunch of filthy redskins.

The cabin was occupied, no doubt about that, because smoke coiled up from the stone chimney at one end of the rough log structure.

One man, maybe two, no more than that, Deaver thought. And some of those old fur trappers had plenty of bark on them. But even two men wouldn't be a match for him and his companions, no matter how tough they were.

He didn't see a barn or corral, but there might be a lean-to shed around back of the cabin, that is, if the trapper even owned a mule or a horse. They could investigate that later, after they had made . . . arrangements . . . to stay here and wait out the storm.

Deaver stopped and waved Manning up beside him. He pointed out the cabin.

"I knew it!" Manning said. "I knew we'd find a good place to stay."

It was sheer luck and Deaver knew *that,* but he didn't say anything about it to Manning. Let him think whatever he wanted to.

"We'll leave all the horses here," he said. "Make sure those pack animals are tied securely to trees. I don't want them wandering off with those guns on their backs."

Manning nodded.

"I'll see to it, Willie."

"Then we'll slip up on the place. I'll kick the door open, and you go in first."

Manning looked like he wanted to ask why didn't they reverse those chores, but he didn't say anything. He was a smart man, at least part of the time, thought Deaver as they all dismounted.

"I'll be right behind you, and Cy, Darwin, and Fred will be just outside in case we need their help. Got it?"

Manning nodded.

"Yeah. We gonna go ahead and kill whoever's in there?"

"You'll be in front," Deaver said with a grin. "Use your own judgment. Let's go."

After tying the horses' reins to saplings, the five men started forward with Deaver and Manning in the lead. The cabin had some rifle slits in its walls but no windows, so there wasn't much chance of anybody looking out and seeing them coming. The rifle slits were probably covered up inside to keep the cold wind from blowing into the cabin.

As they approached the door, all five of the men drew their pistols. Manning hung back a little to let Deaver get ahead of him.

Deaver hoped the door wasn't barred on the inside. If it was, they probably wouldn't be able to get in.

In that case, they'd just burn the cabin down and let the occupants roast inside. That'd teach 'em.

Deaver lifted his foot and drove the heel of his boot against the door where the latch would be. With a crash, the door swung open. Deaver already darted aside to let Manning rush in first. He stepped over the threshold behind Manning with his pistol cocked and leveled and his finger taut on the trigger.

A woman screamed, and the sound sent a thrill shooting through Deaver. He hadn't expected to find a woman here.

Manning's gun roared while the woman was still screaming. A man howled in pain. Deaver's eyes had a little trouble adjusting after being in the whiteness of the snow-covered landscape outside, but after a couple of seconds he was able to make out the man who lay on the puncheon floor clutching a bullet-shattered shoulder, as well as the woman who knelt beside him, sobbing.

The man was skinny and middle-aged, with a gray beard and a tangle of hair. The woman was somewhat younger, a round-faced Indian. A trapper and his squaw, Deaver thought.

Manning stepped aside to reload his pistol while Deaver pointed his weapon at the couple. A rifle lay on the floor not far from the wounded man. Deaver figured the trapper had reached for the rifle when the intruders burst in, prompting Manning to shoot him.

Deaver toed the rifle, pushing it far enough away the trapper wouldn't be tempted to make another try for it.

"Settle down, you two," he said. "We're not here to hurt anybody."

That was an outright lie, and probably everybody in the cabin knew it.

"Who . . . who are you?" the trapper demanded through teeth clenched with pain. "What do you want?"

"Just a place to get out of the storm," Deaver said. "Maybe a little food. You got a shed here?"

The man glared at him and said, "Out back."

Deaver said to Manning, "Tell the boys to take the horses around back and tend to them."

"Sure, Willie," Manning said. "You all right in here?"

"There won't be any more trouble,"

Deaver said.

Manning went out of the cabin. The door swung back and forth a little on its leather hinges as the wind blew in, bringing snowflakes with it and putting a chill in the air despite the flames burning brightly in the fireplace at the side of the cabin.

"Here's the way it's gonna be," Deaver said quietly to the trapper. "Your woman's gonna fix us something to eat, and if you've got any whiskey here, we want it, too."

"Just take what you want and go, damn your eyes," the trapper growled.

Deaver shook his head.

"I told you, we're not going anywhere until this snowstorm blows over. Then after we've eaten and warmed up . . . what's your woman's name, anyway?"

The trapper didn't answer for a moment, but then as he stared down the barrel of Deaver's pistol, he said reluctantly, "She's called Meadow Lark."

"Meadow Lark," Deaver repeated. "That's a right pretty name. Well, then, as I was sayin', after we've eaten we'll all take turns pleasurin' ourselves with Meadow Lark. If you want, I'll let you live so you can watch, or —"

He didn't get any farther than that. Despite the trapper's wounded shoulder, he

176

lunged up off the floor, bellowing in anger and outrage.

That was just what Deaver expected him to do. Deaver squeezed the trigger, and the pistol roared and bucked in his hand as he shot the trapper in the head. The impact drove the man back down on the floor in a limp heap. He didn't even jerk.

The squaw screamed again and threw herself on top of him as if to shield him, but it was far too late for that. The trapper was already dead.

Manning ran in.

"You all right, Willie?" he asked.

"Yeah," Deaver said. He started reloading his pistol. "Fella got a mite too feisty. I had to shoot him."

"Oh. Well, I expected as much."

"Get the horses taken care of?"

"The boys are workin' on it."

Deaver nodded and tucked his pistol behind his belt. He stepped forward, bent down, and grabbed hold of Meadow Lark's arm.

"Come on, squaw," he said as he started to haul her to her feet. "You got work to do."

She came up a lot faster than he expected, and as she turned toward him he caught the glint of firelight reflecting on the knife she held. He didn't know if she had taken it off the dead trapper or if she'd had it on her the whole time, but it didn't matter. He flung himself backward to avoid the knife as she slashed at him. The blade came within inches of opening up his gut.

Manning's pistol blasted. The woman reeled back, blood welling from the hole in her chest. She dropped the knife and collapsed. After a second, her raspy breathing stopped.

"You stupid son of a bitch!" Deaver yelled. "What did you do that for?"

"She tried to kill you!" Manning protested.

"I could have taken that knife away from her," Deaver said coldly. "Now we'll have to cook for ourselves, and we won't be able to pass the time sportin' with her while we wait for the storm to blow over."

"Sorry, Willie," Manning said. "I reckon I wasn't thinkin'."

Deaver shook his head and sighed.

"These things happen, I suppose. Let's drag the bodies well away from the cabin. The wolves will have themselves a feast tonight, and I don't want 'em keepin' me awake with all their growlin' and snappin'."

CHAPTER 17

The snowstorm lasted two more days. Snow wasn't falling constantly during that time. There were a few breaks, but they didn't last long before more flakes began to spiral down from the gray sky. By the time it was over, more than two feet of snow rested on the ground, and the drifts were two or three times that deep.

Also by the time the storm was over, Preacher and Raven's Wing were well acquainted. They spent the long hours wrapped in thick fur robes and wrapped in each other as well.

Since Raven had laid in plenty of food, the only reason Preacher set foot outside the lodge was to get more firewood and to clear snow off the grass in Horse's pen so the big gray stallion would be able to graze. On those occasions he saw a few of the Assiniboine moving around the village, but not Two Bears.

179

That was good, Preacher thought. He had never in his life run from trouble, but sometimes if you just left a problem alone, it went away on its own.

He didn't really expect that to happen with Two Bears, as deep-seated as the man's anger seemed to be, but it was possible.

Preacher didn't see Lorenzo, Audie, or Nighthawk, either, and he wondered how the wound in the Crow's side was healing. He was confident Nighthawk was all right. Most people who lived in these mountains had iron constitutions, and the Crow was no exception. Nighthawk was as tough or tougher than anybody Preacher had ever met.

On the morning of the third day, Preacher saw sunlight peeking through the cracks around the flap over the lodge's entrance when he awoke. That meant the storm was over, at least for now.

He shifted a little, intending to slip out of the robes without disturbing Raven, who still slept.

But she let out a drowsy little moan of protest and asked, "Where are you going?"

"Sun's shinin'," Preacher told her.

"That means nothing. The clouds and the snow may come back."

"Yeah, but they ain't here now. I ought to

get dressed and go outside to check on things."

He leaned over to plant a kiss on the sleek skin of her bare shoulder. The rest of her was bare, too, and he was sorely tempted to just keep kissing and see what he could find, especially when she squirmed closer against him.

"If there was trouble, you would know it." She nuzzled her face against his broad, hairy chest and murmured, "Stay here with me."

No man in his right mind could argue with a plea like that, and Preacher had always considered himself eminently sane. He supposed it wouldn't hurt to linger in the lodge for a little while longer . . .

It was mid-morning when he pushed the entrance flap aside and stepped out, wearing a thick sheepskin coat over his buckskins. His breath fogged thickly in the cold air as he looked around the village. More people were moving around now in the sunshine, mostly women, but he saw Audie and Nighthawk walking toward the creek. His long-legged strides quickly allowed him to catch up to them.

"Mornin'," Preacher said. "How're you fellas doin'? Make it through the storm all right?"

"Yes, indeed," Audie said with a big smile.

"Winter in these parts may be fierce at times, but it certainly has its pleasures as well."

"Umm," Nighthawk said.

Preacher chuckled.

"How about you, old-timer? That wound in your side healin' all right?"

Nighthawk nodded his head gravely.

"Seen Lorenzo?" Preacher went on.

"I happened to see him poke his head out of his lodge earlier this morning," Audie said. "He looked around, then pulled his head back in like a prairie dog ducking back into its hole. He appeared to be all right, just not ready to come out and face the world yet."

"The old codger," Preacher said with a smile. "I reckon that Honey Gal's been warmin' his bones."

"Undoubtedly." Audie hesitated, then went on, "Preacher, I saw Two Bears this morning, as well. He was looking at your lodge, and he didn't appear to be happy."

Preacher sighed.

"I was hopin' he might've got over bein' mad by now."

"I don't think that's the case."

"Well, that's just too damned bad. I didn't do nothin' wrong, and neither did Raven."

"I completely agree with you, but I'm not

the one you have to worry about."

"I ain't worried about Two Bears," Preacher said with a snort.

"I didn't mean it that way. But you know that trouble may come from this."

"Let it come if it's goin' to," Preacher said.

They had reached the creek, which had frozen over during the storm. The ice on its surface wasn't very thick, though. Audie was able to chop through it with a tomahawk, and once he had, he and Nighthawk dropped fishing lines through the hole. With any luck, they would come up with some nice trout.

Preacher didn't have any fishing gear and didn't feel like it anyway, so he said so long to his friends and ambled back up to the village. He wanted to check on Horse this morning. Dog had spent most of the storm curled up inside the lodge, so Preacher knew the big cur was all right.

Horse tossed his head in greeting, the way he did every time he saw Preacher.

"You'd like to get out and run for a while, wouldn't you?" the mountain man asked as he patted the stallion's shoulder. "That sounds good to me, too, but I don't reckon you could do it in this deep snow. As soon as the weather clears up some, we'll sure give you a chance to stretch your legs."

When Preacher turned away from the brush corral, he found Two Bears standing there, scowling at him. The snow and the warrior's natural stealth had kept Preacher from hearing his approach.

"You should leave this village," Two Bears said without preamble. "You are not welcome here."

Preacher grunted.

"That's not the way it seems to me. Bent Leg said it was fine for me and my friends to winter here."

"Bent Leg is an old man. He thinks like an old man."

"Yeah, well, you go tell him how old and decrepit he is," Preacher suggested. "See how well he takes to it."

"You think because you helped my people, that gives you the same rights as an Assiniboine warrior."

"Seems like I helped more than just your people. I recollect —"

Preacher stopped short. He had been about to remind Two Bears of how he'd saved his life during that last fight with the Gros Ventre. But he was certain Two Bears recalled that as well as he did, and throwing it in his face would be too much like boasting. Preacher had never been a boastful man.

The flush that spread over Two Bears' features told Preacher that the man knew quite well what he was talking about, anyway. Two Bears repeated stubbornly, "You are not welcome here."

"That comes as a surprise to me. Raven's Wing has made me feel mighty welcome the past few days."

That was boasting, too, Preacher supposed, but Two Bears had irritated him so much he didn't care anymore.

The verbal thrust went home. Two Bears' lips drew back from his teeth in a snarl, and he leaped at Preacher with blinding speed, hands outstretched to grab him.

Preacher twisted in an effort to avoid the lunge, but Two Bears snagged his coat with one hand and slung him against the brush corral. Preacher rebounded from it, but Two Bears was ready and tackled him.

Both men sprawled in the snow, thrashing around so that a cloud of the white stuff rose in the air around them, almost like fog. Two Bears seemed intent on getting both arms around Preacher in a crushing grip, but the mountain man writhed free and hammered punches to the warrior's head and body. Caught up in the grip of his anger, Two Bears was able to shrug off the punishment Preacher was dealing out to him.

All right, Preacher thought, if Two Bears wanted to wrestle, they would wrestle. He slid to the side, and when Two Bears came after him, Preacher grabbed him around the neck and rolled. They went over and over in the snow, and when they stopped, Preacher was behind Two Bears with an arm looped around his neck. He clamped down hard, cutting off Two Bears' air and forcing his head up and back.

Preacher planted a knee in the small of Two Bears' back and bore down hard. He knew that if he heaved now with all his strength, he could break Two Bears' neck and there was nothing the warrior could do to stop him.

For a second, in his own anger, he came very close to doing just that.

Reason asserted itself at the last moment, cutting through the red rage that filled Preacher's head. Two Bears was an annoying jackass, but he wasn't evil. He had just made the mistake of falling in love with the wrong woman and being too blasted stubborn to admit it.

He didn't deserve to die for that mistake.

Besides, no matter how friendly Bent Leg was toward Preacher, and no matter how much he had helped the Assiniboine, the mountain man wasn't one of them. Two Bears was right about that. If he killed Two Bears, who would probably be the chief of this entire band someday, Bent Leg would probably have to banish him and his friends from the village. That was the least it would take to satisfy the anger of Two Bears' fellow warriors. They might even insist that Preacher be put to death.

He wasn't going to put Lorenzo, Audie, and Nighthawk in that much danger just because of some squabble over a woman.

Preacher kept the pressure on Two Bears' throat until the warrior was only half conscious. Then he let go and pushed himself to his feet. All his attention had been focused on keeping that grip on Two Bears, so he wasn't aware until he stood up that their fight had been noticed. Quite a few of the Assiniboine were standing nearby watching, as were his three friends.

And Raven's Wing, standing there with a thick fur robe wrapped around her and a worried look on her face.

Preacher brushed snow off his coat and buckskins and said, "Sorry, Bent Leg. I didn't mean for this ruckus to start up again. I hoped Two Bears had gotten over it."

"He is a proud man," Bent Leg said as he stepped forward. He reached down, took hold of Two Bears' collar, and lifted the groggy warrior with a strength that belied his age. "He will not get over it, as you say."

"Then maybe it would be better if I leave here," Preacher said. He didn't want to take that step — he didn't relish the idea of having to find some other place to spend the winter after the cold weather had already descended on the land — but as long as Bent Leg allowed Lorenzo, Audie, and Nighthawk to remain, Preacher supposed he could handle that solution.

Raven's Wing stepped forward and said, "No! If you force Preacher to leave, I will go with him."

Bent Leg frowned at her.

"You are like a daughter to me, as you well know, but you will not tell me how to make my decisions as chief of our people."

Her chin came up defiantly as she said, "Make whatever decision you deem best, uncle . . . and so will I."

Preacher grimaced. He hadn't set out to cause trouble within the chief's family, too. Somebody needed to talk a little sense into all these folks.

Two Bears pushed himself to his feet. He pointed a finger at Preacher and said in a hoarse voice, "I challenge you, white man!"

Preacher shook his head.

"Don't do that."

"You will meet me in a fight to the death, or else everyone in these mountains will know that the man called Preacher is a coward!"

Bent Leg pursed his lips and said, "Choose your words wisely, Two Bears. Preacher's courage has never been cast in doubt."

"I cast it so now," Two Bears insisted. "Unless we settle this as two men should."

Bent Leg drew in a deep breath and let it out in a sigh.

"So be it," he said. He looked at Preacher. "You have been challenged to a fight to the death, with my niece Raven's Wing as the prize. What say you, Preacher?"

Two Bears hadn't exactly put up Raven's Wing as the stakes in this deadly wager, Preacher thought, but everybody knew that was what he meant.

Including Raven's Wing, who had gone as pale as her natural coloring would allow.

Preacher wished like blazes that Two Bears hadn't pushed things this far . . . but now that he had, there was no honorable way to back down.

"I accept Two Bears' challenge," he said.

"No!" Raven's Wing cried, but no one paid any attention to her now.

Bent Leg nodded.

"Agreed. The combat will take place three days from now, when the sun rises." He looked at his niece. "Until then, you will see neither Preacher nor Two Bears."

She opened her mouth, probably to argue, but stopped short at the stern look on Bent Leg's face. Protesting now might just make things worse, and she seemed to realize that. Her mouth closed into a firm, angry line as she stepped back.

"Everything has been said that needs to be said," Bent Leg snapped. He waved an arm. "Everyone go back to whatever you were doing."

As the crowd broke up, Preacher went over to Lorenzo, Audie, and Nighthawk. He watched Two Bears walk off, still casting resentful glances over his shoulder at the mountain man. Bent Leg ushered Raven's Wing away.

Preacher figured it would be a good idea for him to stay away from the lodge they shared for a little while, to give her time to gather up her things. She would probably move into Bent Leg's lodge with the rest of his family for the time being.

"Well, you seem to have got yourself in

quite a mess," Lorenzo said. "We're gonna get kicked out of this village and I'm gonna have to leave my Honey Gal in the middle of the damn winter."

"It's Preacher's life that's at stake, Lorenzo," Audie pointed out. "If he gets killed, that's worse than us having to find some other place to stay."

"If I get killed, you won't have to leave," Preacher told them. "Bent Leg's an honorable man. He'll let you stay here, and you'll be fine."

"We'll see," Lorenzo said. "After all we been through together, I ain't sure I could stay under circumstances like that, Honey Gal or no Honey Gal."

Preacher clapped a hand on the old-timer's shoulder.

"Maybe it won't come to that," he said.

But the only way he could prevent it was to kill Two Bears, and he didn't want to do that, either.

When he was stalking those Gros Ventre in the badlands, he had thought that he was caught between a rock and a hard place.

Now he really was.

Chapter 18

By the time the snow finally stopped and the sun came out, Willie Deaver was more than a little crazy from being cooped up in the little cabin with his four companions. That was too many men for such a small space, especially when they didn't have anything with which to occupy their time.

Deaver had mentally cursed Manning more than once for shooting that squaw. They could have kept her alive for several days and had their fun with her.

Instead he'd been forced to listen to Fred Jordan and Cy Plunkett recounting endless filthy stories about the women they'd had in their lives. Deaver had been around, and even he didn't think some of the things they talked about were possible.

Darwin Heath, at least, knew how to keep his mouth shut. He didn't say much of anything and in fact slept most of the time they were there.

Deaver and Manning played poker with a greasy deck of cards they'd found among the trapper's gear. They bet and lost fortunes they didn't have yet, and ultimately called it even.

Finally the sun came out, warmed the air a little, and started to melt the snow.

The five men had to wait another day for things to clear off enough for them to leave the cabin and resume their journey. The ground was muddy now from the melted snow and sucked at the horses' hooves as they rode away. Deaver wasn't going to miss this place, that was for sure.

They rode all day. Deaver had been to their destination before, and he was pretty sure he knew how to find it again. He had a good instinct for directions and knowing where he was.

But he was just uncertain enough to make him nervous, and so he was glad that afternoon when he spotted smoke rising into the sky on the other side of a ridge in front of them. Soon they would be where they were going.

Deaver pointed out the smoke to the others, and after a short but necessary stop to take care of some business, they pushed their horses a little harder in their eagerness to reach their destination. They had been so close when the storm blew in, Deaver thought bitterly. Less than a day's ride away.

But now they were here, or almost, anyway.

They found a trail to the top of the ridge, crossed it, and descended into a narrow valley on the other side. The smoke came from several campfires burning among a cluster of wood, mud, and hide lodges. The snow had been deep here, too. Some drifts still remained in the shaded areas underneath trees.

A number of barking and snarling curs bounded out from the village to dance and snap around the horses. Deaver kicked at one of them that came too close, saying, "Get away, you damned beast!" The toe of his boot caught the dog in the side and sent it rolling. When it got up it slunk away, whimpering.

The commotion brought warriors out of their lodges to see what was going on. Many of the men carried bows and arrows, and a few held old trade muskets. Their coppery, hawk-like faces wore suspicious expressions.

As Deaver and his companions reined in, one of the men separated himself from the others and strode forward. He was lean as a whip, and his face bore the pockmarks of the disease that the white men had brought

looked like the redskins were about to pull any sort of double-cross, they would open fire. Each man had a loaded rifle and four loaded pistols, and they could deal out a lot of damage in a hurry, enough to cripple any pursuit by the Gros Ventre.

And the first one to die would be Snake Heart. Deaver would see to that himself.

But if the Indians played square with him, he would play square with them. He said to Manning, "Break out one of those rifles, Caleb."

Manning dismounted. He and Jordan lifted one of the crates down from the horse that had been carrying it, and Manning pulled the lid off of it. He took out one of the rifles and unwrapped it.

Deaver heard murmurs of appreciation from the warriors when the gleaming brass-work and polished wood came into view. He took the rifle from Manning and turned to offer it to Snake Heart.

Deaver could tell that the Gros Ventre chief was trying to act unimpressed, but he saw the unbridled lust — if you could call it that — in Snake Heart's eyes and knew better. Snake Heart was a killer, and he wanted this instrument of death with a fierce passion.

Snake Heart reached out to take the rifle.

He hefted it, examined the flintlock and pan. He cocked it and squeezed the trigger. The rifle wasn't loaded, of course, so it just snapped; but again the assembled warriors murmured at the sound, obviously impressed. Those old pieces of junk they had probably misfired as often as they fired. Maybe more often.

"Load it," Snake Heart said as he thrust the rifle back at Deaver.

Using his own powder and shot, Deaver took the weapon and loaded and charged it. When it was ready to go, he handed it back to Snake Heart. For a second he thought about how Manning had pointed one of the rifles at Odell St. John.

Snake Heart didn't care about trying to be funny, though. He just cared about killing his enemies. He lifted the rifle, cocked it, and aimed it at the same dog Deaver had kicked. The animal was sitting about twenty yards away licking itself.

The rifle boomed.

Snake Heart grunted in satisfaction as he lowered the weapon.

"Meat for stew," he said.

"Whatever you say, Snake Heart," Deaver agreed. "But what did you think of the way it shoots?"

Snake Heart nodded.

"Very good. You say you have one hundred of them?"

"That's right. Enough for every warrior in your village to have one, with some left over."

"With many left over," Snake Heart said with a scowl. "We have lost quite a few men in recent raids on our enemies. But with these guns, we can avenge our fallen warriors. In the spring, the Assiniboine women will wail and cover themselves with ashes as they mourn their dead husbands and fathers and sons and brothers."

"Assiniboine?" Deaver repeated. "That's who you're at war with?"

Snake Heart pointed toward a ridge that lay in the distance to the east.

"On the other side of that ridge is the valley of Bent Leg, the Assiniboine. Long have we warred with each other. But now we have the means to wipe them out at last."

"Bent Leg," Manning said. "That sounds familiar. Ain't that —"

Deaver lifted a hand to stop him from saying anything else. He knew Manning was right. As soon as he had heard the name of the Assiniboine chief, Deaver had remembered what Blind Pete told them before they pinned his hands to the floor with knives and set the trading post on fire.

Preacher and those bastards with him intended to spend the winter with Bent Leg's band of Assiniboine.

"You plan to attack them in the spring?" he asked Snake Heart.

The Gros Ventre chief said, "Yes. We will kill them all."

"Why not do it now?"

"It is winter," Snake Heart said with a frown. "We do not make war in winter."

"You said a while ago that you'd lost some warriors in recent raids."

"The last raids before the snows began to fall. In fact, snow was on the ground when our warriors failed to return."

"So you don't know for sure they're dead."

"They are dead," Snake Heart said in a voice as hard as flint. "If they were not, they would be here with the prisoners I sent them to capture."

"All right," Deaver said. "I believe you. You really need to settle that score with the Assiniboine, and there's no need to wait until spring to do it."

Snake Heart frowned and shook his head, clearly confused.

"Why not attack them now?" Deaver went on. "You know how these storms are. It'll be a few days before another one blows in. Maybe a week or more. That's plenty of time for you to get over to that other valley and raid the Assiniboine. They won't be expecting you at this time of year."

"No," Snake Heart said slowly, "they would not be."

"It's perfect," Deaver urged. "You have these new rifles, we'll bring you the rest of the powder and shot . . . and I'll tell you what, we'll even go along with you to help you."

"You would make war on the Assiniboine with us?"

"Yes," Deaver said. "To show you that we are truly your friends."

And once that news spread among the tribes, he could set up a steady flow of rifles from Canada, in return for an equally steady flow of pelts to him and his partners. He might wind up as rich as some of those blasted fur tycoons back East, Deaver told himself.

That wasn't all, though. Something almost as important might come out of this proposed alliance with the Gros Ventre. If Deaver and the others went on the raid with Snake Heart's warriors, they could make sure that Preacher and his friends died. Being shown up like they had been at Blind Pete's had festered inside Deaver for weeks now. That insult cried out for vengeance . . .

and throwing in with these redskins was the perfect way to get it.

"All right," Snake Heart said as he came to a decision. "You will join us, and we will not wait for spring. Assiniboine blood will flow like a river."

And so would Preacher's, Deaver vowed to himself.

Better watch out, mountain man. We're comin' to get you.

CHAPTER 19

At first Preacher wondered why Bent Leg had decreed that his showdown with Two Bears would take place in three days. Then he realized the chief had given it that much time in hopes that some other resolution would present itself. Bent Leg had to be wondering if he could get away with simply declaring that from now on, Raven's Wing would be Two Bears' woman.

Raven's Wing wouldn't want to go along with that, but she might not have any choice.

The weather stayed fairly pleasant, warm enough to melt all the snow except for a few patches here and there where the deepest shade lurked. Preacher, Lorenzo, Audie, and Nighthawk did some hunting and came back with a couple of good-sized bucks to add to the village's supply of meat for the winter.

As usually happened when something unpleasant was looming, the time seemed to pass more quickly than it should have. The days went by in a hurry, and then it was the night before Preacher and Two Bears would meet in a fight to the death.

Preacher and Lorenzo were in the mountain man's lodge that evening. As they sat by the fire in the center of the lodge, Lorenzo asked, "Are you gonna kill him, Preacher?"

"Two Bears, you mean? That's the idea. Either I kill him or he kills me."

"Well, if those are the only choices, I'm hopin' he's the one who winds up dead. But I was thinkin' maybe you could just beat him but not kill him. That'd be just as good, wouldn't it?"

Preacher shook his head.

"That'd be an even worse insult to Two Bears. He'd just come after me again and again until one of us is dead."

"That's a damned shame. You really think the rest of this bunch will let us stay here for the winter if you kill him?"

"Two Bears' friends may not like it, but Bent Leg will insist on it. To do anything else would be dishonorable for him. The same thing means that if I'm the one who winds up dead, you and Audie and Nighthawk will be fine. This is between me and Two Bears, and nobody else has got anything to do with it."

Lorenzo sighed.

"You know a lot more about how these redskinned folks live than I do, so I'll take your word for it and hope you're right. I sure wish it hadn't come to this, though."

"You and me both," Preacher said.

Lorenzo left a short time later, after wishing him luck come morning. Preacher let the fire burn down and rolled up in his blankets, but he didn't really expect to fall asleep easily. He wasn't scared or even worried — whatever happened would happen, and life would go on for somebody — but like Lorenzo, he regretted that the situation had developed in the first place.

Because he was thinking about that, he was still awake when the hide flap over the lodge's entrance stirred. Preacher's hand moved almost imperceptibly, sliding under a bearskin robe to close around the butt of the pistol he had put there earlier. His other weapons were also placed around the lodge where he could get to them in a hurry if he needed them.

This wasn't an enemy who had come to call, though. By the faint light rising from the fire's embers, Preacher recognized the slim figure of Raven's Wing as she stole into the lodge.

He sat up, causing her to stop short and let out a gasp of surprise.

"What are you doin' here?" Preacher asked. "Bent Leg said you weren't to see me or Two Bears until after the fight. If he found out about this, he could use it as an excuse to call things off and have me killed."

"He would not do that," Raven said. "He knows that I would never forgive him if he did."

Preacher grunted.

"I reckon you've got a different opinion than I do about how much ol' Bent Leg'd be worried about that."

She came across the lodge and dropped to her knees in front of him.

"He will not find out I'm here."

"I hope you're right about that. Why *are* you here?"

"I think we should leave this place, you and I."

"Leave the village? Leave your people?" Preacher shook his head. "I can't ask you to do that."

"You are not asking me! *I* am asking *you.*"

"That would make me look like I was runnin' away, like I was too scared to face Two Bears. I can't do that."

"You and I would know that is not true," Raven argued. "And we would be together.

What else is more important than that?"

Plenty of things, Preacher thought, but she probably wouldn't appreciate it if he said that.

He realized that she was taking things a lot more seriously between them than he ever had. She was a smart, attractive young woman, and he was more than happy to spend the winter with her . . . but he wasn't going to marry her. He had met one woman in his life who he might have considered marrying, and that hadn't worked out well. He didn't intend to ever have to mourn another woman the way he had mourned Jenny.

Raven's Wing likely wouldn't understand any of that, though, even if he had been the sort to talk about such things, which he wasn't.

Instead he said, "I'm sorry. I can't do it."

She took a deep breath.

"Then you must kill Two Bears. Or he will kill you."

"I know that."

She leaned closer, put her hands on her shoulders. He felt her warm breath on his face.

"And tonight . . . tonight you must love me."

"Not a good idea," Preacher forced himself to say. Raven's Wing was hard to resist, as always. "You should leave now, before Bent Leg figures out you're gone."

She shook her head.

"He sleeps. When he does, the mountains could get up and walk around, and he would not know it."

"What about his wives?"

"My aunts?" She smiled. "They want me to be happy."

"So they're helpin' you get away with this. But you don't know that Two Bears or some of his friends ain't keepin' an eye on my lodge. He might've seen you come in here."

"If he had, don't you think he would have made it known by now?"

She had a point there, he supposed.

"No one knows I am here, Preacher," Raven went on. "No one but you. And truly, do you wish to send me away?"

She had pulled up the skirt of her buckskin dress when she dropped to her knees on the robe in front of him. Now she reached down, grasped the garment's hem, and peeled it up and over her head. Preacher's jaw tightened as he saw the reddish glow from the embers playing over her skin.

"No," he growled. "I'm not gonna send you away."

But even as he reached for her, he still

thought this probably wasn't a good idea.

Raven's Wing slipped out of the lodge some time during the night. Preacher knew when she left, but pretended to be asleep. In a way he was glad they'd had at least one more night together.

After several days of welcome sunshine, the morning of the third day dawned with a thick overcast covering the sky. When Preacher stepped out of the lodge and looked up at the gray clouds, he thought that within another day or two the snow would return. He wondered idly if he would be alive to see it.

Bent Leg had said that the showdown would take place when the sun rose this morning. The overcast made it difficult to tell for sure, but Preacher thought that time had already come and gone. Close enough, though, he thought.

The people of the village were converging on a large open area near the creek. There would be plenty of room there for the battle between Preacher and Two Bears. The Assiniboine gathered in a half circle, with the stream cutting off one side of it.

Preacher carried his rifle and two of his pistols as he approached the battleground with Dog padding along behind him. He

saw Lorenzo, Audie, and Nighthawk waiting at the edge of the crowd and angled
toward them.

Audie said, "Preacher, I've wracked my
brain trying to think of a way to avoid this
bloodshed, but I just haven't been able to
come up with anything."

"That's all right," Preacher said with a
smile. "Sometimes things just got to be,
whether you want 'em to or not." He looked
over the crowd. "I don't see Raven's Wing."

"She's in Bent Leg's lodge," Audie explained. "She won't come out until the fight
is over, Bent Leg says. I don't know if that
was her decision or his."

It didn't matter either way, Preacher
thought.

He handed his rifle to Nighthawk.

"I want you to hang on to this for me," he
told the Crow. "If I don't come back to get
it later . . . well, you just keep hangin' on to
it, all right?"

Nighthawk nodded and said, "Umm."

"I appreciate that," Preacher said. He
turned to Audie and pulled the pistols from
behind his belt. "I'll trust you with these."

Audie took the guns as if being handed
them was an honor.

"Thanks, Preacher. I'll take good care of
them."

"I know you will." To Lorenzo, he went on, "There's another brace of pistols in the lodge where I've been stayin'. They're yours if I ain't around no more."

"Now, don't go to talkin' like that," the old-timer said. "We all know you're gonna be just fine. Fine and dandy."

"I hope you're right," Preacher said with a smile. "But if I ain't, I'll be dependin' on all you fellas to see to it that Dog and Horse are took care of proper-like."

Audie nodded.

"Of course, Preacher."

The mountain man scratched at his beard-stubbled jaw.

"I reckon that takes care of everything. All the rest of my possibles, divvy 'em up amongst yourselves however you see fit. And don't never forget . . . you fellas are the best friends a man could ever have."

He shook hands with them one by one, and each handshake ended in a back-slapping embrace.

Then a murmur from the crowd made Preacher look around. He saw Two Bears striding toward him, followed by Bent Leg. The warrior carried a knife.

Preacher drew his own knife. He faced Two Bears, who regarded him with a cold scowl. Preacher kept his own expression neutral. He didn't hate Two Bears, not by a long shot. But he couldn't turn his back on the warrior's challenge, either.

Bent Leg snapped an order, and the crowd parted to let Preacher and Two Bears walk into the open area where they would do battle. As the Assiniboine closed ranks around them again, Bent Leg said to Two Bears, "Do you withdraw your challenge?"

"I do not," Two Bears snapped without hesitation.

The chief looked at Preacher.

"And you still wish to answer it?"

"Not much else I can do," the mountain man drawled.

Regret flickered for a second in Bent Leg's eyes, but other than that he maintained the same stony expression.

"Very well," he said. "Each of you has a knife. These are the only weapons permitted. You will fight to the death, and if one surrenders . . . his life will not be spared."

"Can't put it any plainer than that," Preacher said. "Bent Leg, thank you for the hospitality you and your people have extended to me and my friends. I ask that you continue to honor it for them."

"Of course. You have my word." Bent Leg looked at Two Bears. "Do you wish to speak?"

"No," Two Bears said. "I wish to kill."

Bent Leg sighed and inclined his head. He backed away. Preacher and Two Bears raised their knives and began a slow, wary circling as each man looked for an opening, an advantage that could be seized.

Suddenly, Two Bears leaped forward and slashed at Preacher with the knife. The mountain man twisted away, moving with blinding speed.

And because of that, Preacher's back was to the creek when a rifle shot suddenly blasted and what felt like a giant fist slammed into his body.

CHAPTER 20

The impact drove Preacher off his feet and sent him rolling across the ground. He was so stunned that he was only vaguely aware of hearing more shots, mingled with shouts of surprise, anger, and fear.

He tried to push himself up, but pain radiated out from his left side where he had been struck and made that arm useless. It collapsed under him and he fell. That just made him hurt worse.

But he knew he had to get up. If someone was attacking the Assiniboine village, as seemed likely from all the chaos going on around him, he would make an easy target for the raiders just lying on the ground like this.

Suddenly a strong hand closed around his arm and hauled him upright.

"Go!" a voice urged him. "Head for the lodges!"

It took Preacher a second to realize that

the voice belonged to Two Bears.

He wasn't surprised that the war chief was trying to save his life. Two Bears wanted to be the one to kill him.

He felt the hot wetness on his side as he stumbled toward the lodges. He had dropped his knife when he was shot, so he had to get his hands on some other weapons. Two loaded pistols waited in his lodge.

Preacher would have fallen a couple of times if Two Bears hadn't gripped his arm to steady him. Hoofbeats pounded, causing Preacher to jerk his head around to see what was going on. He saw men on ponies riding through the village, firing what looked like new rifles. They were gunning down every Assiniboine they saw: men, women, and even children. Other members of the band went down screaming under the hooves of the raiders' ponies.

"Preacher!"

The mountain man looked around and spotted Lorenzo, Audie, and Nighthawk standing together, fighting some of the raiders at close quarters. Lorenzo was the one who had shouted his name, and the old-timer was being hard-pressed to hold off a pair of attackers who flailed at him with tomahawks. He blocked the blows with his rifle, but any second now, one of the 'hawks was going to get through and cleave his skull.

Preacher tore loose from Two Bears and lunged toward the melee. His left arm still hung useless, but there was nothing wrong with his right. As one of the raiders lifted his tomahawk to strike again, Preacher reached up and locked his right hand around the man's wrist. A savage twist snapped bones and made the man cry out in pain as he dropped the tomahawk.

Preacher snatched the weapon out of midair and drove it deeply into the side of the raider's neck. Blood spouted in a crimson fountain as Preacher wrenched the tomahawk free. He swung it in a backhand that ripped across the other raider's face, leaving it a gory ruin.

"Praise the Lord!" Lorenzo said. "I thought I was a goner for sure!" He looked down at Preacher's bloodstained shirt. "You're hurt!"

"I'm all right," Preacher said. And for the moment he was, because he was so caught up in the battle that his mind was forcing his body to do things it shouldn't have been capable of.

More raiders crowded between him and Two Bears, causing him to lose sight of the war chief. With his three friends at his side,

Preacher began fighting his way across the village. He wanted to reach Bent Leg's lodge and make sure Raven's Wing was all right.

The other men had emptied their guns, including the ones Preacher had given them, and there was no time to reload in the middle of this pitched battle. Instead, Preacher fought with the tomahawk he had grabbed, and Lorenzo, Audie, and Nighthawk used knives and employed their empty guns as clubs. The Crow had a tomahawk of his own, and he wielded it with deadly efficiency, cleaving skulls and slashing throats.

This was up-close killing, the sort that left a man splattered with his enemies' blood. Because of that, Preacher got a good look at the men with whom he struggled, and there was no doubt in his mind that they were Gros Ventre. Snake Heart had lived up to his name and sent another raiding party against the Assiniboine, even though such things traditionally were not done after the first snowfall.

But tradition and treachery were two different things, Preacher thought as he tried to catch his breath during a momentary lull in the fighting around him.

Something else bothered him even more.

The Gros Ventre were armed with shiny new rifles, not the old, unreliable trade muskets they were supposed to have. The firepower that gave them made a difference, too. They had inflicted a lot of damage on the Assiniboine with those first couple of volleys. The timing could not have been better for them. Most of Bent Leg's people had been assembled to watch the battle between Preacher and Two Bears, and they hadn't been expecting an attack. They were perfect targets.

Screaming in hatred, several Gros Ventre warriors kicked their horses toward the little knot of defenders. Audie finally had managed to reload the pistols Preacher had given him, and both guns roared as he fired. Two of the charging raiders were blown backward off their ponies.

Nighthawk leaped high and dragged another man to the ground. The desperate struggle between them ended a heartbeat later with Nighthawk's tomahawk buried in the raider's skull.

Preacher did the same, pulling a man from horseback and bludgeoning him with the tomahawk, but as he straightened, a runaway horse rammed into him with its shoulder and knocked him spinning off his feet. He rolled across the ground and looked up just in time to see another horse about to trample him.

This was no Indian pony, and Preacher's eyes widened in surprise as he saw the face of the rider. The man was white, with ugly, rawboned features and a shock of yellow hair under his hat. Preacher just had time to recognize him before one of the horse's shod hooves clipped him on the head as he tried to fling himself out of the way.

But even though he knew he had seen the man before, he couldn't put a name with the face, and there was no time to think about it. The hoof's impact was stunning, even though the blow was a glancing one. Blood flooded into Preacher's eyes, blinding him with a crimson wave. He struggled desperately to hang on to consciousness, but that was a fight he was destined to lose.

Oblivion claimed him.

As awareness began to seep back into Preacher's brain, at first he knew only that he hurt. In fact, he seemed to be engulfed in pain from head to toe.

But his head and his side hurt especially bad, and gradually Preacher remembered that he had been kicked by a horse in one place and shot in the other.

Clearly, neither of those injuries had

proved fatal, or else he wouldn't feel like this. He didn't know what was on the other side of the veil or what sort of torments a soul might endure there, but he was pretty damned sure that death was the end of *this* world's pain.

With an effort, he forced his eyes open, then experienced a moment of panic when he still couldn't see anything. Darkness still enfolded him. He tried to move . . .

Then a voice said, "He's awake," and whatever was covering his face went away. Light struck him like a physical blow. He flinched.

"Take it easy, Preacher," the voice went on, and now the mountain man recognized it as belonging to Audie. He experienced a moment of relief that his friend was still alive.

Something cool wiped across his forehead. A wet cloth had been draped across his face when he regained consciousness, he realized. His squinted eyes began to adjust to the light. He made out several figures leaning in around him.

"We figured you was dead for sure, all covered up with blood like you was." That was Lorenzo.

"Umm," added Nighthawk.

Audie said, "Head wounds often bleed

profusely, even they're not really as serious as they appear."

"Does that mean like a stuck pig?" Lorenzo asked.

"Exactly."

"Well, that was the way you looked, all right, Preacher," Lorenzo said. "Bleedin' like a stuck pig."

Audie continued wiping the wet cloth across Preacher's forehead.

"You actually did lose quite a bit of blood from that wound in your side, too," he said. "But I stopped the bleeding, cleaned it, packed it with moss, and bound it up securely. I'm sure you'll hurt like blazes for a while, but barring unforeseen circumstances, I think you'll be fine in a few days. The rifle ball just creased you."

But even a minor wound like that had been enough to knock him down, make him lose that blood Audie spoke of, and render his left arm useless for a while. As he thought about that, Preacher made a conscious effort to flex the fingers of his left hand. He was glad when they responded and he felt them clenching and unclenching.

He could tell now that his shirt was off and his torso was tightly bandaged. The wrappings kept him from drawing a deep breath. He had to lie there breathing shallowly.

From the feel of it, he was stretched out on a bearskin robe. He saw the curving roof of an Assiniboine lodge above his head. The entrance flap was tied back so that light spilled into the lodge.

That light was gray and weak, despite its apparent brilliance when Preacher first opened his eyes. The sun was obscured by clouds, which meant, he hoped, that this was the same day the Gros Ventre raiders had attacked the Assiniboine village.

He started to push himself into a sitting position. At first Audie said, "Preacher, you should just lie there and rest."

Then, as he saw that the mountain man wasn't going to listen to him, he said, "Nighthawk, give me a hand with him."

The Crow's strong arm went around Preacher's shoulders and gently lifted him. Once Preacher was upright, his head spun crazily for a moment. It seemed like the entire earth had suddenly started revolving in the wrong direction.

The sensation eased and his head calmed down. He lifted a slightly trembling hand and touched his forehead. A bandage was wrapped around it, too.

"When that horse's hoof nicked you, it

opened up a good-sized cut," Audie explained. "You'll have another scar to add to your already extensive collection, I'm afraid. But again, I've cleaned and bandaged the injury, and I'm confident that given your hardy constitution, it'll be fine with time."

Preacher nodded. He felt an urge to stand up, but before he could do so, a dark figure appeared in the lodge's entrance, blotting out the weak light for a moment.

"Preacher lives?" Bent Leg asked as he came into the lodge, followed by the larger, burlier form of Two Bears. Preacher was glad to see that both of them appeared to be all right.

"Yes, he regained consciousness a few minutes ago," Audie said in answer to the chief's question. "He's still very weak, but —"

As if to contradict what his friend was saying, Preacher pushed himself to his feet. He swayed a little, but he caught himself before Nighthawk had to grasp his arm to steady him.

Bent Leg took hold of Preacher's right arm and squeezed.

"It is good that you are alive, old friend," he said. "When I saw you covered with so much blood, I feared that you had departed this world for the realm of the spirits."

"And I feared that I had been cheated out of killing you," Two Bears added with a scowl.

"Enough!" Bent Leg snapped at him. "I told you, the battle between the two of you is over! We have more important things to worry about now, like going after the hated Gros Ventre and rescuing our people from them."

Preacher's eyes widened at those words.

Bent Leg saw his reaction and nodded.

"They killed many of us," the chief said in a voice choked with sorrow, "and took a dozen prisoners, including my niece."

Preacher started to shake his head.

"That's right," Two Bears said. "Raven's Wing is now a prisoner of the Gros Ventre once again. But this time it will be I who saves her."

Preacher didn't give a damn who saved her. He just wanted her brought back safely to her home.

"Wait a minute," Audie said. "Preacher, you haven't said anything since you regained consciousness." The diminutive fur trapper sounded worried. "I've heard about men who lost the ability to speak after they suffered a blow to the head. Can . . . can you still talk, Preacher?"

In a rusty, strained voice, Preacher said,

"I . . . can . . . talk. And I'm . . . goin' with you . . . after the Gros Ventre. We got to . . . get those prisoners back. And . . . one more thing."

"What's that?" Audie asked.

"I'm gonna kill . . . Willie Deaver."

CHAPTER 21

"Deaver," Audie repeated, obviously not recognizing the name at first. Then understanding dawned on him and was visible in the way his eyes widened. "That reprobate we clashed with at Blind Pete's Place!"

Preacher nodded and rasped, "Yeah. I caught a glimpse of him durin' the fightin'. In fact, it was his horse that kicked me in the head."

"You are talking about a white man?" Two Bears asked. "It was the Gros Ventre that attacked us!"

Bent Leg lifted a hand and gestured for his war chief to step back.

"Several of my warriors mentioned they thought they saw a few whites with Snake Heart's men. This man Deaver you mention could have been one of them, Preacher."

"He was one of 'em, all right," Preacher said with a nod. His voice was stronger now but still had a rasp to it because of his dry throat. "I need some water."

"I'll fetch it," Lorenzo offered. He hurried out of the lodge with a water skin and headed for the creek.

"Somethin' else I noticed," Preacher went on. "The Gros Ventre had plenty of rifles, and they looked and sounded like they were good ones. They looked new to me, in fact."

With a grim expression on his weathered face, Bent Leg nodded.

"I saw this, too. Never have Snake Heart's men been so well armed."

Audie said, "I can think of a possible explanation for that, Preacher. Blind Pete said that Deaver and those men with him were pretty bad sorts. Suppose they got their hands on some rifles and traded them to the Gros Ventre."

"That's just what I was thinkin'," Preacher said. "And then they came along while Snake Heart and his warriors tried 'em out."

"Yes, that makes sense to me," Audie agreed.

Lorenzo came back from the creek with the water. Preacher took the skin from the old-timer and lifted it to his mouth. He hadn't realized how thirsty he really was until he started to drink. He tipped his head back and let the cold water from the stream flow down his throat.

When he finally lowered the skin, he wiped the back of his other hand across his mouth and said, "Just let me get my gear together, and I'll be ready to ride out with the rest of you fellas."

"Wait just a minute," Audie objected. "You suffered two wounds in that fight, Preacher, and lost a considerable amount of blood. You're in no shape to go chasing off after the Gros Ventre. You need to stay here and rest."

Out of respect for his friend, Preacher let Audie finish. Most men, he would have interrupted and told them to go to hell.

But when Audie had spoken his piece, Preacher said, "I'm goin', and there ain't no use in arguin' with me. If you want to help, round up my guns for me, while I put on a shirt that ain't covered with dried blood."

Audie frowned up at him.

"You're a very stubborn man, do you know that?"

"So I've been told," Preacher said as he summoned up a smile.

"Wait," Two Bears said. "I have not said that any of you white men can ride with us to rescue Raven's Wing and the other prisoners. *I* am war chief here."

The look he gave Bent Leg was an open

challenge.

Preacher swallowed a curse. The last thing they needed to have to deal with right now was Two Bears' hurt feelings. Not when the lives of Raven's Wing and those other prisoners were at stake.

Instead of confronting Two Bears, Preacher turned to Bent Leg and asked, "How many warriors did you lose in this raid?"

"Ten men were killed, another dozen wounded. Seven of them are hurt badly enough that they cannot ride."

"So you're down fifteen warriors," Preacher said. "The four of us can't replace them . . . but I reckon we're a start."

Two Bears opened his mouth to say something again, but Bent Leg silenced him with a lifted hand. Two Bears might be the war chief, but Bent Leg was the ultimate authority in this village.

"Preacher and his friends will go with us," Bent Leg decreed.

"You're riding with the war party?" Preacher asked the old chief.

Bent Leg nodded.

"Every man who is able will go. Only the wounded, the old men, and the boys will stay. They will be enough to protect the village."

Preacher hoped Bent Leg was right about that.

"How many men did the Gros Ventre have?"

Audie answered that question.

"I estimate between forty and fifty."

"And how many of us can we muster?"

"Maybe thirty," Audie admitted. "Counting the four of us."

"So we'll be outnumbered."

"And outgunned," Lorenzo reminded them. "Those savages got all them new rifles."

"Well . . ." Preacher shrugged. "Won't be the first time I've gone into a fight with the odds against me, and I'm still here."

"Your luck came close to running out this time," Audie said.

Preacher shook his head.

"I don't believe in luck. I believe in powder and shot and cold steel."

Even though several hours had passed since the raid on the Assiniboine village, a feeling of exultant triumph still filled Willie Deaver. Not only had the Gros Ventre inflicted a lot of damage on their traditional enemies and carried off a dozen prisoners, so they were well-pleased with the rifles the white men had brought them, but just as important to

Deaver, he had settled the score with the mountain man called Preacher.

It would have been nice if they'd been able to kill the midget and the Crow and the black man, too. Maybe they really were dead; Deaver didn't know, because he had never spotted them in the chaos of battle.

But he *knew* Preacher was dead. The mountain man probably had been mortally wounded by that first shot Deaver had fired to begin the attack, and then a few minutes later fate had smiled on him and placed Preacher directly in the path of his horse.

Deaver had ridden right over him, then reined in and twisted in the saddle to look back and see Preacher sprawled on the ground in the stillness of death with blood covering his entire head.

Deaver would have pumped a rifle ball into the varmint just to make sure, but at that moment one of the Assiniboine had charged him and he'd had to blow the redskin's brains out instead. By the time he looked for Preacher again, the struggling human tides had cut him off from view.

Despite that, Deaver was confident that his enemy was dead. He felt it in his bones.

He felt something else in his bones, too, whenever he looked at one of the captives the Gros Ventre had dragged away from the village. The Assiniboine woman was a mighty good-looker, with hair the color of midnight framing a frightened but still beautiful face.

Maybe he would ask Snake Heart if he could have the woman, Deaver thought. Call her a sort of bonus to go with the pelts that the Gros Ventre were trading for the rifles.

That idea intrigued Deaver, and he wasn't the only one with such thoughts lurking in his head, he realized as Caleb Manning urged his alongside Deaver's mount and asked, "What do you think, Willie? Some of those Injun gals look pretty good for savages, don't they?"

"You just feel that way because the nearest white woman's all the way back in St. Louis," Deaver said. He didn't want Manning horning in on his plans. "I don't reckon Snake Heart would like it too much if we started messin' with the prisoners. He figures they're his by right of capture."

"Well, sure," Manning agreed. "But that don't mean he might not feel generous enough to let us have the use of a few of 'em. After all, we brought him the rifles he used to damn near wipe out those other redskins."

Deaver wasn't sure the Assiniboine were

anywhere near wiped out. Sure, quite a few of them had fallen to the rifle shots, but with all the confusion, it was difficult to tell just how many had been killed . . . and how many were left alive to maybe give chase to the Gros Ventre raiders.

"I'll see what I can talk Snake Heart into once we get back to his village," Deaver said. "Maybe you're right and he'll be feelin' generous. But the main thing is to get those pelts he promised us and to get out with our own hair."

"Well, sure," Manning said.

"And if this setup works out for us the way I think it might," Deaver went on, "we'll all be rich enough to go back to St. Louis and buy us any woman we want. Hell, we might even go back east and get us some of them Philadelphia or Boston women."

"Now you're talkin'," Manning said with a grin.

Deaver turned in his saddle and looked behind them as a chilly wind tugged at his hat. The Gros Ventre war party was stretched out in a line, with a dozen warriors riding double because a prisoner was perched on the pony's back in front of each of them. The women had wailed and cried at first, but they had fallen silent when their captures threatened to slit their throats and dump them beside the trail.

Somewhere back there, the Assiniboine might be coming after them already, Deaver mused. He hoped not, but even if that turned out to be true, Snake Heart's men probably outnumbered the pursuers, and they were damned sure better armed with those new rifles. If there was another fight, Deaver was sure his newfound allies would emerge triumphant again.

It would be better if things didn't come to that, though, and as the raw wind sent a shiver through him, he thought that it would be a lucky break for them if the snow came back sooner than expected. All the storm needed to do was hold off until the Gros Ventre were through that notch in the ridge and into the badlands beyond. Then there could be a blasted blizzard as far as Deaver was concerned. If the snow was heavy enough, it wouldn't take long for drifts to block the notch and prevent the Assiniboine from coming after them.

He glanced at that good-looking prisoner again and wished the Assiniboine woman was riding with him. He could have used that opportunity to get better acquainted with her.

But the time was coming, he told himself. He just had to be patient.

And then that pretty little redskin gal would be his to do whatever he wanted to with her. He would enjoy himself one hell of a lot.

But she probably wouldn't.

By the time Preacher had pulled on a clean buckskin shirt over his bandaged torso, Audie and Nighthawk had returned to the lodge with his rifle and the pistols he had given to Audie earlier. His other two pistols were still there in the lodge, ready to be gathered up with the rest of the gear.

"Nighthawk, can you go saddle Horse for Preacher?" Audie asked.

The Crow nodded and said, "Umm." He left the lodge while Preacher was loading the pistols.

"I still think this is a bad idea," Audie went on. "You should be lying down and resting for the next week, at least."

"You ever know me to take it easy for that long, Audie?" Preacher asked.

"Well . . . no."

Preacher smiled.

"Shoot, here a while back I had to chase down some varmints while I had a busted arm. If I can do that with one wing, I can manage with a little scratch and a bump on this hard ol' noggin o' mine."

"Those injuries are more than a scratch and a bump, and you know it."

Preacher shrugged.

"Maybe, but I'll be all right."

"You won't have it any other way, will you?"

"Nope."

From the lodge's entrance, Lorenzo said, "And I been ridin' with Preacher long enough to know that arguin' with him ain't gonna do no earthly good. I done told you that before, Audie."

"Yes, I know."

Preacher tucked the loaded pistols behind his belt and picked up the other brace of firearms. He would carry them in the holsters strapped to his saddle.

The three men left the lodge. Nighthawk was waiting outside with Horse and the other three mounts. He passed out the reins, then the four men walked toward the area near Bent Leg's lodge where the rest of the war party was assembling. Dog strode alongside Preacher.

"You are ready to ride?" Bent Leg asked when the visitors came up.

"More than ready," Preacher replied for all of them.

"You had better be able to keep up, white man," Two Bears said. "We will not wait for you, and we will not turn back to take care of you."

"I wouldn't expect it," Preacher said, "but I reckon I'll still be goin' as long as you are, old son." He swung up onto Horse's back and settled himself in the saddle. "As long as it takes to bring Raven's Wing and the other prisoners back safely to their home."

Chapter 22

The bandage around Preacher's head made it difficult for him to wear his usual broad-brimmed felt hat. Audie loaned him a coonskin cap instead. The cap wouldn't put as much pressure on the head wound.

An hour after leaving the Assiniboine village, Preacher shrugged into the sheepskin coat he had brought with him. The air was getting downright chilly. He looked at the sky.

Snow up there. How soon it began to fall could have an impact on the pursuit.

When the Gros Ventre rode out of the Assiniboine village, they had been headed due west. There wasn't any doubt that they were going to go through the notch into the badlands and then make their way across that rugged stretch back to their own stomping grounds. So the Assiniboine headed for the notch as well, taking the trail that had been carved out over the years by their ponies.

A heavy snowfall might block that gap in the ridge, which ran for twenty miles or more, Preacher recalled from previous visits to these parts. If the pursuers couldn't get through the notch but had to go the long way around instead, they wouldn't have any chance of catching the raiders before the Gros Ventre got back to their village. That would complicate any effort to rescue the prisoners and make it much more difficult.

So Bent Leg and Two Bears, who could read the weather as well as Preacher could, kept the war party moving as quickly as possible. The long hours in the saddle made Preacher's side ache, but there was nothing he could do about that. As long as the wound didn't break open and start bleeding heavily again, he could put up with a little pain.

Snow began to fall in mid-afternoon, lightly at first, then faster and thicker, but not too bad. The war party had already started to climb the wooded slopes toward the notch, and as Audie rode alongside Preacher, he said, "I think we're going to make it. At the rate the snow is falling, it'll be morning before there's any danger of the gap being blocked, if then."

"That's as long as the snow don't get any

worse," Preacher pointed out.

"Yes, of course, but even if it does, I think we're going to be close enough that we can make a run for it and get through in time."

"I hope you're right," Preacher said. "The last little while, though, I've started havin' a funny feelin' on the back of my neck, like we might have some trouble waitin' for us that we don't know about yet."

From Preacher's other side, Lorenzo said, "I trust those instincts of yours, Preacher. I reckon we better keep our eyes open."

"We're doing that anyway," Audie said. "But I agree with you, Lorenzo. In situations such as this, Preacher is nearly always —"

Audie was about to say *right,* Preacher figured, but the sudden boom of a gunshot interrupted him.

More shots followed, one on top of another, and rifle balls began to whip through the trees around them. A man yelled in pain. Two Bears bellowed orders, telling his men to find cover.

Preacher and his companions dismounted quickly and knelt behind thick-trunked pines. A rifle ball smacked into the tree where Preacher had taken cover and knocked a big chunk of bark off it. He crouched a little lower and searched for the source of the shots.

"Anybody see those damn bushwhackers?" he called to his friends.

"I think they're in a clump of rocks about a hundred yards up the slope," Audie replied.

Preacher risked a look and saw gray fringes of powdersmoke floating in the air above the boulders Audie had mentioned. Audie was right. That had to be where the hidden riflemen were holed up.

"You reckon it's some of them Gros Ventre?" Lorenzo asked.

"More than likely," Preacher said. "Snake Heart must be pretty smart. He knows it's a race between them, us, and that snow, so he left some men behind to slow us down and give them more of a chance to win."

The rest of the war party had scattered and taken cover behind trees as well. The ambushers had done a good job of choosing their hiding place. They were able to lay down fire all across the rough trail leading toward the notch and keep the Assiniboine pinned down.

Some of Bent Leg's warriors sent arrows arching toward the boulders, but at this range if any of them hit their target, it would be just pure luck. Preacher, Lorenzo, Audie, and Nighthawk opened fire on the rocks, but most of their shots ricocheted harm-lessly.

"Hold on!" Preacher called to his compan-ions. "We're just wastin' powder and lead. They're dug in up there, and there ain't much we can do about it from where we are."

He looked along the line of trees where the war party had taken cover, and his heart leaped into his throat when he spotted Bent Leg lying behind one of the pines with Two Bears working over him. It was obvious that the chief was wounded.

"You fellas make it hot for those varmints for a minute," Preacher told his friends. "Bent Leg's been hit. I'm gonna go see how bad it is."

As soon as Audie, Nighthawk, and Lo-renzo had reloaded their rifles, Audie said, "All right, Preacher, go!"

They opened fire as the mountain man sprinted toward the tree where Bent Leg lay. Audie fired first, then Nighthawk, then Lorenzo, spacing out their shots to give Preacher as much time as they could.

By the time Preacher reached the tree, Two Bears had Bent Leg sitting up with his back propped against the trunk. Preacher knelt behind a nearby tree, since that one wasn't big enough to shield all of them.

"How bad is it?" he called to Two Bears, who was wrapping a strip of cloth around Bent Leg's upper right arm.

Bent Leg answered the question himself before Two Bears could.

"I live," he said. "I can fight."

Two Bears grunted and shook his head.

"His arm is broken. I will bind up the wound, then tie branches on it as splints."

"My arm is not —" Bent Leg started to say, then he stopped and groaned as Two Bears straightened his arm. From the look on the chief's face, Preacher knew that bones were grinding together in there as Two Bears worked them back into place.

"You cannot go on," Two Bears said as he started looking around for broken branches he could use as splints. "You must go back to the village."

"The warriors of the Assiniboine need their chief!" Bent Leg protested.

"And they will still need their chief when they return," Two Bears said.

Preacher picked up a couple of branches and tossed them over to Two Bears.

"Use those," he suggested. "They look like they'll keep that arm straight until he can get back to the village and the women can take care of it properly."

Two Bears gave Preacher a curt nod,

which was as close as he was going to come to saying thanks, the mountain man thought. That was fine with him. He didn't need or want Two Bears' gratitude. The only thing that mattered was rescuing those prisoners.

When Two Bears had the chief's broken arm splinted, Bent Leg leaned back against the tree and sighed.

"You will lead the war party now," he told Two Bears.

Two Bears nodded again and said, "Of course. We must get around the men Snake Heart left behind."

The snow continued to fall, slowly but steadily getting thicker. White had already started to accumulate on the ground and on the tree branches.

Two Bears went on, "I will circle around and attack them from behind."

"By yourself?" Preacher asked. "They'll kill you if you do. Half a dozen rifles against a tomahawk and a knife ain't my idea of a fair fight."

Two Bears glared at him.

"Then what do *you* think we should do, white man?"

"Let me and Nighthawk go," Preacher suggested. "I'll give him my two extra pistols. If we can get amongst 'em before we open fire, we'll make the odds look a heap better in a hurry."

Bent Leg looked up at Two Bears and nodded.

"It is wise," he said. "Preacher and the Crow are known for their stealth."

"No one is stealthier than Two Bears!"

"Maybe not," Preacher said, "but I reckon Nighthawk has probably handled pistols more than you have."

Two Bears didn't like it, but he couldn't argue with the logic of Preacher's argument.

Preacher caught Nighthawk's attention and motioned back the way they had come from. As the Crow began to withdraw, Preacher said, "Dog, you come with me, too," and slipped through the trees. The Gros Ventre continued firing from the rocks, but to be honest, they weren't the best shots in the world, Preacher thought. A lot of the balls went high, whipping through the branches and dislodging some of the snow that had started to deposit on the boughs.

A couple of the Assiniboine had taken charge of the horses and led them back away from the standoff. Preacher told Nighthawk, "Come with me," and went to Horse. He drew the two extra pistols from their sheaths and handed them to the Crow.

"They're loaded and charged, and I know

you know how to use 'em," Preacher went on. "You and me are gonna circle around and hit them varmints from behind. Those pistols are double-shotted, and so are the ones I'm carryin'. Hell, when we cut loose our wolf, we might just take down the whole bunch with one volley."

It would take a lot of luck to accomplish that, but it wasn't out of the question. At the very least, they could do enough damage with the four pistols to make the odds a lot closer to even. Preacher was more than willing to take his chances in almost any hand-to-hand fight.

Moving quickly on foot with Dog trotting along beside them, Preacher and Nighthawk made their way through the woods at right angles to the trail they had been following. The going was rough because of thick brush, but the two men were good at finding openings where none seemed to exist.

When they had covered several hundred yards, Preacher turned back toward the ridge. The growth would make it hard for the Gros Ventre to spot them now. Preacher blinked away snowflakes that landed on his eyelashes and melted as he and Nighthawk started up the slope.

The shooting continued, rifles cracking in the rocks and down below in the trees as

Lorenzo and Audie kept up a return fire. But here in this snowy wilderness, the reports seemed almost muffled somehow. It was as if nature was trying to impose winter's peace on the land, but man kept stubbornly resisting it.

Preacher gradually maneuvered himself and Night hawk above the Gros Ventre bushwhackers hidden in the boulders. They went to their bellies and crawled through the snow until they came out on a jutting lip of land that overlooked the cluster of rocks.

From the sound of the shots, Preacher had estimated that there were six Gros Ventre riflemen. A quick head count confirmed that. All the raiders seemed to be uninjured, which meant that none of the arrows or rifle shots fired from below had found their marks. That didn't surprise Preacher.

He put his mouth close to Nighthawk's ear and said, "We need to get down there closer. These pistols ain't accurate for distance work."

Nighthawk nodded but didn't say anything. He gestured toward the slope in front of them, which was pretty steep as it led down to the rocks where the Gros Ventre were crouched.

"Yeah, I see what you mean," Preacher

agreed. "If we slide down, we'll be right in the middle of 'em by the time they know we're comin'."

Nighthawk nodded gravely.

"And I don't need to be doin' much jumpin', anyway, on account of this crease in my side," Preacher went on. "So this'll work out for the best. You ready?"

Nighthawk took the pistols from behind his belt and cocked them by way of answer.

With a tight grin on his face, Preacher slipped closer to the edge. He swung his legs around so he could slide down feet first. He motioned for Dog to stay. When the time came, he would give the big cur the order to attack.

Nighthawk moved up beside Preacher and nodded again to indicate his readiness. Preacher cocked both of his pistols and lifted them. He used his legs to pull himself forward, and suddenly his weight tipped him in that direction as well. He started sliding down the hard-packed slope toward the rocks.

Instinct must have warned one of the Gros Ventre warriors. He glanced around as he reloaded his rifle, then yelled in alarm and leaped to his feet. He swung his rifle up, but before he could fire, Preacher was practically on top of him. The pistol in the mountain man's left hand roared, and the raider was thrown back as both balls from the weapon smashed into his chest.

The fight was on.

CHAPTER 23

As Preacher reached the bottom of the slope, he swung his right-hand pistol toward a spot behind a particularly large boulder where three of the Gros Ventre crouched. He pulled the trigger, and the weapon went off with a deafening boom as the extra-heavy charge of powder detonated.

Two of the three raiders went down. One of them had his throat torn out by the shot, while the other doubled over as the second ball punched into his guts.

But that left the third warrior, and he let out a screech of hatred as he jerked his rifle up and fired.

Preacher felt the hot breath of the ball as it went past his beard-stubbled cheek. He yelled, "Dog!"

The big cur sailed off the top of the slope in a leap that carried him right into the man who had just fired at Preacher. The raider tried to scream, but Dog's strong jaws locked on his throat before he could get a sound out. Dog's weight knocked the man off his feet, and the long, sharp teeth finished the job of savaging him by ripping out his throat.

During the brief battle, Preacher had heard Nighthawk's two pistols go off. He swung around now to find out how the Crow was doing. He was in time to see Nighthawk finish off the last of the Gros Ventre with a blow that sent the head of his tomahawk biting deep into the man's skull.

All six of the bushwhackers were accounted for.

The shooting from the trees down below had stopped. Preacher figured Audie and Lorenzo must have heard the pistols and realized that Preacher and Nighthawk had launched their attack.

But just to be sure that nobody got trigger-happy, Preacher shouted, "Hold your fire! Me and Nighthawk are comin' out!"

He stepped away from the boulders where the others could see him and waved to them.

"Come ahead! The varmints have all gone under!"

Within a few minutes, Audie, Lorenzo, and the members of the Assiniboine war party had hiked up the slope to join Preacher and Nighthawk. Bent Leg was haggard from the pain of his broken arm, but still firmly in command.

"None of our warriors were killed in this ambush," the chief told Preacher, "but three besides myself were injured badly enough to go back to the village. You are four fewer now."

"Yeah, well, six of *them* are dead." The mountain man grinned as he waved a hand at the corpses. "We're whittlin' 'em down."

"The snow still falls. Their deaths cost us time we may not be able to afford."

Preacher glanced at the bodies again. Dead men cooled off quick in weather like this. The snow was starting to stick to their faces.

"You're right," he told Bent Leg. "We need to get movin' again."

Two Bears said, "I lead the war party and give the orders, white man, not you."

"Fine," Preacher snapped. "As long as we get those prisoners back safe and sound, I don't give a damn who's in charge."

Two Bears looked like he wanted to say something else, but after a second he turned and called to his men, "Mount up!"

Once the wounded had turned back to the village and the rest of the war party was back on the trail leading up to the notch in the ridge, Lorenzo rode next to Preacher and said, "I'm startin' to pick up some of the lingo, but I couldn't keep up with all the jabberin' goin' on. Who's in charge here, you or Two Bears?"

"Two Bears is the war chief," Preacher said. "He's givin' the orders." He paused. "As long as they're the right ones and don't seem likely to get us killed."

"And if what he wants to do *ain't* the right thing?"

"Then we're liable to have trouble," Preacher said.

Snow had started to collect in the notch when Deaver, Snake Heart, and the rest of the Gros Ventre raiding party rode through it, but the passage was far from being blocked.

A short time earlier, they had heard a lot of shooting coming from down below. Deaver hoped that meant any Assiniboine who were coming after them had been wiped out by the men Snake Heart had left behind. They would know later, when those men either rejoined them . . . or didn't.

For now, Deaver was confident that they were still ahead of any pursuit. Snake Heart seemed to be equally confident, because he called a halt on the other side of the notch so they could rest their horses.

Deaver and his partners dismounted. Caleb Manning came over and asked, "Are you gonna talk to Snake Heart about those women now, Willie?"

"Don't get in such a hurry," Deaver snapped. "I said I'd talk to him when we got back to the Gros Ventre village."

"I know. It's just been a long time since any of us have been with a woman."

Deaver gestured toward the rocky ground, which was rapidly acquiring a coating of snow.

"You reckon this is a good place for carryin' on?" he asked sarcastically.

"Well, no," Manning admitted. "I was just hopin' we could get things settled with Snake Heart, so we'll know what's waitin' for us when we get back to the village."

"Let's just worry about gettin' back there first."

Manning didn't look happy about it, but he nodded.

Despite what Deaver had said to his lieutenant, his eyes kept going back to the Assiniboine woman he found so striking. Like the other captives, she had her hands lashed together in front of her with rawhide thongs, but her legs were free so she could ride.

When the Gros Ventre warrior who had

been riding double with her lifted her down from the pony, as soon as her mocassin-shod feet touched the ground she swung her clubbed hands against the side of his head in an unexpected blow.

The impact made the warrior stagger to the side. The woman seized the opportunity to run. She dashed toward the notch in the ridge.

Deaver wasn't sure where she thought she was going. She couldn't possibly get away. Her path took her fairly close to him, and as the warrior she had struck yelled for her to stop, Deaver took a swift step and reached out to wrap his arm around the woman's waist and jerk her to a halt.

She cried out in frustration, twisted in his grip, and started flailing at him with her bound hands. Deaver got his other arm up to block the blows. She kicked at his shins but couldn't do any damage.

Then she surprised Deaver by yelling at him in English, "Let me go, you bastard! Let me go!"

Deaver threw his head back and laughed.

"Speak the white man's tongue, do you, girl?" he demanded.

The others, white and Gros Ventre alike, gathered around to watch the entertaining spectacle of the young woman struggling against Deaver. It didn't last long, because Snake Heart strode up and barked, "Give her to me!"

Deaver glanced at the reed-thin, pock-marked war chief and saw the jealousy and anger burning in Snake Heart's eyes. He felt an immediate, primitive urge to challenge Snake Heart for this woman.

He couldn't afford to indulge that urge, though, so he shoved her toward the Gros Ventre. Snake Heart grabbed her, sliding one arm around her neck and using his other hand to bring up his knife. The tip of the blade pricked the soft skin under her chin.

"Next time you try to escape, you die," Snake Heart said, using English since that was a common language for them.

Deaver figured that was a hollow threat. Snake Heart wanted the woman; he wasn't going to kill her.

But she probably didn't know that, and no matter how feisty she was, it was hard for anybody to argue with a knife at the throat. Deaver saw the fight go out of her — at least for now — as she sagged slightly in Snake Heart's grip.

"How are you called?" the war chief asked. He pressed a little harder with the knife when the answer was slow in coming.

"I am . . . Raven's Wing," the young woman said, tight-lipped because of the cold steel barely digging into her skin. Deaver knew she didn't want it going any deeper.

"Raven's Wing," Snake Heart repeated. "Never again will you fly like the raven, Assiniboine. Your wings are clipped. You are Snake Heart's woman now."

Well, that was a mighty sorry development, thought Deaver, but he couldn't say that he hadn't seen it coming, even though he had recognized Snake Heart's interest in the woman only moments earlier. That had been enough of a warning, so he knew what was going to happen.

The question now was, what was he going to do about it? The last thing he wanted to do was to fight Snake Heart over the woman. That could ruin the whole gun-smuggling scheme while it was still in its infancy, before he had a chance to grow rich from it.

Anyway, she was just a squaw, he told himself. There were plenty of Indian women out here on the frontier. If he couldn't have this one, he'd just get himself another.

But he sure wished he hadn't looked into those dark, fiery eyes and felt their pull. It had been a long time since he had wanted a particular woman this badly.

"You might thank me for grabbin' her," he pointed out to Snake Heart.

The Gros Ventre looked at him coldly.

"The woman would not have gotten away."

"Maybe not, but I made sure of that. And if you want to pay me back for helpin' out like that . . ."

"What is it you want?" Snake Heart asked impatiently.

This was a chance to make Manning and the others even more loyal to him than they already were, Deaver sensed. He said, "My men have been a long time without a woman. When we return to your village, I know they'd appreciate if they got to spend some time with those prisoners . . . and if you'd allow them to do that, I'd appreciate it, too."

"What about you? You do not want a woman?"

"I didn't say that," Deaver answered, being deliberately vague about it.

He wanted a woman, all right. One woman. The one called Raven's Wing. There was no denying it.

And he promised himself in that moment that he would find a way to have her, somehow. No matter what it took, short of ruining his plans to get rich.

"Very well," Snake Heart said with a nod. "When we return to the village, your men can have their pick of the prisoners . . . except for this one. She belongs to Snake Heart."

You go ahead and tell yourself that, you red-skinned bastard, thought Deaver, even though there was a smile on his face.

Raven's Wing was never going to belong to anybody except him.

Night was not far off when Preacher and his companions reached the top of the ridge and the gap that led through it. Snow had drifted a couple of feet deep in the notch, but it was still passable for the horses.

"Once again we face a journey through the badlands," Two Bears said as the men reined in and looked over the rugged, snow-draped terrain in front of them. "Can your dog follow a scent through this snow?"

"Maybe," Preacher said. "It won't be easy, though."

Frustration made one of the muscles in Two Bears' tightly clenched jaw jump a little.

"We are not going to catch them. We will have to follow them all the way to their village."

Preacher tried not to sigh.

"Looks like you're right. Can you find the place?"

"I can find it."

"Yeah, but can you find your way through the badlands . . . or will we be wanderin' around in there for the rest of the winter?"

"I will lead us through," Two Bears snapped. "And once I have, it will not be difficult to locate the Gros Ventre village."

Audie had moved his horse up alongside their mounts while they talked. Now he said, "Maybe we could trade something to the Gros Ventre for the prisoners. A lot of times that's all it amounts to when they take captives, just something to give them some bargaining power."

Two Bears shook his head.

"Not Snake Heart," he declared confidently. "He has no interest in ransom or in trading with us. His heart is filled with hate, as his name says, and all he wants to do is kill Assiniboine. He will hold them so we have no choice but to come for them, and he believes that when we do, he will kill all of us."

"Well, then," Preacher drawled, "I reckon we'll just have to surprise him."

CHAPTER 24

The rescue party camped just below the notch. It was a long, cold, miserable night as the men huddled in their robes and blankets. With the wind blowing and the snow falling, it was impossible to keep a fire going, so there was no hot food, no chance to warm up next to merrily dancing flames.

The cold made the wound in Preacher's side ache like a son of a gun, and his head throbbed from the wallop it had taken. He was getting too old for adventures like this, he told himself as he lay with a couple of blankets tucked tightly around him and tried not to shiver from the cold.

One of these days he ought to go back home, get some land to farm, maybe find him a widow woman to marry. He could sit on the porch of an evening, smoke his pipe, watch the sun go down, and just enjoy the peace and quiet.

He had to chuckle to himself at that

thought. That was about as likely to happen as it was for buffalo to sprout wings and go flying over the prairie.

For some men, such things were just never going to happen, and Preacher knew he was one of them. Someday he would die with a bullet or an arrow or a knife in him, either freezing on a mountaintop or scorching under a desert sun.

He just hoped that when his time came, he had a weapon of his own in his hand, and the last thing he heard on this earth was an enemy's dying scream.

For a man like him, that would be a good death, a better death than going to meet his Maker lying in a bed somewhere peaceful with a bunch of folks standing around him with glum expressions on their faces.

Of course, given the tumultuous life he'd led, it would more likely be Ol' Scratch waiting for him on the other side of the divide, not St. Peter.

In that case, Preacher would just spit in the son of a bitch's face and keep fightin'.

It was what he did.

And with those thoughts in his head, he dozed off.

When he woke up an unknowable time later, it was to the sounds of men yelling and guns booming.

Preacher had gone to sleep with a pistol in one hand, the other short gun behind his belt, and his rifle right beside him. Dog was on his other side. As he threw the blankets aside and sat up, he saw that the big cur was already standing, ears pricked forward, the fur on his back ruffled, a growl rumbling deep in his throat.

"Sic 'em, Dog!" Preacher ordered. Dog was off like a shot, arrowing toward some struggling figures nearby. Preacher knew that Dog's sensitive nose would tell him which men were friends and which ones were foes.

Snake Heart had struck again, Preacher thought as he uncoiled smoothly to his feet. When the first bunch of ambushers never returned, the Gros Ventre war chief had sent some of his men doubling back to attack the pursuers.

Drawing his other pistol, Preacher strode forward, but he had gone only a couple of steps when a howling figure lunged at him out of the darkness. Preacher ducked as a tomahawk slashed through the air where his head had been an instant earlier. He jammed the barrel of his right-hand pistol against the raider's chest and squeezed the trigger.

The man's body muffled the dull boom

somewhat. The Gros Ventre flew backward and landed in a limp sprawl on the snow. His buckskin shirt was on fire from the burning powder blown out of the muzzle, along with the two heavy lead balls that had punched a fist-sized hole in his chest and smashed his heart into pulp.

Preacher wheeled to his left as his instincts warned him. An arrow cut the air beside his head. He fired the left-hand gun and sent the man who had just launched the arrow spinning off his feet. Preacher shoved the empty pistols behind his belt and drew his knife.

It was close, bloody work, punctuated by screams, shouts, Dog's fierce snarls, and the occasional roar of a gunshot.

When it was over, Preacher's knife dripped red and bodies were sprawled around on the rocky ground with snow collecting on them. Preacher sought out his friends and was relieved to find that Lorenzo, Audie, and Nighthawk were all right.

"It was a near thing," Lorenzo said. "I come mighty close to gettin' my brains bashed out by one o' them Gros Ventre who come after me with a tomahawk. I got my rifle up just in time to jab him in the belly with it and hold him off until I could pull the trigger."

Blood welled from a shallow gash on Audie's forehead. That was the only injury among the four of them.

The Assiniboine rescue party had suffered three more deaths, though.

"One of the men who died was standing guard," Two Bears explained. "It would have been worse if he had not been able to sound the alarm, even mortally wounded."

Six Gros Ventre warriors were dead. Again the Assiniboine had dealt out more damage than they had received. At this rate, the parties would soon be close to the same strength, if they weren't already.

But that didn't really matter, Preacher thought, because as soon as the Gros Ventre reached their village, the odds would go back up again. Frustration gnawed at the mountain man's gut as he thought about the things that might happen to Raven's Wing and the other captives before the rescue party caught up to them.

They pitched the bodies of the Gros Ventre into a ravine for the scavengers. The bodies of the Assiniboine who had been killed were wrapped in blankets and placed in a hollow, and then their fellow warriors piled rocks on top of them to form a cairn. That was all they could do to protect the remains of their former comrades from predators.

No one slept much the rest of the night. For those who did doze off, their slumber was haunted by memories and nightmares.

Crossing the badlands took most of a day, and even though Deaver had been through here before on the way to the Assiniboine village, he knew he would have gotten hopelessly lost in a hurry if he'd had to navigate through these wastes on his own.

Snake Heart seemed to know exactly where he was going, though, and Deaver was grateful for that.

When the raiders camped the night before, Snake Heart kept Raven's Wing close to him, tied hand and foot, but he hadn't tried to assault her. This barren, rocky terrain was too cold and uncomfortable for such goings-on, as Deaver had pointed out to Caleb Manning the previous day. Snake Heart was willing to wait until they got back to the Gros Ventre village for that.

The other raiders were equally patient. The Assiniboine women sobbed softly to themselves, but as far as Deaver could see, they really didn't have that much to complain about so far. Sure, they had been ripped away violently from their homes and families, tied up, and carried into these badlands, but things could have been a lot worse for them.

Things *would* be a lot worse for them. Just give their Gros Ventre captors time, Deaver thought with bleak humor as the group rode out the next morning.

The raiding party was considerably smaller now. Snake Heart had lost some men in the attack on the Assiniboine village itself, and during the pursuit he had left two separate bunches of warriors on their back trail to discourage the Assiniboine.

Surprisingly, none of those men had come back, which likely meant they were all dead. The pursuers were giving a better account of themselves than Deaver expected.

And they were still back there, still coming along doggedly after them. The Gros Ventre got confirmation of that late in the afternoon when they paused on top of a hogback ridge and looked back out over the rugged terrain they had crossed that day, which was now covered with snow. Snake Heart leveled an arm, pointed, and said with bitter anger in his voice, "There."

Deaver looked where the war chief was pointing, and at first he didn't see anything.

Then he spotted some tiny black dots moving against the white landscape and grunted in recognition.

"Riders," he said.

Snake Heart nodded. He had Raven's Wing on his pony today, sitting in front of him with her hands tied again. He hadn't given her a chance to make another break for freedom. Her head was still up, though, and defiant anger still burned in her dark eyes.

He would beat that out of her once she was his woman, Deaver promised himself.

But not too quickly. He wanted to break her spirit, true, but he intended to enjoy himself while he was taming her. Sometimes, the more fight a woman put up, the more he liked it.

"I can see 'em," he told Snake Heart, "but I can't make out any details. Got to be the Assiniboine, though."

Before Snake Heart could reply, Raven's Wing said, "My people will kill all of you. Preacher and Two Bears will lead them, and you will all die."

Snake Heart cuffed her on the side of the head, making her cry out more from surprise than pain.

Deaver had to laugh.

"You think that mountain man's gonna help you?" he asked. "Preacher's dead!"

The stricken look she gave him told Deaver that she cared for Preacher. Hell, for all he knew, she had become his squaw and moved in with him for the winter.

That would make things even better for him when the time came, Deaver thought. His anticipation was growing by leaps and bounds.

Even though Snake Heart had walloped her, Raven's Wing glared over at Deaver and insisted stubbornly, "You lie, white man! Preacher is not dead."

"I put a rifle ball in him myself," Deaver boasted. "And then later during the fightin', my horse trampled him and stove in his skull. He's dead, girl. Don't you make any mistake about that."

Deaver's words did something that all the other mistreatment Raven's Wing had received had failed to accomplish.

They made despair appear in her eyes.

She lowered her head and fought back a sob. When Deaver saw how upset she was, he wished he had told her about Preacher's death earlier. He hadn't known until now, though, of the connection between the two of them.

"You mourn over a white man?" Snake Heart said disgustedly. "They are even more disgusting than the Assiniboine! If you allowed a white man to touch you, truly you are fit to be only the lowest of slaves."

If he felt that way about her, Deaver thought, then maybe he wouldn't be so determined to hang on to her for himself. And Deaver didn't care who she'd been with. He just wanted her.

Snake Heart pulled his horse around. "They cannot catch us," he went on. "We will be back in our village by nightfall, and once we are there, no one will dare to come after us. The Assiniboine are finished. They might as well turn around and go home."

Deaver didn't really expect that to happen, but he wasn't particularly worried about the pursuit, either. With their numbers and their superior firepower, the Gros Ventre could hold off any attack by a party of Assiniboine bent on taking revenge and rescuing the prisoners.

As the raiders rode on, Manning said quietly to Deaver, "I'm sure lookin' forward to gettin' there, Willie, now that Snake Heart's promised us some time with those squaws. This is gonna be some night."

"Yeah," Deaver said. But maybe not for him, though. He might have to wait a while to get what he really wanted.

It was going to be worth the wait.

The snow was still falling when the pursuit resumed that morning, but it stopped by midday, although the sky remained overcast. Once again the pursuers relied on Dog's keen nose to guide them, because the snow had blotted out the tracks of the Gros Ventre as it fell.

Two Bears was convinced that he knew his way through the badlands, but Preacher could tell that the war chief was glad they had Dog along, too. Sometimes the big cur lost the scent, but he always found it again, and the paths he took agreed for the most part with the way Two Bears thought they should go.

Preacher rode with Lorenzo, Audie, and Nighthawk. Lorenzo had bound up Audie's head wound with some strips torn off his shirt.

The old-timer asked, "Since we ain't likely to catch 'em before they get back to their village, what do you reckon we'll do once we get there?"

"Snake Heart is bound to have left some of his warriors behind," Audie said, "which means that his force will be considerably stronger than ours again. And since they'll be expecting trouble, I don't think a direct attack would prove to be successful."

"Umm," Nighthawk said.

"That's true," Audie agreed. "They might kill the captives rather than letting us rescue them. Snake Heart is certainly cruel enough to do just that."

"They ain't gonna kill nobody," Preacher said harshly. "I'm thinkin' me and Nighthawk will get into the village and free the prisoners. Then the rest of the bunch can attack as a diversion while we get the gals outta there."

"Lemme get this straight," Lorenzo said. "You're gonna turn them women loose and then we take off for home, right?"

"That's about the size of it," Preacher said.

"Well, what's to stop this Snake Heart fella from comin' after us? Seems like we're liable to just take turns chasin' each other back and forth across those blasted badlands!"

"I can't vouch for the rest of the Gros Ventre," Preacher said, "but I'm gonna see to it that Snake Heart don't come after us."

"How do you plan on doin' that?" Lorenzo wanted to know.

"By killin' him, of course," Preacher replied in a hard, flat voice.

"Oh." Lorenzo nodded. "Well . . . I should'a knowed it, I reckon, and never asked the question in the first place!"

CHAPTER 25

Dog wasn't infallible. He led them down a few false trails, a few dead ends that required the members of the war party to turn around and retrace their steps until Dog picked up the scent again.

But the big cur led them through this snowy, trackless wasteland better than anybody else could have, Preacher thought. And for damn sure better than Two Bears, although Preacher didn't bother voicing that opinion even to his friends, who would have agreed with him. No point in it.

They came to the end of the badlands as the light was fading from the overcast sky. Preacher was glad to see some trees again after the seemingly endless expanse of rock and bare ground. He had no idea what had caused the lack of vegetation, or what calamity had scored and scoured the ground behind them, but during his long years of wandering he had encountered similar blighted places elsewhere on the frontier, stretches of barren wasteland in country that was green and lush everywhere else.

At the moment, the terrain in front of them wasn't green but rather white because it was covered with snow, but at least it didn't have great gashes in the earth running through it anymore.

"How far is the Gros Ventre village from here?" Preacher asked Two Bears as the group stopped to rest the horses.

The war chief shook his head and said, "We cannot reach it by nightfall."

"Can you find it in the dark?"

"Perhaps."

Audie said, "Maybe it would be better to wait for morning."

"No," Two Bears said flatly. "I will not leave our women in the hands of those savages that much longer."

"If we try to find the village tonight and wind up getting lost, it might take us that much longer tomorrow to find it," Audie pointed out.

"I agree with Two Bears," Preacher said, and the war chief looked a little surprised by that. "We know the general direction they were goin'. If we keep headin' that way, we ought to smell their smoke sooner or later."

Lorenzo said, "They'll be waitin' for us,

won't they?"

"More than likely," the mountain man replied.

"Then I think we should go on, too. Gives 'em less time to get ready for us that way."

Two Bears nodded.

"The black white man is right."

"Well, I appreciate somebody realizin' that for a change, but about that black white man business —"

"We go," Two Bears went on as if he didn't even hear Lorenzo.

With a sigh and a shake of his head that brought a grim chuckle from Preacher, Lorenzo repeated, "We go."

Darkness closed in quickly once the riders entered the trees. The snow muffled the hoofbeats of the horses, and the cold, the gloom, and the quiet created an eerie atmosphere that sent shivers creeping up Preacher's spine.

He was a practical, hard-headed man, but like most hombres who lived in these mountains, he had a superstititous streak in him, too. He wasn't afraid of anything that walked on two or four legs, but as the riders wound their way through this snow-draped forest, it was like they were traversing a land of the dead. All the sin-shouters claimed that hell was fiery hot, but to Preacher's mind it had always seemed just as likely that it would be cold.

It didn't help matters that there were no animals around. Preacher told himself they are all hunkered down in their dens and burrows waiting for warmer weather to show themselves again, but a little voice in the back of his head warned him that they had all fled this area because they knew something bad was going to happen soon.

Preacher tried to banish those thoughts from his mind, but it wasn't easy. He had come to the valley of the Assiniboine hoping to spend a nice, peaceful winter, but instead there had been one outbreak of trouble and violence after another, as if those things had followed him north from Santa Fe. He knew it wasn't true, but it seemed like that, anyway.

With all those uneasy thoughts rattling around in his head, it came as a relief when he lifted his head, sniffed the air, and caught a faint tang of wood-smoke. A fire meant there was somebody alive in these parts.

Unless it was the pits of Hades he was smelling, that mocking voice told him.

"Can't be," he growled. "I don't smell no brimstone."

"What?" Lorenzo asked from beside him. "Brimstone? What you talkin' about,

Preacher?"

The mountain man laughed.

"Nothin'. Forget it. I didn't even know I said that out loud."

"Man goes to talkin' to hisself, it generally ain't a good thing. It's even worse if he starts answerin'."

"I reckon that's true." Preacher nudged Horse for ward until he came alongside Two Bears. "I smell smoke."

The war chief nodded.

"So do I. The Gros Ventre camp is ahead of us. We will be there soon."

"Probably be a good idea to stop and figure out exactly what we're doin'," Preacher suggested.

He thought Two Bears might get stiffnecked and refuse to consider that idea simply because Preacher was the one who brought it up. But after a second, Two Bears nodded and said, "Yes, we should talk. You and the Crow are not going into the Gros Ventre village."

"Blast it —" Preacher began.

"You and I are going," Two Bears went on. "And this time you will not persuade me otherwise."

Preacher frowned in thought. He had seen Two Bears in action and knew the man could handle himself in a fight. Two Bears would have never become the war chief of Bent Leg's band if that were not the case.

But being good at brawling didn't mean Two Bears could sneak into an enemy camp without being seen or heard. Preacher knew from experience that Nighthawk was capable of that.

He shook his head and said, "The lives of all those prisoners depend on us gettin' in there without the Gros Ventre knowin' about it."

"You think I cannot do it?" Two Bears demanded.

"I didn't say that. But I don't *know* that you can, and that's a whole other thing. I ain't sure I want to risk everything on —"

"On my abilities?" Two Bears said as he reined his pony to a halt and glared over at Preacher. "Is that what you are saying?"

Preacher stopped Horse as well, and the rest of the rescue party followed suit.

"If you want the bold-faced truth, that's exactly what I'm sayin'," Preacher told Two Bears. "I've seen enough to know that you're a fine warrior, but sneakin' ain't the same thing as fightin'."

"You should call it skulkin', Preacher," Lorenzo suggested. "Sneakin' don't sound as good."

"Skulking isn't usually an admirable activ-

278

ity, either," Audie pointed out.

Preacher ignored the conversation. His attention was focused on Two Bears. Even though it was too dark to get a good look at the war chief's face, he could tell by the tense set of Two Bears' body that the man was angry.

"I tell you, I can do this thing," Two Bears said. "I would not lie out of stubborn pride. Not with the life of Raven's Wing riding in the balance."

Preacher frowned. Two Bears had a point there. The man genuinely cared for Raven's Wing. It was a question of whether his affection for her was greater than his dislike for Preacher.

The mountain man was willing to bet that it was, he decided. He said, "All right. The two of us will go in there and free the prisoners. As soon as we've got 'em clear, we'll give the signal to attack. That sound good to you?"

"I believe it will work," Two Bears replied. "But one of us must make sure that Snake Heart dies. Without him to lead them, there is at least a chance the Gros Ventre will not pursue us. They probably have little appetite for fighting in weather such as this."

"I reckon you're right," Preacher said. "Let's go get the lay of the land."

The rescue party rode on, the snow muffling the hoofbeats of the horses. With Preacher, Two Bears, and Dog leading the way, they had no trouble following the trail of campfire smoke that guided them toward the Gros Ventre village.

When the smell became strong enough to tell them that the village was close, Two Bears called a halt.

"Preacher and I will scout," he said. "The rest of you stay here for now."

Preacher wasn't sure, but he thought that might have been the first time Two Bears had used his name. Usually the war chief just called him *white man* and said it with a sneer on his face and in his voice.

"I think Audie should come with us, too," Preacher suggested.

"I appreciate the vote of confidence, Preacher," Audie said, "but I really don't think I'm in the same league as the Ghost-killer when it comes to stealth."

Preacher shook his head.

"I didn't mean you'd slip into the village with us," he explained. "But when Two Bears and me get those prisoners loose, we're gonna need somebody close by to turn 'em over to. I reckon that'd be a good job for you. You can hustle 'em away from the village and make sure they're safe, while

Two Bears and I go back to help with the killin'."

"I see," Audie said. "That makes sense. I'm ready whenever you are."

Nighthawk lifted Audie down from his horse. Preacher told Dog to stay with the others.

On foot now, Preacher, Audie, and Two Bears stole through the pine forest, making their way even closer to the Gros Ventre village.

Knowing that Snake Heart would have posted guards around the encampment, they moved as silently as they could, eventually dropping to hands and knees to crawl forward.

It was too dark to see much, but Preacher heard the tiny hiss Two Bears made and took it for a command to stop. He dropped onto his belly in the snow. Beside him, Audie did the same. Two Bears was just ahead of them.

A moment later, Preacher heard what had alarmed the war chief. Footsteps sounded nearby. They were quiet, as if the man was trying not to make too much noise, but even with snow on the ground, it was impossible to walk around out here without making some sound.

That was one of the guards, Preacher

thought, as he and his companions lay there absolutely silent and utterly motionless. The man was about ten feet away and coming closer.

If he discovered them, they would have to kill him quickly and without any fuss. They couldn't afford for him to sound the alarm now. Soundlessly, Preacher moved his hand to his knife and gripped it.

Then the guard turned, walking at right angles to the way he had been going, so he passed them only a few feet away without ever knowing they were there.

Preacher would have heaved a sigh of relief, but he was afraid it would make too much noise.

Instead, he lay there with Audie and Two Bears until the guard was out of earshot, and then they resumed their stealthy crawl.

A few moments later, Two Bears signaled another halt. He tapped Preacher on the shoulder. Preacher crawled forward as Two Bears parted some brush to reveal a tiny gap they could use to spy on the Gros Ventre village.

Several campfires burned, casting a flickering glow over the scene. At first glance, the place wasn't much different from the Assiniboine village. The same sort of wood and earth and hide lodges were scattered around a fairly level clearing in the woods. Even though Preacher couldn't see it, he knew there would be a stream somewhere close by so the villagers would get water.

By this time of night all the women and children were asleep, but several warriors were still moving around, checking on horses or taking care of other chores.

The hide flap over the entrance to one lodge was pushed back, and a man stepped out of the dwelling. Two Bears touched Preacher's shoulder and put his mouth close to the mountain man's ear as he whispered, "Snake Heart."

The fella even looked a little like a snake, Preacher thought . . . lean and evil. The Gros Ventre chief turned to say something to someone inside the lodge, and as he held the flap back, Preacher looked inside and saw a couple of white men.

Although quite a bit of time had passed since the encounter at Blind Pete's, Preacher recognized them as Willie Deaver and Caleb Manning. So he hadn't imagined seeing Deaver during the fight back at the Assiniboine village. The man really had been there.

Preacher saw something else in the lodge that interested him. Several long crates had been dragged into the structure. Preacher caught just a glimpse of them before Snake Heart let the hide flap fall closed and stalked off toward another lodge, but that was enough.

Preacher had a hunch he was looking at crates full of new rifles like the ones the Gros Ventre had used in their raid.

And if that was true, it made things very different indeed.

CHAPTER 26

The Gros Ventre who had remained behind in the village were happy to see the raiders when they returned. Women, children, and the warriors who had not ridden with Snake Heart came out to welcome them. Dogs leaped around and barked, which added to the tumultuous greeting.

The women of the village were especially excited to see the prisoners. They gathered around, spitting on the Assiniboine captives and hitting them with sticks. Most of the prisoners cringed and tried to get out of the way as the Gros Ventre women carried out this mistreatment with fiendish glee.

But not Raven's Wing, Willie Deaver noted.

No, Raven's Wing never flinched. She stood straight and proud and looked like she wanted to spit right back in the faces of her tormentors.

Watching that, Deaver wanted her

even more.

When the Gros Ventre women had their fill of making life miserable for the prisoners, the Assiniboine women were herded into a single lodge. Packing them in like that would make it easier to stand guard over them.

Deaver had already dismounted and turned his horse over to Manning. He went to find Snake Heart and remind the chief of their bargain.

"You said my men could have their choice of the prisoners for the night," Deaver said.

Snake Heart regarded him with a cold stare.

"I remember what was said. My men wish to have their time with the captives as well."

Anger welled up inside Deaver. He kept it under control, but he didn't think it would hurt to let a little of it out.

"Blast it, we had a deal —"

Snake Heart lifted a hand to stop him.

"Our deal involved rifles and pelts," the Gros Ventre said. "That arrangement is concluded. Anything else you and your men may get is a matter of generosity on my part."

"Fine," Deaver snapped. "You got what you wanted. You can afford to be generous."

"I suppose," Snake Heart said with a

shrug. "There are five of you. I will give you two women. For the night, you understand, not permanently."

That was better than nothing, Deaver supposed.

"All right," he said, although Snake Heart hadn't exactly asked him if he agreed. "My men can take turns. They won't care that much." He chuckled. "It won't be the first time."

"What about you?" Snake Heart asked, evidently curious. "You will not take part?"

Deaver hesitated. This was the tricky part. He didn't know how far he could push things. While they were on their way back to the Gros Ventre village, Snake Heart had staked his claim on Raven's Wing, but then later he had seemed less interested in her.

She had been put in the lodge with the rest of the captives, too. Deaver wondered if that meant Snake Heart had decided she was no different from the rest of the Assiniboine women.

Finally he said, "I'm the chief of my men, and I don't share with them. I want a woman of my own."

That ought to put it on terms that Snake Heart could understand, he thought.

Snake Heart's eyes narrowed suspiciously. "Is there one particular woman you want?" he asked.

This was the moment of truth, Deaver told himself.

And yet he saw something in Snake Heart's eyes that he didn't like, some reptilian menace true to the man's name. Too much was at stake to rush things.

He shook his head and said, "Not really. I just don't want to share with my men."

"I will think on it and tell you my decision later," Snake Heart said with a curt nod. He pointed. "Those two lodges are for you and your men."

"Fine." Although the word tasted a little bitter in his mouth, Deaver forced himself to add, "Thanks."

In the fading light, the members of the raiding party dispersed to take care of their ponies and return to their lodges. Deaver rejoined his men and waved a hand toward the two dwellings Snake Heart had pointed out to him.

"That's where we'll be staying," he told them. "Caleb and I will be in one of them, you three in the other one."

Even though he had told Snake Heart that he didn't want to share a woman with his men, he was willing to share a lodge with Manning, and for good reason.

He knew Manning was ambitious, and it

never paid to trust an ambitious man too much. If he claimed one of the lodges for his own and made the other four share, they might resent that. Deaver didn't want Manning sitting in there with Plunkett, Heath, and Jordan fanning that resentment. A three-two split was more natural.

"How long are we going to be staying here, Willie?" Darwin Heath asked. "Our business with the Gros Ventre is finished, isn't it?"

"I don't really want to leave with this much snow on the ground," Deaver said. "We'll wait until the weather gets better before we pull out."

"We need a place to spend the winter," Fred Jordan said. "Why not here?" He grinned his big grin. "Plenty of fine-lookin' squaws to keep us warm durin' those cold nights."

"That sounds good to me, too," Cy Plunkett put in.

"You let me worry about that," Deaver snapped. "I do the thinkin' for this bunch, remember?"

"The boys aren't tryin' to cause trouble," Manning said smoothly. "They're just concerned about our long-term plans. You can't blame 'em for that."

Comments like that were just the sort of

thing that worried Deaver where Manning was concerned. He said, "I'm not blaming anybody. We'll work it all out." He forced a smile onto his face. "I've never let you boys down so far, have I?"

"That's the God's honest truth," Plunkett said. "You've been a bloody good leader, Willie. Bloody good."

"Let's keep it that way," Deaver said with a nod. "Come on. I'll bet Snake Heart's gonna send some squaws pretty soon with something for us to eat."

There was a surprise waiting in the lodge that Deaver intended to share with Manning. The crates containing the extra rifles were being stored there. Seeing them made Deaver feel better for some reason, even though the weapons belonged to the Gros Ventre now.

As Deaver predicted, a couple of women brought pots of stew to the lodges. The men gathered in Deaver's lodge and dug in with their hands, Indian-fashion. Manning took one of the jugs of whiskey from the crates and passed it around, and they washed the food down with swigs of the fiery stuff.

Deaver explained that Snake Heart had promised them two of the Assiniboine prisoners for the night.

"Do we get to pick the two?" Jordan asked.

"If we do, I've got a couple in mind," Plunkett added.

Deaver shook his head.

"Nothing was said about that. I reckon you'll have to make do with whatever shows up. And you'll use the other lodge for whatever goes on, too."

Jordan grinned at him.

"Turnin' into a prude in your old age, Willie?" he asked.

Deaver grunted disdainfully.

"Not hardly," he said. "But I've got other things on my mind tonight, boys. This is just the start of big things for us. Just the start."

When they were finished with their supper, Plunkett, Jordan, and Heath went back over to the other lodge, leaving Deaver and Manning alone.

Manning sat on one of the crates, patted it affectionately, and said, "Come spring, are we gonna have St. John deliver another load of these rifles to us, Willie?"

"That's the idea. We won't have any trouble finding some more savages willin' to trade pelts for them." Deaver grinned. "Who knows? Maybe we'll go see the Assiniboine and offer to trade with them."

"Arm both sides in this feud, you mean?"

Manning threw back his head and let out a hearty laugh. "Oh, I like that idea, Willie. I really do."

Someone pushed back the hide flap over the entrance. Snake Heart stepped into the lodge. Deaver and Manning stood up to greet the Gros Ventre chief.

"The prisoners will be brought soon," Snake Heart said. "Two for the other men, and one for you, Deaver."

Deaver bit back a curse. He would have just as soon Snake Heart hadn't said that in front of Manning. The others would have found out about the arrangement anyway, of course, but Deaver wished he'd had a chance to soften them up a little first.

He could tell from the way Manning's eyebrows arched in surprise that the man intended to make something of it the next time he got a chance to talk to the other three alone.

Deaver figured he could smooth over any hurt feelings . . . this time. The money they would make off those pelts would help considerably.

In the future, though, he was going to have to give some thought to eliminating any potential problems he might have with Manning.

The easiest way to do that, of course,

would be to eliminate Manning.

"Thanks, chief," Deaver said now.

Snake Heart gave them a curt nod and turned to leave the lodge. He stopped in the entrance and looked back at them.

"When enough of the snow melts to make travel easier, you and your friends will leave our village," he said. "Our business with you is done. You will not spend the winter with us, as the white men were with the Assiniboine."

The contempt in Snake Heart's voice made it clear what he thought of that practice.

"Fine," Deaver said. "For now, we appreciate your hospitality."

Snake Heart just grunted and left the lodge, letting the flap fall closed behind him.

"Sounds like you've got a good deal for yourself, Willie," Manning said when the chief was gone.

"I had to do something to make him respect me," Deaver said. He didn't like feeling the need to explain himself to his lieutenant. "Otherwise he might have tried to take advantage of all of us."

Manning nodded slowly.

"That makes sense . . . I guess."

Deaver wanted to respond angrily to that, but he kept a tight rein on his temper.

"Of course it makes sense," he said. "You know I always have what's best for all of us in mind."

Manning just nodded again and said, "Uh-huh."

Before either of them could say anything else, Deaver heard someone sobbing outside. He stepped over to the entrance and shoved the flap back.

Half a dozen Gros Ventre warriors herded along three of the Assiniboine captives. Deaver was disappointed but not surprised to see that Raven's Wing was not among them.

One of the warriors pointed at Deaver and then nodded toward the prisoners. Deaver interpreted that to mean that he was supposed to choose one of the women.

He looked them over and saw that they were all about the same, reasonably attractive but not nearly as appealing as Raven's Wing. He was prepared to let the other men have the two best-looking of the trio, but there really wasn't enough difference in them for that.

Almost at random, he walked over to one of the women and reached out to put a hand on her shoulder. She let out a sob and tried to twist away from him, but Deaver tightened his grip on her.

"No point in worryin' about it, darlin'," he told her, even though she probably didn't speak a word of English. "You're comin' with me."

Manning had hurried over to the other lodge and called for Plunkett, Jordan, and Heath to come out. The men had big smiles on their faces as they emerged from the lodge, even the normally dour Darwin Heath.

Big, bluff Fred Jordan took the arms of the other two captives and steered them into the lodge. Plunkett and Heath followed them into the dwelling.

Manning hesitated.

"I'll see you later, Willie," he said. "You enjoy yourself. I intend to."

"Yeah," Deaver said. He pushed the woman toward the lodge. "Let's go."

The warriors who had delivered the prisoners trooped away as the white men went into the lodges with the women. Deaver closed the entrance flap and tried not to think about Raven's Wing.

It was impossible to put her out of his mind, though. Even as he motioned for the woman to take off her buckskin dress and said, "Get your clothes off," he thought about how exciting it would be if Raven's

Wing were the one stripping naked in front of him.

The Assiniboine woman was still sobbing quietly. That was going to get tiresome in a hurry, Deaver decided. He would tell her once to shut up, and if that didn't work, he would see if his fist could make her stop crying. He was willing to bet that it could.

So when he stepped closer to her and her eyes widened, at first he thought the reaction was because she was afraid of him.

They he realized that she was surprised instead, and not only that, she was looking at something over his shoulder, rather than staring at him.

He barely had time to think about that — and what it might mean — before something crashed into the back of his head and sent him spiraling forward into darkness.

CHAPTER 27

After Snake Heart left the lodge where Deaver and Manning were, Preacher, Audie, and Two Bears backed away through the brush until Preacher thought it was safe to whisper again.

"Did you see what was in there with those two varmints?" the mountain man asked.

"It looked like boxes of some sort," Audie replied.

"Crates full of new rifles would be my guess."

Audie caught his breath.

"Deaver and his friends are running guns to the Gros Ventre?"

"That's the way it looked to me," Preacher agreed. "It would go a long way toward evenin' up the odds if our Assiniboine pards had some of those rifles."

Audie didn't reply for a long moment, then, "Preacher, you're not suggesting that we try to steal one of those crates of rifles, are you? Because getting into the village and back out again with something like that seems impossible, even for the Ghostkiller!"

"It might be for one man, but there are three of us. And I ain't sayin' we'd lug out a whole crate. We cut a hole in the back wall of the lodge, one man goes inside and passes the rifles back out to another man, who passes them on to the third fella, and he caches 'em in the woods until we can fetch the rest of our bunch."

"Hmm," Audie said.

"Now you're startin' to sound like Night-hawk," Preacher said, grinning in the darkness.

"It might work," Audie admitted. "You'd need a lot of luck, though."

"A man always needs luck."

"I thought you didn't believe in it, only in powder, shot, and cold steel."

"Blast it, don't go usin' my own words against me. Are you in or not?"

"Of course I'm in," Audie snapped. "Don't think for a second that I —"

Audie didn't finish, because at that moment Two Bears whispered, "Someone else comes."

At first Preacher thought the Assiniboine war chief meant that another guard was approaching, but then he heard voices and realized that something was going on again at the lodges.

The three men pulled themselves forward through the brush until they could see again. They watched as several Gros Ventre warriors prodded three crying captives up to the lodges. Deaver and Manning came out of their lodges, and their three friends emerged from the other lodge to join them.

It was obvious what was about to happen. Preacher heard Two Bears breathing hard and thought that the enraged war chief might jump up, charge out of the brush, and ruin everything. He was prepared to make a grab for Two Bears in case he needed to hold him back.

Two Bears got control of himself, though, and whispered, "We can get behind the lodges while no one is paying attention."

"That's just what I was thinkin'," Preacher whispered back. "Come on."

Moving as quickly as they could risk, the three men began circling the village. When they reached a spot that commanded a view of the back of the lodges being used by Deaver and the other gunrunners, Preacher looked around as best he could.

Men were still talking in front of the lodges, but he didn't see anybody else moving around. The village was mostly quiet now. The Gros Ventre warriors who had gone on the raid would be with their wives, celebrating their safe return home.

He drew his knife, pointed to himself, then to Two Bears, then to Audie. He would go first and sneak into the lodge where the rifles were being stored.

That meant he would probably have to kill Deaver and Manning. That prospect didn't bother Preacher a bit. The challenge would be to dispose of the varmints without raising enough of a ruckus to alert the Gros Ventre.

The trees and brush grew to within twenty feet of the lodge. While he was crossing that space and cutting an opening into the rear wall, Preacher would be visible to anybody who happened to look in this direction. It was a risky proposition, but he had to take the chance.

He crawled toward the lodge, the heavy hunting knife gripped tightly in his hand.

The light was bad back here, with only a faint glow from the campfires that reached this far, and he had that on his side, anyway. He could still hear voices from in front of the lodge and knew that Deaver and Manning hadn't come back in yet.

Moving quickly, Preacher chopped and gouged at the rear wall of the lodge. He didn't want to make a big hole, because his enemies might notice that when they came in. All he needed was a gap big enough to fit his shoulders through.

While he was wielding the knife with his right hand, he used his left to pull away the branches he cut and scoop dirt out from under the wall. In a matter of minutes he had a big enough opening to slither through.

This was another risky moment, while he was crawling through the hole. The flap hung closed over the entrance, and the lodge was empty. Preacher pulled himself through, grabbed a bearskin robe, and threw it over himself as he pressed his body against the wall where he had cut the opening.

He hoped that would be enough concealment to keep Deaver and Manning from noticing that anything was wrong.

Breathing shallowly, Preacher lay there, and he didn't have to wait very long. He heard someone come into the lodge.

A moment later, a voice he recognized as Willie Deaver's said, "Get your clothes off."

Silently, Preacher pushed the bearskin robe aside and stood up. Deaver and one of the Assiniboine captives were the only people in the lodge other than him, and Deaver had his back turned. Manning must have gone with the other men. That was a stroke of luck, and Preacher didn't intend to waste it.

Gripping the knife tightly, Preacher stepped closer to the man. He was about to plunge the blade into Deaver's back and pierce his rotten heart, at the same time clapping his other hand over Deaver's mouth so there would be no outcry, when suddenly he changed his mind.

Instead he lifted the knife, and as the prisoner caught sight of him over Deaver's shoulder and her eyes widened in surprise, Preacher struck.

He hammered the brass ball at the end of the knife's handle into the back of Deaver's neck. Preacher put all his strength behind the blow, knowing that if it landed correctly, it would instantly knock Deaver out cold and make him collapse like a puppet with its strings cut.

Deaver went down, all right. His knees folded up and he hit the ground, unconscious. The woman opened her mouth, and Preacher stepped forward quickly and covered her lips with his free hand in case she was about to yell in surprise. He didn't want that.

"It's all right," Preacher whispered to her

in Assiniboine. "Don't yell. I'm here to help you."

She seemed to understand what he was saying. After a moment she nodded, and he took his hand away from her mouth. He remembered seeing her around the Assiniboine village, and obviously she knew who he was.

"Preacher!" she whispered. "That terrible white man said you were dead!"

She pointed at Deaver's limp form sprawled at their feet.

"Reckon he was wrong, wasn't he?" Preacher said with a grin. He pointed to the hole he had cut in the wall of the lodge and went on, "You can crawl out there and take off for the woods, just be quiet about it. There's a rescue party not far off. Two Bears and Audie are out there, and they'll help you get back to the others."

She was crying with relief now, but she said, "The other captives —"

"I know," Preacher told her. "We'll get 'em all free as quick as we can. Right now you can help by gettin' out of here, so we'll know you're safe, anyway."

She nodded and went to the opening he had made. She was able to crawl through it, even though she was stockier than the lean mountain man.

Without wasting any time, Preacher tied Deaver hand and foot and cut a piece off one of the bearskin robes to cram into the gunrunner's mouth as a gag. Then he used his knife to pry the lid off one of the crates.

The long wooden box wasn't filled with rifles, but it held more than a dozen of them, along with kegs of powder and shot. Preacher took a couple of the rifles and carried them to the hole in the back wall.

"Two Bears!" he called softly.

"Here," the Assiniboine war chief replied.

"Did the woman get away?"

"Audie is showing her the way back to the others."

Preacher slid the two rifles out through the opening.

"Take these," he said. "I'll have some more here by the time you get back."

Keeping an eye on Deaver, Preacher worked for the next few minutes with swift but unrushed efficiency. Everybody in the Gros Ventre village believed that Deaver was in here enjoying himself with the Assiniboine captive, so it was unlikely anyone would intrude for a while.

But it wasn't impossible, so Preacher didn't want to waste any time. He emptied the crate of rifles, and Two Bears passed the weapons on to Audie. Preacher shoved a keg of powder and a keg of shot through the hole as well, then opened one of the other crates. It contained eight rifles.

Deaver hadn't budged or made a sound since Preacher had knocked him out. The mountain man began to wonder if he had killed Deaver after all. He had changed his mind at the last minute and struck with the knife's handle instead of its blade because he wanted to question Deaver and find out where the rifles came from. It might be important to know if this was an isolated incident or if someone was trying to organize a continuous flow of guns to the hostile tribes.

By the time Preacher had emptied the second crate of rifles, Deaver was starting to stir. Preacher knelt beside the man and pressed the tip of his knife to Deaver's throat.

The touch of cold steel made Deaver's eyes fly open. Preacher leaned over him and said quietly, "Don't bother tryin' to yell or get loose. You ain't goin' nowhere, mister." A grin stretched across the mountain man's face. "Surprised to see me, ain't you? You thought you'd trampled me back yonder in Bent Leg's village. But stubborn varmints like me are hard to kill."

Anger and hatred blazed in Deaver's eyes.

Preacher knew that if the man were loose right now, Deaver would do his best to kill him. Preacher didn't intend to let that happen.

"You got two choices," Preacher went on. "You can cooperate and tell me what I want to know, or I'll just go ahead and cut your throat right now. It's up to you, Deaver."

Deaver glared at him for a few seconds longer, then moved his head slightly in a nod. That made the knife point dig a little deeper into his skin.

"All right," Preacher said. "I'll take that as you sayin' you'll tell me what I want to know. I'm gonna pull that gag out of your mouth, but if you try to make a peep before I tell you to, it won't take but a second to shove this knife right through your gizzard. You won't get a single sound out."

Preacher took hold of the gag but didn't remove it yet.

"Here's what I want to know," he said. "Where did those rifles come from, and are there any more headin' this way?"

He tugged the chunk of bear hide out of Deaver's mouth.

The man grimaced and used his tongue to work bits of coarse fur out of his mouth.

"You son of a bitch," he said in a choked voice. "I'll kill —"

Preacher leaned on the knife. A thin line of blood trickled from the wound it made in Deaver's throat.

"That ain't answerin' my questions," the mountain man said. "And you done used up all the patience I got for you. I'll ask you one more time . . . Where'd the guns come from?"

"England," Deaver spat out. "We got 'em from an Englishman named St. John."

That didn't surprise Preacher at all. He knew that the British government still harbored a lot of resentment toward its former colonies. Not only that, but the British fur-trading companies operating in Canada were jealous of all the pelts being taken here in the Rockies by Americans. Several times in the past, Preacher had run into British agents trying to cause trouble for the mountain men and disrupt the American fur trade.

Arming the Gros Ventre and the other tribes that hated the whites, such as the Blackfeet, would go a long way toward accomplishing that aim.

"You got more rifles comin' in?" Preacher asked. "And remember, if I think you're lyin' to me, I won't have no reason not to go ahead and kill you."

"The ones we brought here are all of them

for now," Deaver said. "Maybe we might get some more in the spring. We'd have to set up a new deal, though."

Preacher's instincts told him that Deaver was speaking the truth.

"You better go ahead and kill me," Deaver went on. "If you don't, I swear I'll hunt you down, and next time I'll make sure you're dead."

A grim smile touched Preacher's mouth.

"You know, I was just thinkin' the same thing," he said.

But before he could exert even the small amount of pressure needed to send the blade slicing deep into Deaver's throat, a footstep sounded behind him as someone threw back the hide flap over the lodge's entrance and stepped inside.

"Sorry to bother you while you're busy, Willie," Caleb Manning said, "but I — *damn!*"

CHAPTER 28

Well, that tore it, Preacher thought as he
whirled toward the entrance. Manning's
bellowed curse was loud enough that somebody had to have heard it.

Not only that, but Manning jerked a pistol
out of his belt and brought it up to fire as
Preacher's arm whipped around and sent
the knife flickering across the room in a
deadly throw. The blade buried itself in
Manning's chest and knocked him backward just as he pulled the trigger.

The pistol boomed and sent a ball smashing through the roof of the lodge. The real
harm was in the noise, though. If Manning's
yell hadn't woken up the Gros Ventre village, the shot had done it for sure.

There was no time now to worry about
Deaver. Preacher left the man where he was
lying. Deaver shouted curses after him as
Preacher ran out of the lodge, pausing only
long enough to reach down and grab his

knife, ripping it out of Manning's chest. Manning lay on his back, dead eyes staring sightlessly at the top of the lodge.

Preacher sheathed the knife and pulled both pistols from behind his belt as he ran out of the dwelling. Gros Ventre warriors were coming out of some of the other lodges, looking to see what all the commotion was about. When they spotted Preacher, they yelled warnings and grabbed for weapons of their own.

A thrown tomahawk flew through the air only inches from the mountain man's head. Preacher ignored the man who had thrown it, since he wasn't armed anymore, and thrust a pistol toward another bare-chested warrior who had his arm drawn back to fling a tomahawk. The pistol roared and blew the Gros Ventre warrior off his feet before he could make the throw.

Preacher could have fled toward the woods then, but instead he ran deeper into the village. Somewhere among this cluster of lodges were Raven's Wing and the rest of the Assiniboine captives. If he could find them, he might still be able to free them and get them away during the confusion.

Shots rang out behind him, but when Preacher didn't feel the impact of lead balls smashing into his body, he glanced over his shoulder and saw tongues of orange muzzle flame spurting from the shadows under the trees.

His heart leaped at the sight. Audie and Two Bears had gotten those rifles into the hands of the rescue party, and now they were joining the fight. Preacher saw several of the Gros Ventre go down, probably with no idea what had hit them.

The unexpected attack threw the village into even more confusion. Men shouted, women screamed, and dogs barked frenziedly. One of the Gros Ventre grabbed at Preacher and got a broken head for his trouble as the mountain man slammed the empty pistol against his skull.

"Raven's Wing!" Preacher shouted. "Raven, where are you?"

He didn't know if she could hear him with all the racket going on, but he probably wouldn't have time to check all the lodges for the prisoners. And even though the rescue party had the advantage of surprise right now, that wouldn't last. They were still heavily outnumbered, and if the Gros Ventre were able to get over their confusion and get organized, they could fight off the Assiniboine attack.

"Preacher!"

The sound of a woman's voice screaming

his name made him jerk his head around. He looked for Raven's Wing, knowing that she was the one who had called him.

"Raven!"

"Preacher!"

There! The shout came from a lodge to his left. But as he veered in that direction, a pair of Gros Ventre warriors armed with bows sent arrows flying toward him.

Preacher flung himself down and felt pain shoot through him from his wounded side as he landed on the snowy ground. The arrows sliced through the air above his head. As he lay on his belly, he tilted up the left-hand pistol and pulled the trigger. Both balls ripped into the groin of one of the bowmen.

They were armed with bows because they had been guarding the lodge where the prisoners were being held, Preacher realized. Even though he had done for one of the men, the other was still on his feet and had another arrow nocked. He let fly, forcing Preacher to roll aside. The arrow buried itself in the ground next to the mountain man.

Before Preacher could get up, a familiar figure rushed past him. Nighthawk drove his tomahawk deep in the Gros Ventre's skull before the man could get another arrow ready to fire.

Preacher scrambled to his feet, ignoring the pain in his side, and said, "Nighthawk, the women are in that lodge! Get 'em out of there and head for the trees!"

The Crow didn't respond even with his customary "Umm!" He ducked into the lodge.

Preacher knew there was no time to reload. He shoved the empty pistols behind his belt and drew his knife again. A fierce war cry behind him made him swing around in time to see Snake Heart lunging at him. The garish light from a nearby campfire made the chief's pockmarked, hate-twisted face look like something out of a nightmare as he swung a tomahawk at Preacher's head.

Preacher's left hand shot up and grabbed Snake Heart's wrist, stopping the blow in midair before it could land and dash his brains out. At the same time, the knife in his right hand darted at Snake Heart's throat, but the Gros Ventre got his left hand on Preacher's wrist just in time to turn the strike aside.

For a heart-stopping moment, the two men stood there like that, muscles straining against each other, each man knowing that the slightest slip meant sudden death.

Then Snake Heart thrust his foot between

Preacher's calves and hooked it behind the mountain man's knee. A quick jerk threw Preacher off his feet, but his iron grip on Snake Heart's wrist pulled the Gros Ventre down with him.

Preacher landed on his wounded side again. Blinding pain went through him and took his breath away. He didn't loosen his hold on Snake Heart's wrist, though. The two men rolled over a couple of times, and Preacher got a face full of snow. The cold white stuff blurred his vision and choked him for a moment.

Snake Heart wound up on top, and that gave him an advantage. The Indian was thin as a rail, but his rope-like muscles seemed to be as strong as riverboat hawsers. Preacher sensed that his own strength was giving out.

Indians loved to wrestle, and Preacher had spent enough time among them that he had picked up some of the tricks. He flung his right leg up and got it in front of Snake Heart's face. Bucking up from the ground, Preacher threw his strength into the move and used his leg to peel Snake Heart off of him. The chief sprawled on the snowy ground a few feet away.

Preacher rolled onto his good side and tried to get his hands and knees under him so he could push himself to his feet. Snake Heart recovered first, though, and bounded up to aim a vicious kick at Preacher's midsection.

The mountain man twisted his body and reached out to grab Snake Heart's foot before the kick could land. He heaved up on it and sent Snake Heart flying backward. The Gros Ventre came crashing down on his back and was obviously stunned.

Preacher had dropped his knife. He looked around on the ground, spotted it, and grabbed it before he struggled to his feet. The pain made him hunch over as he stumbled toward Snake Heart. He knew he had only seconds to seize this opportunity before the chief recovered.

Too late! Snake Heart snapped a kick at Preacher's groin. Preacher twisted to take the blow on his thigh, but the impact still drove him backward and almost made him fall. Snake Heart leaped nimbly to his feet and charged. He had lost his tomahawk in the fight, but his hands were extended like talons and from the look on his face, he intended to choke the life out of his enemy.

Preacher slashed back and forth with the knife, forcing Snake Heart to haul up short in his attack. Snake Heart gave ground, snarling as he began to circle and search for an opening.

All around the two men, the clamor of battle went on, but neither dared to take his eyes off the other. Suddenly, Snake Heart darted forward again, but the Gros Ventre had made a bad mistake. By delaying his attack for a moment, he had given Preacher a chance to catch his breath, and now the mountain man was able to respond with his usual cat-like speed. His free hand shot out, grabbed Snake Heart's wrist, and jerked the chief toward him.

Snake Heart's eyes widened in shock as Preacher's knife sank itself in his belly. Preacher turned the blade and ripped it upward, opening a gaping wound in Snake Heart's body. The Gros Ventre's entrails began to spill out.

Even mortally wounded, Snake Heart didn't stop fighting. His left hand locked around Preacher's throat in a death grip. Their faces were only inches apart, and as Preacher struggled in vain to draw air into his lungs, he saw the insane light blazing in Snake Heart's eyes. Snake Heart's lips drew back from his teeth in a hideous smile, and it was clear that if he had to die, he intended to drag Preacher right along with him into the spirit world so they could continue their epic battle there.

Preacher pulled his knife out of Snake Heart's steaming, ripped-open belly and swung his arm up and around in a looping blow that brought the blade flashing down on Snake Heart's wrist with all the power the mountain man could muster. The razor-sharp edge cleaved through flesh, muscle, and bone. Preacher put his other hand against Snake Heart's chest and gave him a hard shove. Snake Heart went over backward with blood spouting from his wrist where his hand had been attached only instants earlier.

Preacher ripped the nerveless fingers from his throat and gasped for breath as he tossed Snake Heart's severed hand aside.

He turned away from the dead chief to see how the rest of the fight was going, but as he did the world spun crazily around him. He felt wet heat flooding his side and knew that he had lost a lot of blood again. As his balance tried to desert him and he staggered to the side, a screaming Gros Ventre warrior charged at him with knife upraised for a death blow.

Preacher lowered his head and drove himself forward to meet the attack. The knife went past his shoulder and sliced a painful but shallow furrow in his back. The two men crashed together, and Preacher went over backward. The Gros Ventre landed on top of him and raised the knife again.

A gunshot roared somewhere nearby. The warrior's head exploded before he could drive the blade down into Preacher's chest. Preacher felt the warm shower of gore and brains splattering across his face.

Then utter darkness came down around him, and when he tried to breathe there was nothing there, no blessed air to fill his lungs. Only a black, terrible weight that blotted out everything else, including Preacher's consciousness.

CHAPTER 29

The first thing he was aware of was motion.

The second was that he was sick.

Preacher hadn't had time to eat much in recent days, but as his belly convulsed, it emptied itself of everything that was in it. The motion stopped, and after a moment he felt himself being lowered to what felt like the ground. It was cold. That was snow, he thought. Its frigid touch felt good on his face.

"Well, that's one way to wake up," Lorenzo said. "I ain't sure Nighthawk cared much for it, though, seein' as how he was the one carryin' you."

Preacher forced his eyes open. A number of men stood around him, vaguely visible in the gray light of dawn. Nighthawk was using handfuls of snow to try to clean off his buckskins where Preacher had thrown up on them.

"Umm!" the Crow said in emphatic response to Lorenzo's comment.

Audie bent over Preacher and studied the mountain man with a concerned expression on his face.

"You've been unconscious for a long time," Audie explained. "How do you feel, Preacher? Can you see all right?"

A terrible taste filled Preacher's mouth. He turned his head to the side and tried to spit, but without much success.

"Gimme . . . some snow," he husked.

Audie pressed a handful of snow into Preacher's palm. He brought it to his mouth, gulped it down, rolled it around, and spat it out. That helped a little.

"I feel like . . . I been busted apart . . . and put back together wrong."

"I'm not surprised," Audie said. "The wound in your side opened up again during the fighting, and you lost quite a bit of blood. Plus with that head injury, you were in no shape to be doing all that brawling anyway. Any normal man who had to endure as much punishment as you do would be dead three or four times over, Preacher."

"Help me . . . sit up."

"I'm not sure that's a good idea."

"Blast it . . ."

"All right, take it easy," Audie said quickly. "I know better than to argue with you.

Nighthawk, Lorenzo, give me a hand here."

Together they lifted Preacher into a sitting position. That caused another wave of dizziness to go through him, like the one he had experienced before he passed out.

When the feeling subsided, he managed to ask, "Where are we? What happened?"

"We whipped them Gros Ventre, that's what happened," Lorenzo replied with a note of pride in his voice. "Beat 'em so bad, they ain't even chasin' us."

"Is that true?"

Two Bears came over to join them. The war chief nodded and said, "It is true. Because you killed Snake Heart, the Gros Ventre lost their will to fight, at least for now. We go back to Bent Leg's village, where we will be safe for the rest of the winter." He held up one of the new rifles. "And well armed, so the Gros Ventre will think twice about attacking us again!"

"In all the confusion, we were able to grab even more of those rifles," Audie put in.

Preacher nodded, satisfied in knowing that at least some of the weapons intended by the British to be used against their enemies would now be used to defend the friends of the American fur trappers instead. If there was such a thing as poetic justice, this was a good example of it.

"What happened . . . after I passed out?" he asked. "I remember not bein' able to get my breath . . ."

"There was a good reason for that," Lorenzo said. "We found you with one of them varmints draped over your face, and he was dead as he could be. Reckon it was just good luck the son of a gun didn't suffocate you!"

Preacher recalled the Gros Ventre warrior who had been about to stab him.

"Somebody shot him in the head," he said. "Who was that?"

Audie grinned.

"I'll take credit for that shot, thank you very much. I didn't mean for him to fall on top of you like that, however."

Preacher gripped his friend's shoulder.

"Thanks," he said simply. Among men such as these, that was enough.

Another thought occurred to him, prompting him to look around the place where they had stopped. The sky was brighter now, even though the sun still wasn't up.

"The prisoners!" he said, alarm in his voice because he didn't see any of the women. "Where are they? Did we get 'em all?"

"I sent them ahead with some of the warriors," Two Bears said. "We freed them."

His normally dour face grew even more bleak. "Except for Raven's Wing."

Preacher's head jerked up.

"She . . . she didn't make it?" he rasped.

Audie said, "We didn't find her, Preacher. We don't know what happened to her. She wasn't with the other women when we freed them."

Preacher's head throbbed from the punishment he had taken. He would have liked nothing more right now than to stretch out and go to sleep.

But he forced his brain to work instead and asked, "The women who'd been brought to Deaver and his men . . . you got them out, too?"

"They're all right," Audie assured him. "The only one we couldn't find was Raven's Wing. One of the women said . . ." He hesitated as if he didn't want to go on. "One of them said that Snake Heart came to the lodge where they were being kept and took her with him, not long before the trouble started."

So Snake Heart had claimed her as his own, Preacher thought. Given Raven's beauty and defiant nature, it wasn't surprising that the Gros Ventre chief had chosen her.

But Snake Heart was dead now. Preacher

had killed him. There was no doubt about that. No one could have survived the wounds that the mountain man had inflicted on him.

"She must've been in Snake Heart's lodge when the commotion broke out," Preacher said. "If he ran out and left her there . . ."

"She would have tried to escape," Two Bears finished the thought for him. "She would have seized the chance."

"So she's liable to be wanderin' around in the woods somewhere by herself?" That possibility brought Preacher to his feet. All the weakness from his injuries was forgotten now. "We got to find her. If we don't, the Gros Ventre might capture her again."

"If she is free, she will make her way back to Bent Leg's village," Two Bears said. "There were other prisoners. We must make sure they reach their homes safely."

Preacher heard the pain in Two Bears' voice. The woman he loved was missing, but as the war chief of the Assiniboine he had a responsibility to the other captives they had rescued. Those women all had people who loved them, too.

"Where are we?" he asked. "Have we crossed the badlands yet?"

Two Bears shook his head.

"It is not far."

"You really think she can get through there on her own? She might get lost and wander around until the Gros Ventre find her, or she starves to death. There are wild animals in these mountains that might get her, too."

Two Bears said, "You are not telling me anything I do not already know, white man."

"Listen here," Preacher said. "You fellas go on to Bent Leg's village. I'll go back and find Raven's Wing." Something nuzzled his hand, and he looked down at the big cur. "Dog and me'll find Raven's Wing."

"You ain't goin' nowheres by yourself," Lorenzo said. "I come this far with you, Preacher, and I intend to stick."

"And with those injuries you've suffered, you'll need someone with medical knowledge around, in case you need to be patched up yet again," Audie added. "I'll go with you, too."

Nighthawk nodded and said, "Umm."

"I am war chief here —" Two Bears began.

"And I ain't Assiniboine," Preacher stopped him. "Neither are my friends. We'll do what we please."

Audie said, "Even though you're in no shape to —"

Preacher silenced him with a look.

Two Bears took a deep breath and gave

them a curt nod.

"Very well. But I will come, too."

"You have those women to take home," Preacher said.

"My warriors can do that without me," Two Bears insisted. "Everyone knows your fame, Ghostkiller. But *I* know these mountains better than you."

Preacher wasn't so sure about that, but he didn't see any point in arguing. Two Bears was right about one thing: since the Gros Ventre weren't pursuing them, the other Assiniboine warriors could handle things from here and take the former prisoners back to Bent Leg's village.

"All right, the five of us will find Raven's Wing," he said.

"Now that we've got that settled," Audie said, "you'd better let me have a look at your side, Preacher. I should probably bind that wound up again."

"Sure." Preacher sat down on a deadfall. "You can use some snow to clean it. We ain't got any time to waste, though. Not with Raven's Wing still in danger."

While Audie worked on the wound in Preacher's side, the mountain man thought about everything that had happened in the Gros Ventre village.

"What happened to Deaver?" he asked.

"Anybody see him? I killed Manning, but Deaver was still tied up in the lodge where he was stayin', the last I saw of him."

"Stocky fella with hair like straw?" Lorenzo asked.

Preacher nodded.

"That's right."

"I didn't see him," Lorenzo said. "Come to think of it, I didn't see any white men while the fightin' was goin' on."

"Neither did I," Audie said. "They must have decided to lie low. After all, it wasn't really their battle."

Preacher scratched at his bearded jaw and frowned in thought. He had tied Deaver pretty securely, but he supposed it was possible the man had gotten loose.

Another possibility occurred to him, and it sent a chill down his backbone.

"You don't reckon those varmints got their hands on Raven's Wing, do you?"

Two Bears stood straighter, stiffening in obvious horror at the idea.

"I don't think it's likely," Audie said as he drew a fresh dressing tight around Preacher's torso to cover the wound in the mountain man's side, "but I don't suppose we can rule it out."

"Get that finished up, Audie," Preacher snapped. "We got to get movin'. The sooner we find Raven's Wing, the better."

But even as he spoke, a persistent voice in the back of his head warned him that it might already be too late.

Sometimes, if a man was patient enough, luck smiled on him even when it looked like everything was going straight to hell, Willie Deaver thought.

He lifted a hand and touched the tiny, scabbed-over wound on his throat where Preacher had pressed the knife. Deaver knew he had been very, very close to death, close enough to look the bony old bastard in the eye.

And now, less than twelve hours later, he had the woman and a small fortune in pelts, and his worries about Caleb Manning getting too ambitious and double-crossing him were gone.

Manning was dead.

Preacher had killed him.

The thought still made Deaver want to laugh.

Instead, he tightened his arm around the trim waist of Raven's Wing as she rode in front of him. Her hands were tied together, and although she had spat angry words at him for a long time, she had finally run out of energy and breath. Now her head drooped forward in despair as the four men rode south through the pine-forested hills.

Yes, luck had been with Deaver. Tied up in the lodge after Preacher killed Manning and rushed out, as the tumult of battle rose outside he had yelled the names of Plunkett, Heath, and Jordan, hoping that one of them would hear him. After a few minutes, Plunkett had looked into the lodge. His eyes were wide with surprise and fear.

"Cut me loose, damn it!" Deaver had ordered the Englishman. "We've gotta get out of here!"

If Preacher was there, some of the Assiniboine warriors probably were, too. That would explain the gunshots and the rest of the ruckus. Deaver had known that his life and the lives of his friends wouldn't be worth a plugged nickel if the savages from the other tribe got hold of them.

Their only hope of survival was to get away from the village during the chaos that gripped the place.

That was what had happened. As soon as Deaver was free, he and Plunkett hurried out, met up with Heath and Jordan, and went for the horses, staying in the shadows as much as possible so they wouldn't be noticed.

The pelts had already been bundled up

and were ready to load onto the pack animals. Deaver wasn't going to leave them behind unless it was a matter of life and death. As things had worked out, they had been able to lash the pelts onto the pack horses and lead them and their saddle mounts away from the village without anyone bothering them.

That was what they were doing when Deaver literally ran into Raven's Wing, who was fleeing from the battle, too.

That was the moment when Willie Deaver realized fate was on his side after all. Everything he wanted out of this deal had been delivered to him. True, the weather wasn't very good and there was still snow on the ground, which would make their escape a little harder, but Deaver could deal with that.

"Honey, when we get where we're goin', we're gonna have ourselves a fine old time," he said to Raven's Wing now. "You just wait and see."

She lifted her head and turned it to look back at him in the gray light. He had never seen a more bleak expression in his life.

She'd get over that, he told himself. Just give him a little time, and he would win her over.

And if he didn't . . . well, he would enjoy

330

himself anyway, even though she might not.

Only one question remained to be answered, and he knew that sooner or later he would have to deal with it, probably sooner.

Where the hell were they going?

CHAPTER 30

The five men led their horses through the woods, since that was quieter than riding. Even though the Gros Ventre had been discouraged by Snake Heart's death to the point that they hadn't given chase to the Assiniboine, Preacher knew they would still fight if they got a chance to attack their enemies. He didn't want to give them that chance.

The sun was well up by the time they reached the vicinity of the Gros Ventre village. A warm breeze blew through the valley from the south. The snow had started to melt, although there was still a lot of the white stuff on the ground. It would take days for all of it to melt, and when it did, things would be a soggy mess around here.

Preacher called a halt when they smelled the smoke from the fires in the Gros Ventre village.

"You fellas wait here," he told the others.

"Dog and me will do a little scoutin'."

"I can come with you," Two Bears said.

Preacher shook his head.

"Not this time. No offense, Two Bears. You done just fine when we snuck up to the village last night."

"I do not need your praise, white man." The war chief wore his usual scowl when he spoke.

Preacher tried not to sigh. Seemed like Two Bears was just bound and determined to be an unpleasant son of a gun right to the end, no matter what happened. Well, so be it, the mountain man thought. A fella didn't have to be friendly to be a valuable and dependable ally.

"Just stay here," Preacher said. "Dog and me know what we're doin."

Two Bears scowled, but didn't continue the argument.

"We'll circle the whole village and see if Dog can pick up a scent," Preacher went on. "At the same time I'll have a look and make sure Deaver and his bunch ain't still there."

"What if they are?" Audie asked.

"Then Raven's Wing is probably out somewhere by herself, which is the best thing we can hope for, because Dog can track her for us. If we don't find any trail at all, that means she's still in the village . . . one way or another."

Preacher's grim expression made it clear what he meant. Raven's Wing could have been killed in the fighting.

But he wasn't going to let himself believe that as long as there was reason to hope otherwise. With a curt nod of farewell, Preacher moved off through the trees on foot with the big cur padding alongside him.

The two of them were like shadows drifting through the pines, making no sound and not disturbing the underbrush. Usually when Preacher needed to approach a place with such stealth, he waited for the cover of darkness. He didn't have that luxury this time, since Raven's life might be in danger.

The smell of smoke grew stronger, and Preacher began to hear voices. He dropped to one knee in the snow and wrapped an arm around Dog's neck.

"Find Raven's Wing," he whispered to the big cur. "Find her!"

When he released his hold, Dog moved off through the trees, nose to the ground. This wasn't the first time they had conducted such a search. The shaggy, wolf-like canine knew what to do.

Preacher followed, still being careful not to make any noise.

Dog circled the village, never getting too close to the lodges. He went to the north, never stopping or even slowing. He must have come across scents that would have sent other dogs following them eagerly, but not this Dog. He was intent on his mission.

Preacher wasn't surprised when Dog didn't pick up Raven's trail north of the village. It was unlikely she would have fled in that direction. Of course, in the confusion of battle, anything was possible, but he thought they stood a better chance of finding her trail south of the Gros Ventre encampment.

That was exactly what happened. Dog suddenly stiffened and snuffled the ground more intently. He turned away from the village and padded along with his nose down, practically scraping through the melting snow, mud, and old pine needles.

Preacher felt his spirits rise. Dog had spent quite a bit of time around Raven's Wing, and he knew her scent. His reaction was proof that the young Assiniboine woman had made it out of the Gros Ventre village the previous night. So were the small, moccasin-shod footprints he spotted here and there. Preacher let the big cur follow the trail until he was confident that it was leading almost due south.

He was about to call out softly for Dog to stop, so they could go back to where Two Bears and the other men waited, when Dog abruptly stiffened and planted his feet. The hair on the back of his neck rose as he growled.

"What the hell?" Preacher muttered. Raven's Wing's scent wouldn't have caused Dog to react like that. He came up beside Dog and dropped to a knee to study the ground.

Instantly, he saw the hoofprints, along with some bigger footprints left by boots. Preacher's keen eyes roamed over the marks on the ground and read them as if they were letters in a book. Four men had come along here leading seven horses.

Four *white* men, because Indians didn't wear boots like that, and they didn't ride shod horses.

The mountain man's pulse hammered with alarm inside his head. The men had come along and stopped here for a few moments. The droppings from the horses told him that. Where the two trails merged, the snow was scuffed and scattered, as if there had been a brief struggle.

Preacher knew exactly what had happened here. He could see it in his head as clearly as if his eyes had witnessed it.

Raven's Wing had been fleeing from the Gros Ventre village, which was about half a mile behind Preacher and Dog, when she'd run into four men also leaving the village. Preacher had no doubt those men were Willie Deaver and his confederates, minus Caleb Manning, whom Preacher had killed in Deaver's lodge.

And they had taken her prisoner, Preacher thought, as anger filled him. Raven's Wing had escaped from the village only to find herself a captive again, probably in even more danger.

"Yeah, I don't blame you for growlin'," Preacher told Dog. "You smell Deaver's stink, don't you?"

He straightened and went forward, following the tracks on the ground. He didn't need Dog's nose now. The prints were still plain to see in the melting snow, although they were beginning to blur a little.

The men had continued to lead their horses, and Raven's Wing trudged along with them. After several hundred more yards, Deaver must have decided that they were far enough from the village to risk mounting up. The footprints disappeared, but the hoofprints continued. They were riding now.

And Raven's Wing was probably riding

double with Deaver, Preacher thought. The idea of Deaver putting his hands all over her made the flames of anger burn even brighter inside Preacher.

His brain stayed cool and steady, though. He couldn't afford to give in to his emotions. Instead he told Dog, "Go find Audie and Lorenzo and the others and bring them back here. I'll go ahead and follow the trail on foot. Go find Audie!"

Dog looked up at him for a second, as if telling him to be careful, then bounded off through the woods.

Preacher stood there, rubbing his angular jaw as he looked down at the prints on the ground. Then he drew in a deep breath and started following them. He didn't know how long it would take to catch up to Deaver and the others, and he didn't care.

He would follow them as long as it took to get Raven's Wing away from them.

Deaver was no closer to figuring out his next move when he called a halt that evening so the group could make camp in some foothills, but at least they had put quite a few miles behind them. They had reached the southern edge of the mountains in which the valley of the Gros Ventre lay. A broad, snow-covered basin flanked by other ranges lay in front of them.

"Do you think it's safe to have a fire, Willie?" Plunkett asked as they dismounted. "I wouldn't mind brewing up a pot of tea."

"Go ahead," Deaver told the Englishman. "Keep the fire small, though."

"Will do, boss."

Raven's Wing still sat on the horse. Deaver told her to get down, and when she didn't move but just stared straight ahead, he reached up, put an arm around her waist, and dragged her to the ground.

That seemed to wake her from her trance. She twisted in his grip and struck wildly at his face. Deaver laughed as he warded off the blows with his other arm. He jerked her tight against him.

"You go ahead and fight," he told her with a sneer. "I don't mind. In fact, I like it."

That took the spirit out of her again. She sagged in his grasp.

"Heath, bring me some rope from our supplies," Deaver said.

The dour-faced Darwin Heath complied with the command. He brought the rope to Deaver, who took it, attached it to the bonds around the prisoner's wrists, and then tied the other end around a tree.

"This way you can't try to run off," he told Raven's Wing. "The sooner you realize there's not a damned thing you can do, the better off you'll be, gal."

She just gave him a hooded, baleful stare from under the sleek black hair that had fallen in front of her face.

Plunkett soon had a small fire going. The men tended to the horses, unsaddling the ones they had been riding and lifting the bundles of pelts down from the pack animals. While this was going on, Raven's Wing stood with her back stiff and her eyes downcast.

Plunkett melted snow for water and brewed tea. Deaver didn't care for the stuff himself, so he nipped from one of the jugs of whiskey they had brought along. The liquor kindled a warm glow inside him but didn't muddle his mind.

After they had made a meager supper from their supplies, Deaver took a piece of antelope jerky to Raven's Wing and held it out to her.

"Better eat something," he told her. "You've got to keep your strength up."

She didn't take the jerky, didn't give any sign that she had even heard him.

"It's your choice," Deaver said with a shrug. "You might as well realize, though, it's gonna take a damned long time for you to starve yourself to death. And I'm not gonna feel sorry for you and take it easy on you while that's goin' on, either."

Raven's Wing still didn't reach for the jerky.

"Suit yourself," Deaver said. He put the jerky in his mouth and started gnawing on it right in front of her. She would change her tune once her belly had been empty for a few days, he thought.

Plunkett let the fire burn down to embers. They still gave off a little heat for the men who gathered around them.

Deaver sensed that something was on the minds of the other men. After a few minutes, Fred Jordan confirmed that by saying, "I've been thinkin', Willie . . . I realize that when we rode out, we were just tryin' to get away from the Assiniboine, but where are we goin' from here?"

Darwin Heath said, "The storms are just going to get worse and last longer. We need a permanent place to spend the winter."

"I've been thinkin' about that, too," Deaver said, "and I've got an idea."

It had come to him late in the afternoon, and while he didn't know how well it would work out, at least it was a possibility.

"I think we should go back to Blind Pete's," Deaver said.

That statement caused puzzled frowns to

appear on the faces of the other three men.

Plunkett said, "But we burned Blind Pete's. Burned the bloody place down right around him, like you told us to."

Deaver nodded.

"I know that. But I'll bet the fireplace and the chimney are still standin', and it won't take long to throw together a nice big cabin around them. There's plenty of water and game in the area. We'd make out all right. But if I'd known we'd be coming back this way so soon, I would have just killed the damned Dutchman and left the place standin'."

"Everybody knows Blind Pete," Heath said worriedly. "What if somebody comes along and wants to know what happened to him and why we're there?"

"What business would it be of theirs?" Deaver snapped. After a second he shrugged and went on, "But we could always say that we found the place that way and don't know what happened to Pete. Nobody could fault us for movin' in and buildin' a new cabin there. It's a good spot."

"That's true," Jordan admitted.

"And who knows, maybe some of the tradin' post didn't burn," Deaver went on. "We rode off and didn't wait around to see. We might be able to salvage some of it."

Plunkett rubbed his chin and narrowed his eyes in thought.

"That's true," the Englishman said. "And I can't think of a place that's any better."

"Neither can I," Heath said.

"If that's what you fellas want to do, it's fine by me," Jordan added.

"It's settled, then," Deaver said. "We'll make for Blind Pete's place."

"There's one thing that's *not* settled," Jordan said. He exchanged glances with Plunkett and Jordan.

Trying not to let his irritation show, Deaver asked, "What are you talkin' about, Fred?"

Jordan lifted a hand and pointed at Raven's Wing, who still stood stiffly near the tree she was tied to, not looking at her captors.

"I'm talkin' about that squaw, Willie," Jordan said. "Do you still intend on keepin' her all to yourself, or are you gonna share her with your friends and partners like a good fella?"

CHAPTER 31

Preacher knew from the horse droppings along the trail that the men he was after were ten to twelve hours ahead of him. That much time wasn't going to be easy to make up, but he kept moving at a brisk pace, hoping to whittle down the gap as much as he could.

It would be better once his friends caught up to him. Then they could head south on horseback, which would make things go a little faster.

The problem was that he didn't know where Deaver and the others were going, so he couldn't follow the trail at night. Dog might be able to track their quarry by scent, even in the dark, but that was too risky. They would have to cut down the lead during daylight hours.

That meant Raven's Wing might have to spend several nights as a prisoner. The thought made Preacher's jaw clench in anger.

Next time he wouldn't hesitate. He would kill that bastard Willie Deaver on sight.

The blood loss he had suffered and the strain of the past few days had drawn Preacher thin and haggard. His reserves of strength were low.

But his righteous rage was strong, and that was enough to keep him moving.

Despite that, he was glad when, around midday, a bark sounded behind him. He stopped and turned to see Dog bounding through the woods toward him. Not far behind the big cur rode Audie, Nighthawk, Lorenzo, and Two Bears. The Crow had hold of Horse's reins and led the rangy gray stallion.

Preacher leaned on his rifle as the men rode up to him. Audie reined in and said, "Good Lord, Preacher, you look like you're on your last legs."

"I'm fine," the mountain man said. "Just lemme rest a minute, and we'll head on after Deaver and that bunch."

"You are certain Raven's Wing is with them?" Two Bears asked.

"I saw the footprints of a woman fleein' from the Gros Ventre village. All the other prisoners are accounted for, so I don't know who else it could've been."

Two Bears thought about that for a moment and then nodded.

"I am satisfied it was her," he said. "And you know the white men captured her?"

"All the signs were there. There was a struggle, and when the varmints mounted up and rode away, Raven's footprints disappeared, too."

Two Bears sighed.

"We must find them as quickly as we can."

"Damn right," Preacher said with a nod. "I'm ready to ride if you fellas are."

He swung up onto Horse's back and settled himself in the saddle. Everyone in the group was an experienced tracker except for Lorenzo, so Preacher was content for the time being to fall back and let someone else take the lead. Two Bears did so, and soon Preacher found himself being rocked to sleep by the stallion's steady gait.

His slumber was light, though, and uneasy, haunted by fleeting nightmares that concerned Raven's Wing. He was just as glad when the terrain grew more rugged and he was jolted awake.

As the afternoon began to wane, the men stopped and Nighthawk dismounted to examine the tracks they were following. After several moments on intense study, the Crow looked up and said, "Umm."

"That's what it looks like to me, too," Audie said.

Lorenzo took his hat off and scratched at his head, running his fingers through his white hair.

"I'm damned if I know how you do that," he said. "It don't sound like nothin' but a grunt to me."

"Nighthawk and I have been riding together for a long time," Audie explained. "He's actually very articulate."

Lorenzo rolled his eyes.

"If you say so. What's he tellin' us now?"

"That Deaver and the others are still about eight hours ahead of us," Audie said.

Nighthawk nodded gravely.

"We'll have to make camp soon," Audie went on. "We can't risk losing the trail in the darkness. If that were to happen, it would just delay our rescue of Raven's Wing that much longer."

"The Assiniboine do not believe in torture," Two Bears said, "but I pray to the spirits that those white men suffer long and painful deaths. If I can, I will make it so."

"Let's just find a place to camp and worry later about how we'll kill those varmints," Preacher suggested.

They made a cold camp and gnawed on jerky for their supper. Although the Gros

Ventre village had been left far behind, everyone knew they needed to take turns standing guard anyway.

"Not you, Preacher," Audie said. "You need more rest."

"Blast it, I don't want nobody coddlin' me," Preacher objected.

"Ain't nobody coddlin' you," Lorenzo said. "There's five of us, and four shifts oughta be enough. Maybe tomorrow night *I'll* be the one who gets to sleep all the way through."

Preacher groused a little more but finally nodded. He spread pine boughs on the cold, muddy ground to make a bed and rolled up on them in his blankets. He had to admit it felt mighty good to rest.

He dropped off to sleep immediately, and this time he was lucky. His sleep was the deep, dreamless oblivion of exhaustion.

Tension gripped all four men around the campfire as Jordan's question hung in the air. Deaver's first impulse was to pull out a pistol and blow a hole right in the middle of the other man's smirk.

But he forced a smile onto his face instead and said, "Ever since we partnered up, it's always been share and share alike, ain't it?"

As he spoke, he glanced at Raven's Wing.

She was pretending not to listen to what was being said, but he could tell from the little tremor that went through her that she knew exactly what was going on.

Looks of relief crossed the faces of the other men.

"It's glad I am to hear that, I am," Plunkett said. "No man wants to have trouble with his partners."

"So it's settled?" Jordan pressed. "We all take turns with her?"

"Sure . . . once we get back to Blind Pete's place."

"Wait a minute," Darwin Heath said with a frown. "Nobody said anything about waiting until we got back there."

"Well, that's the way it's gonna be," Deaver said, his voice firm enough to show that he didn't intend to allow any argument. "Listen, we're gonna be movin' pretty fast for a few days. Anybody who's not standin' guard needs to be gettin' some rest, so we'll be able to stay in the saddle for those long hours. There'll be plenty of time for messin' with the girl once we've got things squared away for the winter."

Jordan gave him a suspicious frown.

"You mean she's not gonna be warmin' your blankets, either, until we get there?"

Deaver hated to agree to that, but it was

one way of postponing trouble. For now, he needed the other three men, and even if he wasn't willing to give them what they wanted, at least he might be able to keep their resentment under control by keeping his own urges suppressed.

"That's what I mean, all right," he said with false heartiness in his voice.

What he really meant was that he would stall them until he no longer needed them, until the cabin was built on the ruins of Blind Pete's place, and then it would be time to dissolve their partnership . . . permanently. Come spring, he would need more men to help him bring in another shipment of rifles, but men who were willing to do just about anything for the right payoff were easy to find, even in sparsely populated mountains such as these.

In the meantime, once he dealt with Jordan, Plunkett, and Heath, he would have the rest of the winter to spend alone with Raven's Wing, just the two of them, snug in that new cabin while the storms raged outside.

Just thinking about it widened the smile on Deaver's face.

"So we're in agreement?" he said. "We'll all keep our hands off the squaw for now?"

Jordan nodded reluctantly.

"I suppose that's fair," he said.

Deaver told himself to keep a close eye on that one. Jordan just might be the type to try a double-cross.

It was a damned shame when a man couldn't even fully trust his own partners, he thought without a trace of irony.

The next three days dragged by for Preacher. Each day he and his companions cut farther into the lead held by Deaver and the other gun-smugglers, but still they hadn't caught up. They left the mountains behind, crossed a long stretch of flats, and trekked over another range of mountains.

That night as they made camp, Preacher realized that they weren't very far from where he had first run into Willie Deaver and the rest of that lowdown bunch.

Blind Pete's Place.

Was it possible Deaver and the others could be making for the trading post? They might need supplies by now. Preacher and his friends were certainly low on provisions. Nighthawk had been able to snare a few rabbits for fresh meat, but the little animals didn't go very far when they were divvied up among five men with healthy appetites.

At least the weather had cooperated. The days had been warm and sunny for the most part, melting the snow and drying up the mud it left behind. That was common at this time of year: a series of increasingly bad storms until winter finally settled in and didn't depart for months.

Preacher had regained some of his strength, too, although the long days in the saddle and the skimpy diet had taken a toll on him. Overall, though, he was better.

Once Raven's Wing was safe and Deaver and the rest of those varmints were dead, he would be even better, he told himself.

He sat down on a log alongside Audie and said, "It occurs to me that we ain't far from Blind Pete's Place."

"The trading post? Do you think we should stop there?"

"What I'm thinkin' is that Deaver and them might be headin' for it," Preacher said.

"Pete wouldn't stand for any trouble. He wouldn't like it that they're holding Raven's Wing prisoner, either."

"They might not actually take her to the tradin' post. Deaver could leave her somewhere close by with him or one of his men to guard her, and the rest of 'em could ride in and stock up on supplies."

"Well, yes, that sounds feasible," Audie said. "We know Pete doesn't have a very high opinion of Deaver and his friends, but he doesn't play favorites. He wouldn't refuse to sell to them." Audie thought it over for a moment, then went on, "Do you think we should head straight there so that maybe we can get ahead of them?"

"I'm not sure we could manage that," Preacher said. "But I'll bet this coonskin cap I'm wearin' that's where they're headed."

"So we need to be careful and not just ride in without checking things out first."

Preacher nodded and said, "That's what I'm thinkin'."

Now that he had come to that conclusion, the hours seemed to pass even more slowly. A part of him wanted to mount up and gallop toward Blind Pete's, right then and there.

But it would be smarter to wait until morning and continue following the trail, Preacher knew.

Even so, his impatience made for a long night.

The next morning, they set out as soon as there was enough light in the sky for them to see the hoofprints they were following. By the time the sun was up for a couple of hours, Preacher had spotted several familiar landmarks. He knew they ought to reach the trading post by the middle of the day.

He was leading the way when he realized that Blind Pete's was on the other side of a ridge that loomed in front of them. Preacher held up a hand to call a halt.

"We'd best do some scoutin'," he told the others. "From the top of that ridge I'll be able to look down and see if the horses we been followin' are in the corral."

"If they are," Two Bears said, "we will ride down and kill the white men."

"Only if they're all there, and Raven's Wing is with 'em," Preacher countered. "If they've got her stashed somewhere, we need to find out where before we kill all of 'em. Otherwise, we're liable to have a mighty hard time findin' her."

Two Bears grunted. Obviously, he was impatient, too, but he would have to keep his impulsive nature under control. Otherwise, they might be needlessly risking Raven's life.

"Audie, you and me will go first," Preacher went on. "The rest of you wait here."

Nighthawk said, "Umm," and nodded, as if saying that he would enforce Preacher's decision.

"Dog, stay," Preacher told the big cur. Then he and Audie rode toward the ridge.

It took them a while to work their way to the top of the rugged slope. They dismounted before they reached the crest, with Preacher helping Audie down from his horse, and went the rest of the way on foot, carrying their rifles. When they made it to the top, they dropped to their bellies and crawled forward until they could look down on the far side into the valley where the trading post was located.

Preacher's jaw tightened and his breath hissed between his clenched teeth in surprise when he saw the burned ruins of Blind Pete's Place. The stone chimney and fireplace still stood, as did half of one wall, but the rest was just debris. What the hell had happened here?

What really took the mountain man's breath away, though, was the sight of Deaver and the other three men, their saddle mounts and pack animals, and sitting on the nearby stump of one of the trees Horst Gruenwald had cut down when he built the place . . .

Raven's Wing.

She was alive.

That knowledge made Preacher's heart leap. He had thought she was still alive, but it was nice to have confirmation of that. Now he could start thinking about ways to rescue her from her captors.

The sound of a gun being cocked behind

him made him roll over quickly and reach for one of his own pistols.

He stopped the motion without drawing the weapon, because he found himself staring down the broad barrel of a blunderbuss capable of blowing his head clean off.

CHAPTER 32

"Gott in Himmel!" a thick, Teutonic voice exclaimed. "Preacher?"

The mountain man looked up into the beefy, unshaven face of Horst Gruenwald, better known as Blind Pete. Pete wore buckskins now, instead of the homespun shirt, corduroy trousers, and canvas apron he had usually sported in the trading post.

That wasn't the only difference. His left hand had strips of cloth bound tightly around the palm to form a wide, thick bandage that left his fingers free. The fingers didn't move, though. They were held together and hooked into a claw-like shape that clenched around the musket he held.

Pete's right hand was gone, and in its place was an iron hook bound to his forearm with rawhide. He had used the hook to cock the musket, and now it rested on the trigger, ready to pull it.

Pete lowered the weapon, though, as he

recognized the two men.

"*Und* Audie," he went on. "What are you doing here? I thought you went to spend the winter with the Assiniboine, *ja?*"

"Never mind that," Audie said. "What happened to you, Pete?"

Pete nodded toward the burned-out remains of his trading post and said, "That *verdammt* Willie Deaver and his friends happened. The same day you fellows had that trouble with them, they came back later that night and attacked me." Pete scowled and looked embarrassed at the same time. "I am sorry, Preacher. They forced me to tell them where you planned to go."

"That's all right, Pete," Preacher assured him. "They must've treated you awful bad to make you talk."

"They pinned my hands to the floor with knives and then set the place on fire to burn down around me."

"Good Lord," Audie muttered.

"But I did not die as they hoped," Pete went on. "The knives were turned so that I was able to cut myself loose with them."

"You mean you cut your hands wide open to get loose," Audie said.

Pete nodded and said, "*Ja.* It was very bad, but better than burning. I crawled out of the flames. A day or two later, some trappers found me nearby, unconscious. They treated my wounds as best they could, but my right hand could not be saved. I had them take a tomahawk and chop it off."

Preacher could only imagine what that had been like. He wasn't sure but what he would have preferred dying to losing a hand like that.

"By then the ashes had cooled enough that I was able to find this hook in the rubble. I knew it was there, and I hoped it had not melted in the flames. I was fortunate that it hadn't. My new friends helped me, gave me some clothes and this gun, and in return I promised to repay the favors once the trading post is rebuilt."

"You're going to start it up again?" Audie asked.

"*Ja,* of course. What else would I do? But I must wait for spring. Until then, I will watch over the place." Pete nodded toward the ruins again. "And that is how I came to see those . . . those monsters ride up again, with some poor Indian woman as their prisoner."

"Her name is Raven's Wing," Preacher rasped. "She's from Bent Leg's village, where we were stayin'."

"It's a long story," Audie added. "I'll see if I can boil it down for you."

He did so, filling Pete in on everything that had happened since they had left the trading post several weeks earlier.

"Where are these trappers who helped you?" Preacher asked when Audie was finished with the tale.

"They were on their way out of the mountains with a load of pelts," Pete explained. "They could not stay. They wanted to get away before the winter closed in. I didn't blame them for that. I was just grateful for the help they gave me."

"Well, you're not by yourself now," Audie said. "We'll help you, Pete."

"But first we got to deal with Deaver's bunch," Preacher said.

With anger burning in his eyes behind the thick spectacles, Pete nodded and said, "*Ja.* I will fight at your side, *mein freund.*"

The three of them looked down at the trading post again. Deaver and his friends were poking around through the ruins, obviously looking for anything they could make use of. Preacher didn't know how long they intended to stay there, but they didn't seem to be in any hurry to leave.

An idea came to him. Launching an all-out attack on Deaver and his friends was too dangerous. Raven's Wing might get hurt if she was still there when rifle and pistol balls started flying around.

But Preacher thought he knew of a good way to take their enemies by surprise, and that might give them a chance to get Raven's Wing out of harm's way before all hell broke loose.

"Pete, there's a way you can help us, all right," he said slowly, "and I think you're gonna enjoy it."

Deaver had hoped that more of the trading post would still be standing, but hell, it had been his idea to burn it down in the first place, so he supposed he couldn't complain.

The chimney and fireplace had a layer of soot on them but were otherwise unharmed. The huge, thick stones had come through the flames just fine.

The rest of the building was just rubble except for a small part of one wall. They would have to clear the ground, Deaver thought, before they could build another cabin. He hoped the good weather held for a while longer.

First, though, he wanted to see if there was anything in the ruins they could salvage.

"You sit down right there on that stump," Deaver ordered Raven's Wing. "If you so much as stand up without me tellin' you to, you'll be sorry. Got it?"

She didn't respond, but he knew that she heard and understood.

She had started eating again during the trip here, just as he had thought she would. She hadn't said a word, though, and he might have thought she was mute if he hadn't heard her cussing him out so bad right at first.

Her spirit wasn't completely broken. From time to time Deaver caught her looking at him with such animal-like hatred that he knew she would have cheerfully carved him into little pieces if she could get her hands on a knife.

He didn't intend to let that happen.

"What are we lookin' for, Willie?" Jordan asked as they poked around in the ashes.

"Knives, axe heads, shovels, anything that didn't burn that can still be useful," Deaver said.

He himself was looking for something else, though, and when he didn't find it, a puzzled frown appeared on his face.

"You fellas come over here," he called. When the other three men had joined him, he gestured toward the area at his feet and went on, "Isn't this about where we left Blind Pete staked to the floor?"

"I dunno, Willie, it's hard to tell with the rest of the bleedin' building gone, you know?" Plunkett said.

"You thought you'd find his bones?" Heath asked.

"That's right," Deaver said. "Have you seen any bones anywhere?"

All three men replied that they hadn't.

"Shouldn't they be here?" Jordan asked worriedly. "I mean, he was burned up. He couldn't just walk off."

"No, but a wolf or some other animal could have dragged the carcass out of here," Heath suggested.

Relief went through Deaver at those words.

"Sure," he said. "That's bound to be what happened. Some varmint got a bait of roasted meat. For a minute there . . ."

The other three looked at him, waiting.

Deaver gave a curt wave of his hand.

"Never mind," he said. "Just get back to lookin' around."

For the rest of the day, though, despite what he had said about Heath's idea, he kept glancing over his shoulder.

By nightfall, they had found a few things that might come in handy, but for the most part, the trading post and everything in it had been destroyed. That was a shame, but it couldn't be helped. Anyway, they still had some supplies and could make them last for quite a while if they made the effort to stretch them. And there was plenty of game around here to provide fresh meat.

Plunkett built a fire in the fireplace and began brewing tea, as well as using an iron pot they had found in the rubble and cleaned out to cook some stew. Jordan and Heath had cleared an area in front of the hearth for their bedrolls. Even now, the smell of old ashes hung in the air, and while Deaver didn't like it, he didn't know of anything he could do about it.

Deaver noticed the looks that Jordan kept casting at Raven's Wing, and he knew that tea wasn't the only thing brewing. There might be another confrontation as well.

Deaver didn't want to make a move against his companions until after the cabin was built, but if things came down to it, he could put the cabin up by himself. He wasn't afraid of hard work. He could tie Raven's Wing every morning so she couldn't escape, and in a few weeks he would have a decent shelter for them.

But the storms might get bad again before then, Deaver reminded himself. The sooner the cabin was put up, the better.

Maybe he could tolerate letting them amuse themselves with the squaw for a little while, he thought. If he had to. Then he could kill them and have the cabin — and the woman — to himself.

While they were eating, Jordan said, "Willie, I've been thinkin' about that deal we made a few days ago. This is where we're spendin' the winter, right?"

"That's right," Deaver said. Looked like his suspicions were correct.

"Well, then, since we're not goin' anywhere else, seems like there ought to be enough time for us to start enjoyin' ourselves."

"We still have a cabin to build —" Deaver began.

"We can get it built during the daytime," Heath said as he cast a hard look at Deaver.

"That's right, Willie," Plunkett put in, and he looked just as intent as the other two.

Deaver bit back a curse. He had run out of time. He had to make a decision right now about what he was going to do.

But before he could, an eerie, wailing sound floated out of the darkness around them.

All four men jerked their heads up. Even Raven's Wing looked startled.

"Bloody wolf!" Plunkett muttered. "That sounded close."

"That *was* close," Heath said, "but it was

no wolf —"

"It was some sort of animal," Deaver said as he got to his feet. "It had to be."

Jordan's eyes were wide with fear.

"I don't know," the big man said. "It sounded like . . . like . . ."

The wail came again. All four men were standing now, looking around wildly.

The noise sounded a third time, even closer, and this time the horrible wail turned into words. Thick, guttural words that Deaver didn't understand, but he had heard something like them before. His heart hammered so hard it felt like it was going to explode right out of his chest.

Then a bulky figure with an ash-begrimed face stepped into the flickering light of the fire and lurched toward the men with a bloody palm outstretched, crying, "Death! Death!"

Plunkett screamed.

"It's Blind Pete, come back from Hell!" he screeched.

The men were so shocked that for a second they didn't even grab for their pistols and rifles, but just stared at the grisly apparition instead.

Then, abandoning the shambling gait that had brought him into their camp, Pete suddenly pivoted, lunged toward Raven's Wing, and grabbed her, lifting her from the stone where she sat and diving back into the shadows.

That broke the terror spell, and Deaver bellowed, "Kill him!"

Guns began to roar.

It wasn't a fair fight, and Preacher didn't give a damn about that. Deaver and his bunch had long since forfeited any right to fairness. Audie, Nighthawk, Lorenzo, and Two Bears opened fire, and a couple of the men crumpled as rifle balls tore through them.

The biggest member of the gang somehow avoided being hit, though, and so did Deaver, who twisted aside just as Preacher's shot whipped past his ear. Satan himself had to be watching over that son of a bitch, Preacher thought as he dropped the empty rifle and yanked out his pistols.

Deaver wasn't staying to fight, though. A huge bound carried him out of the light from the fire in the fireplace and sent him plunging into the darkness after Pete and Raven's Wing.

Preacher ran after them. As he dashed through the ruins of the trading post, from the corner of his eye he saw Two Bears locked in a fierce, hand-to-hand struggle with the biggest of the gun-smugglers.

At the same time, one of the wounded killers pushed himself up and tried to level a pistol at Two Bears' back. Preacher couldn't stop to help the war chief, but he called, "Dog!"

The big cur leaped out of the shadows and locked his jaws around the wrist of the man's gun hand. Bones crunched and the man screamed as those incredibly powerful jaws clamped shut.

Preacher didn't know what else was happening back there because he had to concentrate on finding Pete, Raven's Wing, and Deaver. He heard a struggle up ahead. Pete cried out in pain.

"You're not a damned ghost!" Deaver shouted. "But you're about to be dead!"

"No!"

That was Raven's Wing. Preacher held his fire. He couldn't shoot blindly for fear of hitting her or Pete. His eyes were adjusting to the shadows now, and he spotted Deaver struggling with Raven's Wing. They were fighting over something . . .

It was Pete's hook, Preacher realized, and Raven's Wing suddenly had it in her hands. Those hands were tied together, but they were able to grip the hook as she swung it at Deaver with desperate strength.

Preacher heard the grisly *chunk!* as the hook lodged in Deaver's throat.

Deaver staggered back from her, making gagging sounds as blood bubbled from his ruined throat. Preacher saw the dark flood flowing down over Deaver's throat. He stepped closer, gripping one of his pistols now, and said, "Deaver!"

Deaver reeled around toward him.

"I ought to just let you bleed to death," Preacher said, "but I'm damned sick and tired of this."

The pistol in his hand roared and blew half of Deaver's head away. The carcass hit the ground with a soggy thud.

Pete had fallen during the struggle. He climbed back to his feet and went over to Deaver's body, bending down to pull the hook free with his bandaged left hand.

"Steal a man's hook right off his arm, will you?" he grated. "You got what you deserved, *ja.*"

Raven's Wing ran to Preacher. She couldn't hug him, since her wrists were still lashed together, but he put his arms around her and drew her against him.

"It's over," he told her. "For good this time."

She looked up at him and with concern in

her voice asked, "Two Bears?"

"Let's go find out," he said.

Two Bears was all right. Lorenzo related in colorful fashion how the Assiniboine war chief had gotten his hands around the neck of his opponent and choked the life out of him. Preacher had cut Raven's Wing loose by then, and she went to Two Bears and laid a hand on his arm.

"Thank you for coming all this way after me," she said.

Two Bears scowled.

"As the war chief of Bent Leg's people, it was my duty," he said.

Preacher knew good and well it was more than that, though, and so did everybody else here, including Raven's Wing.

After everything they had gone through, he didn't want more trouble with Two Bears . . . and he thought he saw a way that it might be avoided.

At Pete's suggestion, they withdrew a few hundred yards from the ruined trading post and made camp in the trees.

"The smell of the ashes is bitter to me," the trader explained, and Preacher could certainly understand why he felt that way.

Nighthawk and Two Bears dragged away the bodies of the renegade white men, leaving them for the scavengers a good distance away from the trading post. The horses and the pelts remained behind, the animals picketed where they were, and the pelts stacked in the cleared area next to the fireplace.

The next morning, everyone gathered near the chimney that reared its sturdy height into the mountain air.

"Pete," Preacher said, "the fellas and I have been talkin', and we decided that if you'll have us, we'll winter here this year and help you rebuild your tradin' post. We'll work when the weather permits and have a good start on it by next spring, so it won't take long to finish up."

The German blinked back tears of gratitude and said, "You would do this for me?"

"Sure," Preacher said. "We had a hand in what happened here, even though it wasn't intentional, so the least we can do is help you put it right."

"Absolutely," Audie added. "It's an eminently sensible solution."

Nighthawk opened his mouth to speak, but before he could, Lorenzo said, "Umm." When they all looked at him, he spread his hands and asked, "What? I've been around this big galoot long enough I reckon I'm startin' to pick up a little of that Crow lingo."

That brought laughter from everyone, even Nighthawk.

A little later, Raven's Wing caught Preacher alone and said quietly to him, "I thought you would return to Bent Leg's village with us."

"I know, but I ain't sure that's such a good idea," he said as he scratched his jaw. "You and Two Bears belong there, so you got to go back, but the rest of us really ought to stay and help Pete get back on his feet. Audie says he can fix that hook better on his bad arm and maybe even do somethin' for that other hand of his."

"I hope so. He is a good man."

"Yep," Preacher agreed.

"And so are you. You and Two Bears have fought side by side for so long, you want peace between you."

She was a smart woman, Preacher thought.

"Seems like it works out best that way," he said softly.

"Best for Two Bears."

"And for you, too," Preacher insisted. "Shoot, come spring, I'd be gone anyway. Shiftless fella like me never stays anywhere for long."

"The winter is long," she said.

"Spring will be here before you know it," Preacher said.

She took his hand and squeezed it.

"You saved my life more than once," Raven's Wing said. "I will honor your wishes, Preacher." She smiled. "But you do not know what you are giving up."

Oh, he knew, all right, Preacher thought. And she was right about one thing.

It was gonna be a long, cold winter.

He was already looking forward to spring, when he could answer the call of the frontier once more.

The employees of Thorndike Press hope you have enjoyed this Large Print book. All our Thorndike, Wheeler, and Kennebec Large Print titles are designed for easy reading, and all our books are made to last. Other Thorndike Press Large Print books are available at your library, through selected bookstores, or directly from us.

For information about titles, please call:
    (800) 223-1244

or visit our Web site at:
    http://gale.cengage.com/thorndike

To share your comments, please write:
    Publisher
    Thorndike Press
    10 Water St., Suite 310
    Waterville, ME 04901